THE KNIFE-EDGE PATH

PATRICK T. LEAHY

Copyright © Patrick T. Leahy, 2019

ISBN: 9789493056336 (ebook)

ISBN: 9789493056329 (paperback)

Publisher: Amsterdam Publishers

info@amsterdampublishers.com

Front cover: Wartime Terminus, by Bert Hardy (Collection Picture Post), Copyright © Getty Images

CONTENTS

ACKNOWLEDGMENTS

Grateful acknowledgment to *Time Life Books, WWII*; *The Rise and Fall of the Third Reich*, by William L. Shirer; *The Ambiguity of Good*, by Saul Friedlander.

For my children, Dan, Tom and Maureen.

PRAISE

"As an ardent, long-time admirer of Pat Leahy's meticulously crafted and at times almost painterly prose, I devoured his latest work in a couple of nights and am still reeling from the experience. In its mining of the human heart's darkest corners, THE KNIFE-EDGE PATH is just a tremendous read: the plotting tight as a harp-string and the characters drawn with such beautiful delicacy, the scope and sense of place genuinely stunning. This is a hugely impressive offering from a writer of significant talent, one that deserves the attention of the widest possible audience. If there's any justice in the world, he'll have a runaway bestseller on his hands." - Billy O'Callaghan, author of MY CONEY ISLAND BABY

PART 1

1

Geli lifted the top off her King Tut humidor, took out the cigarette she'd saved for days. She wouldn't light it up until she got out on the landing. Make this one last down to the end.

The last of her Melachrino Number Twos, cork tipped, that she'd so loved to light up at parties when they would get her into conversations, and she could brag about their being Missie Vassilchikov's brand. The day she'd brought a whole case home from Cairo Gunther chided her about the space they took up in the closet, and she remembered saying, 'Darling, you like them as much as I do. By the time they run out, the war will be over.'

She looked down the length of her dusky bare legs beneath her skirt to the muff mules on her feet. She would be 47 in another year, but men still stared at her, and she knew what they saw. There were still traces of the girl she used to be, and she remembered the shimmering firelight in Hagen, among felled Maypoles, while gongs banged and couples leaped across the flames, and they had crowned her Queen of the May. There'd been her prowess on a bicycle, the races she had shamed the boys into, and Manfred Priepke, their champion, had made the mistake of taking her on.

She took the matches with her and, leaving the door unlocked behind her, stopped a moment in the corridor to light the cigarette, then hurried out onto the landing and sat there, not bothering to pull her skirt down over her knees. The stairway was empty, silent as a tomb.

A plug of ash dropped from her cigarette and splashed across her ankle. She reached down to brush it off. All at once downstairs the gate clashed and a blast of cold air slipped in on a streak of pale light. There was a shuffling at the bottom of the stairway, shoes started upward and she sat still, smelling floral soap before she saw him lumbering upward in a heavy topcoat, tilting side to side. He was almost upon her when she looked up into a pair of pale blue, bulging orbs – jelly-like, as if you had to dive into his watery world to see what he saw just before you drowned.

She scooted a little sideways to let him pass. She'd seen him once before but thought there must be better ones than that. He kept on clumping upward, saying nothing, then as his footfalls reached the landing, and he was behind her, she thought she heard him taking his first step onto the bottom of the next flight up.

"You must be quite cold out here, Madame, dressed like that."

The cigarette between her fingers jerked. She wrenched herself around and saw him twisting toward her on the landing.

"Oh, I'm never out here very long," she said, "and you know – how the smell gets into your furniture, the walls -"

Just then heat seared her fingers and her cigarette fell onto the next step down, showering sparks. Before she could pick it up he lurched down past her with surprising alacrity for a fat man, stomped on the butt and ground it viciously into the worn wood like he was stomping the last few twitches of life out of a centipede.

"There!"

"Oh, dear! That was my last." She reached for the flattened stub.

"No, Madame! Leave that for the janitor. You can't put that filthy thing back on your lips."

She smiled wanly up at him. "Of course you're right. I wasn't going to. You do funny things when you're down to your last smoke." She reached for the butt again. "I'll just drop this in the majolica jar."

He plunged his gloved hand under his blouse, pulled out a platinum cigarette case. She noticed then the lightning bolts of the Death's Head Group of the SS on his collars. His voice sounded decent enough, but God, what would Gunther say?

"Leave it, Madame. Allow me to offer you one of mine." He held out the open case.

"Oh, well, thank you, but I think I'd better get used to going without."

"No, no. I've got plenty more where these came from."

How much easier it might be if he weren't such a toad, she thought. But it was now or never. The words were out before she knew what she was saying, like something so long in the oven it was burning.

"I don't suppose you'd care to join me for a drink?"

He stared down at her. "Well, I - now?"

"At your convenience."

He looked down at her some more. "Do you belong here, Madame?"

She laughed a little, pointed back across the corridor toward

5

the door marked 211. "That's my flat right there. My husband is away at the front."

He stood there in the shadow, motionless. At last he pulled his thick coat sleeve back from the face of his watch. "I almost forgot, I've got a cat to feed. My housekeeper has the night off."

"Ah, so you like cats, sir."

He shrugged, showing the thin leer of a smile. "Not if you ask my housekeeper."

"Oh! Allergic to them, maybe? But how nice of you to put up with one."

He shrugged again, and lifted one foot up onto the next step.

She said, "Well, I'll be up a while longer if you change your mind."

"I normally retire by ten," he said moodily.

"I see. Well, perhaps some other time." She stretched her open hand up to him.

He started to pull off his right glove, then thought better of it as he reached down for her hand. His flaccid squeeze made her look up into his eyes like they were staring from a fish bowl. She traced his mump jowls down to the lightning bolts on his collar, remembering Gunther's admonition once to steer well clear of anybody belonging to the SS The bane of our existence, he'd once said.

"Geli Straub," she said, wagging his hand.

He let go and stood back. "Willy Stumpff."

"Captain," she said. "My husband taught me how to tell the ranks."

His drowsy, lurid smile caressed her with some inscrutable inquiry, and she wondered whether in his mind she was some demimonde who'd sunk quite low enough to let the leash off her husband. He wouldn't be far off, she thought.

"Good night, then, Madame," he said.

"Good night, sir."

As he lumbered upward toward the next level, the smashed butt on the step caught Geli's eye. She reached for it, like being dirty now it was no longer hers. She closed her hand around it and got up.

Back in the warmth of her flat she shut the door behind her and with a sudden shiver thought, my God, what have I done? Probably he won't come, she thought. But if he does...

One bottle of Frascati left in the pantry, a block of Munster from which she'd have to cut away the mold. Barely half a loaf of black bread and three sausages to her name. Yesterday down at Thaleiser's she had bought just one short string of bratwurst. Otto the butcher had handed her the little package over the counter as much as to say what happened to the *pounds* you used to buy, Frau Straub?

She'd lived alone too long. Old newspapers strewn across the piano, dusty paper flowers in the vase beside her monument to Gunther - his portrait in full military regalia, taken in Taranto on their wedding day. She tidied up all around that, then in her bedroom shut the closet door on a heap of soiled clothes. She thought of getting into something more revealing. No, it was enough to leave her stockings off. Her hair looked tousled in the mirror. Let that be. Gunther used to say she looked prettier without makeup. Why did men say that? That one bottle of *Frascati* would hardly be enough to make him feel good, and leave some for the numbing of her own nerves. The chances were he'd never come. He didn't look like the kind of a man who'd had experience with women, unless the housekeeper, well, you didn't have to think too long and hard to guess what kind of 'house' she kept.

She sat on the sofa to wait, glancing at the door from time to time. She waited and waited and then picked up her tattered volume of Rilke's *Das Buch der Bilder*. The words began to sway and blur as she grew sleepy, and the next thing she knew her head jerked up and the clock came into focus, hands showing 10:16. She got up and was about to switch off the lamp when she heard knuckles hitting so lightly on a door she thought it must be coming from across the hallway. The rapping came again, harder.

"Just a moment!" she called out. She hurried toward the door and was about to pull the bolt back when she realized that she was still in her bare feet. The fist on the other side hit again.

"Coming!"

Bare feet might be the best thing she could greet him in, she thought, and feeling breathless she swept the door open.

He stood there now in gabardine slacks, a white shirt open at the collar, arms pumping at his sides like a schoolboy arriving for a term's evaluation. A rivulet of sweat crept down past his ear. His thinning grizzled hair was slicked back with pomade, cheeks freshly shaved and rosily aglow. Gone were his overcoat and the peaked cap. Oddly, though, he'd kept his gloves on.

She stepped aside, pulling the door back. "I'd almost given up on you, Herr Stumpff."

"Well, it's quite late, I know," he said, glancing at her feet. "I hope I didn't get you out of bed."

"No, no. Please come in."

He stepped gingerly across the threshold as if it was a muddy puddle in the street.

Geli said, "May I take your gloves?"

He drew his hands back quickly like a mother who didn't want any strangers touching her baby. "Ah, no thank you. Not at the moment. You see, I have poor circulation." He smiled, then glanced aside at the painting hanging there beside him on the wall. "Ah! The Pastoral Symphony."

8

"Why, you're a connoisseur of art!" she said gaily.

He shrugged. "I was an art dealer before the war." He stepped back from the painting, wincing faintly as his bulging eyes roamed over the fat picnicking nudes, the nonchalance with which a fully clad man with a mandolin sat serenading the heavy naked lumps of flesh under an oak tree.

"I just adore Giorgione, don't you?" she said. "Can't you just see the dust in those old trees?"

Stumpff looked again, this time fingering his chin skeptically. "Actually, I'm rather partial to the nudes of Adolph Ziegler and Julius Engelhard. Our rustic settings are so much more wholesome. Give me Sepp Hilz any day when it comes to unclothed women."

"Yes. My husband used to say that Hilz was one of the finest pornographic painters in Germany today."

The tepid smile on Stumpff's lips froze. "I'm afraid I don't follow you, Madame."

"Well, Gunther thought it was especially true of Engelhard and Breker – how their art inspires our fighting men to do their part for the birth rate when they're home on leave. You know, with the war on, we need all the extra babies we can get."

Stumpff arched one eyebrow, staring at her. "I wouldn't repeat that outside present company."

Geli threw her head back, laughing. "If you promise not to tell on me."

Stumpff moved uneasily, as if he wanted to edge past her. "Who is your husband, Madame, if I may ask?"

"That's him right over there." Geli stood aside, pointing at the portrait on the piano.

Stumpff clasped his hands behind his back and strutted over, taking in the martial beauty of General Gunther Straub's deadly serious pose. He leaned forward, taking a closer look.

"Quite a handsome man, and a *General.*" Stumpff lightly touched the edge of the frame, like a child's fingers on the General's epaulettes.

"Are you surprised?" Geli said.

"Surprised? Oh, perhaps." Stumpff shrugged. "I don't run into General's wives that often."

"Don't be nervous. He's in Russia with Guderian. I've had one letter from him, sent from Smolensk in June of '41. Since then, not a word."

"But that's -"

"Yes, almost three years ago. You fear the worst, but then as long as nobody comes to your door with bad news, you've got a reason to go on hoping. However, when your stipends suddenly run out, that's another story."

He stared at her incredulously. "Your stipends? But if he's still alive, I see no reason why -"

"Oh, don't worry, I marched right down to OKA to inquire. Showed them my papers, but they insisted on seeing our marriage license. I had to come back home to see if I could find it. I looked high and low but it was gone. If Gunther took the original with him, he didn't leave me with a copy. The only thing I had to prove I was his wife was that letter from Smolensk. This smart-aleck little *Deutsches Frauenwerk* seemed to think it was too old to be of value. There was no way of authenticating such a letter. She said come back with your marriage certificate, we might begin to get somewhere. I wanted to smack her smug little face. Not all that little, really."

Stumpff was shaking his head woefully. "Since then the certificate hasn't turned up?"

"No," Geli said, thinking it better to keep her frantic searches through drawers and shoeboxes to herself.

Stumpff shook his head some more. "This all seems quite

irregular to me, Madame. They shouldn't have treated you so shabbily. My only thought is, security restrictions may be keeping your husband's whereabouts under wraps. Things haven't been going all that well for us in Russia."

"Yes, but Gunther's letter got through to me from Smolensk. Then we hear that Guderian, at Moscow's doorstep, turns toward the Ukraine. What could Gunther give away that Goebbels hadn't broadcast to the nation?"

Stumpff rolled his eyes and hooked a finger on his lower lip. "Quite so, quite so. At least you haven't received any official notification of his death. That's something."

"Is it?"

"Mmm. But on this matter of your stipends. There *must* be some way to get to the bottom of that." A lazy, helpless smile moved sluggishly across Stumpff's lips, he sighed and Geli could see that she was wearing him down.

"Enough of my troubles, Herr Stumpff! What about a drink?"

He brightened. "Why, yes. That would be lovely."

"I've got a nice bottle of *Frascati* on ice."

"Oh, splendid. I rarely drink anything stronger than wine."

Geli trotted back into the kitchen, feeling like she ought to tell him they were getting into her last bottle. It lay in a pool of melted water in the icebox. She wiped it down, wondering again whether she should tell him that, after this, there wouldn't be any more. The cork held fast as she tugged, and she twisted on the screw, beginning to get mad. Why was it that the corks in these white wines were always so hard to get out?

She came back with the tray and saw his hand was moving around behind Gunther's picture to the smaller one.

He pulled it out, tucked in his chin and gazed down at her in baggy shorts crossing a plank that spanned a small gorge under the Sphinx near Cairo, hands spread like a tightrope walker, her more sure-footed Egyptian guide behind her. "This is you!" Stumpff turned with the picture in his hand.

"Yes. Not so skinny, then, as you can see."

Still holding the picture, Stumpff glanced up at the tasseled camel's blanket hanging from the wall behind the sofa, then back at the picture. "I've been wondering how you came by all this exotic décor."

"That rug was on my camel, the day I took a tour around the Cheops pyramid."

He set the picture down in front of Gunther's. "Touring Egypt, were you?"

"Not exactly. I might tell you sometime."

"Oh, how mysterious," he said, flattening back a smile.

Geli set the tray on the piano. The bottle began to totter and with lightning speed he steadied it, then with a firm grip around the neck said:

"I wouldn't want to miss my chance to try this stuff that might have ripened under one of your dusty oak trees, Madame."

She smiled.

There was a kind of effeminate strutting in the way he spoke.

"Have you any children, Herr Stumpff?"

"God, no! I never married. There was a woman at one time. She said the child was mine, but I seriously doubted that. The thing was mongoloid. It only lived a few days, mercifully."

"Oh, I'm so sorry."

"Don't be. A thing like that is better off dead. I've never entertained the idyllic fantasies of a family life. And you, Madame?"

"Children weren't at the top of our list when we could see

the war was coming. I'm older than my husband and, well - it's a long time since I was pretty."

He gave her a reproving look. "Not from where I'm standing," he said, reddening a little as he reached for the bottle, then filled her glass and his.

She swung her glass around, held it out for Stumpff to clink.

He did.

They both drank.

"By the time I went to Cairo," she said, "I'd all but given up on children."

"Ah. What took you to Cairo in the middle of the war?"

"Gunther had a chance to go with Rommel to Tripoli after the Tommies finished pushing the Italians all the way across Cyrenaica, but they sent him to Greece instead. I didn't want to stay back in Taranto, doing nothing. He told me I could go to Cairo the hard way, if I wanted to. To him it was a joke, but I took him up on it. The Abwehr needed agents. Being half Italian I could easily pass for a Saracen, so I volunteered. I wanted to use the name of our landlord in Taranto: Berti. But they decided to make me French instead – there were so many of them in Tunis. So I took the name of Mlle Simone Miroux, a woman I'd known in my childhood. They supplied me with a sister living in Paris named Maxine. If anybody tried to check up on me by telephone, a woman would answer, claiming to be Maxine Miroux, and she would vouch for me. I used to want to call that number just for fun, but Gunther warned me this wasn't one of Missie Vassilchikov's masquerade parties."

"So you went?"

"Yes, I went."

"Rather brave of you. How much protection was your darker skin in a city full of Tommies?"

"I stayed in a room in Shepheard's Hotel, teaching French. Then of course there was the belly-dancing."

"My goodness! You taught French *and* belly-dancing?"

Geli felt a little buzz coming on. Things were floating back to her in a haze of cigarette smoke in those strange, troubling days when she'd been happy. "Oh, no. I was the pupil on the dancing. Took lessons from the best of them - first Madame Badia, then Hekmet. The Tommies almost rioted when Hekmet got picked up as a spy. I left before I could find out what they did to her. We'd been friends."

"Making you quite nervous, I should think."

"I made sure she never knew that I was on her side. She only wanted to rid her country of British rule. I was doing my part for the war effort. Trying to impress Gunther, actually. You don't always get loved for showing off, though, do you?"

Stumpff tossed down another gulp, looked at her uneasily, then glanced at Gunther stoically failing to defend himself in the frame he was enshrined in. "So you were quite on your own over there, I take it." He raised his glass to his lips and eyed her over the rim. "Let Rommel finally take Tobruk! You could go back." He sipped and swallowed, smacking his lips with a hiss from the back of his throat.

"No, thank you! Once was enough. I rather fell in love with a certain subaltern. His name was Reggie, a graduate of Sandhurst. He was killed at Halfaya Pass. Hellfire Pass, the correspondents used to call it. I didn't know for almost a month. One of his chums on R&R told me. He'd left all his things in the storeroom at Shepheard's. There were Cunard stickers all over his steamer trunk. In a certain way he was more like my child than a lover. You might say both. After all, I was married."

A sting came into Geli's eyes, bearing the body of the boy she had slept with, then betrayed. He came into her mind and lay there with his inexhaustible devotion to her in bed, with the flies and that god awful desert heat sticking them together, while the paddle-fan on the ceiling turned and turned.

Stumpff squinted at her shrewdly.

She could see that he was getting tight.

"Mmm. Well, I suppose that's one way of doing it – in the line of duty."

"Oh, I don't know. I don't think Gunther would have cared. When he was home he never really looked at me, you know. Not like he's looking at me there. One time I took off all my clothes and did a belly dance in front of him. Put everything I'd learned from Madame Badia into it, and I felt so beautiful. He never quite knew what to do with me. He sat right there in that chair one time and glared at me. He told me once I didn't have an ounce of natural grace. I wasn't really very good in bed, either."

The wine going down Stumpff's throat became a thick, loud glunk. He reached for the *Frascati* on the piano and with a slightly trembling hand sloshed some more into his glass. He set the bottle down too hard on the piano, then remembered hers. "Sorry, Madame." He tilted the bottle stingily over her glass, let a small splash out, then lifted it away as if that was how a lady wanted it. He took a swallow, licked his lips and said, "Well, no regrets, Madame. The information you passed on might have helped to get the Tommy killed. So it came out all right in the end."

"Yes, he got killed, all right," Geli blurted hotly, then lifted her face as if she smelled something, and in her mind she saw the boy again, standing in a doorway, looking out at the promise of a day before the sun came up and a wind full of sand flew in from the desert, forcing her back. He stood out there lost in the dust, trying to come back to her. He'd sworn to her he would, after the battle. The battle was over and soon he would be in her arms again, keeping his promise. He fought the sand and the dust as if he loved her that much – to get back to the place that she had saved for him. He was coming back to her as if the place left in her heart for him could bring back the dead.

The plump, red face was watching her, and she said, "That was the funny thing, how afraid I was that Gunther would be glad I'd cheated on him in the line of duty. I wanted to have something he would think I should be proud of. After all, he was the one who'd said I should go. More worried that I'd upstage him than if some British officer swept me off my feet. So I let a young man die to get one back who didn't really want me."

Stumpff blinked uneasily, looked around as if for a place to hide the red bloom slicked across his face, then shook his head. "Deplorable, Madame," he slurred thickly. "And you! You bearing the brunt of all that danger."

Geli made a move, then, for the little Tutankhamen sarcophagus on the sideboard where she kept her cigarettes. She was halfway there on nerves before she remembered it was empty. She kept on going, anyway, plucked off the lid. "Oh, how stupid of me! Force of habit." She clanked the lid back down.

"I'm afraid I haven't brought any cigarettes with me," Stumpff said.

"No matter, I should quit, anyway. As if I had a choice."

He looked aside, eyes misting over wistfully. "My mother smoked quite heavily. Consequently I was short-changed in the womb. I wanted to be tall, like my uncle, but Mother smoked like a chimney and she made me stay inside when I asked to be excused. I hated her almost as much as the smoke, because I came to think she did it to spite me. Nobody could stop her. I was thirteen before I got up nerve enough to tell her that she looked unsightly with a cigarette dangling from her lips. She

16

slapped my face - my own mother. I was always trying to make a lady out of her, without success."

"I'm sorry," Geli said. "Gunther told me once that not even my Melachrino Number Twos could make one out of me."

He looked her up and down. When he did that it made her laugh, but she quickly clapped her hand over her mouth. He said in a solemn voice, "I wouldn't say they've done you any harm."

"How sweet of you to say." She stepped closer to him. "I could show you how I used to dance in Cairo if you want. Madame Badia put me to work in the Melody Club, the roughest bistro in town. I had to fight off Tommies every night."

He drew in his chin against a choking grin. "Yes, well, no need really, Madame."

She lifted up her arms, weaving from side to side and writhing her hips, remembering the heat and the smell of cigarettes and how the boys, when she got close enough, reached out and tried to touch her through the wire. She put out her hands, made a come-on gesture with her fingers.

Stumpff stared at her as if there was a spider crawling up her neck. He backed away until the bow in the piano stopped him.

Breathing hard, Geli dropped her arms. "I've lost my touch," she said, and tried to smile but the veil slipped.

He turned aside and took the path of least resistance out onto the rug, saying, "I must be going, Madame. It's that hour. The bombing could start in at any moment."

"But we haven't been bombed since -"

"Don't let them fool you, just because they've left *us* alone while they pound Cologne and Magdeburg, Würzburg, Lübeck, the filthy cowards. It's only a matter of time before they get back to us." He was talking angrily, now.

She didn't want to lose him. "But surely not tonight," she said. "It's after dark and we haven't heard a single bomb."

"Let's hope some stray doesn't make a liar out of you, Madame. This air of Cairo won't protect you from a 500-pounder." He started toward the door, swaying off course, then stopped and seemed to think of something. "Don't you have someplace to go when things get bad here in the city?"

"We've got a cottage near Münster, but I think I'd feel much more alone, there, than I do here."

"Better alone than dead, Madame." He suddenly turned and started reeling for the door again.

There was something of a little boy about him, she thought, set loose by the Frascati.

He was almost to the door when she called after him, "May I ask a favor of you?"

His hand was on the knob. He kept it there, cranking his head around. "Cigarettes?"

"Those wouldn't hurt."

"They wouldn't be anywhere near as tasty as the ones you're used to."

"Actually, there was something else."

He turned to face her, looking annoyed. "Well?"

"It's my husband. I thought you might have some connections to help me find out what's become of him."

He blew a sigh that seemed to shrink him, standing there. "I know a couple of people, but I can't make any promises."

"Anything. Anything at all."

"I'm going to be away for a few days, then we'll see. No promises, as I say." He gave a little bow. "Thank you for the company, and your wine."

Without another word he went out, pulling the door shut behind him, softly.

2

She could hear the rain outside, gurgling in the gutter drain. In the window dark scuds drove on above the rooftops and the chimneys. She parted the curtain and looked down into the street at a young woman raising her umbrella. A runabout splashed past. Its occupants stared at the girl through rain-spattered glass before she hurried across toward Thaleiser's and went in. She was so lithe and pretty, the same girl she had seen once on the stairway coming down, cradling a cat in her arms.

She was beginning to despair of seeing Stumpff again. She'd let the days go by during which he was supposed to be away, then she began to wonder if he'd written her off. He must have better things to do than to keep the hounds of hunger from the doorstep of a rather bothersome, dreamy middle-aged woman. The worst was in the evening when he was due home, and she would make sure to be wearing something nice, had rouge on, and lipstick, sometimes a barrette in her hair. What if he *did* take her up on the damsel in distress she'd played for him? The demimonde, an easy mark to do with as he wished. Then what?

She let the curtain go and came back to the sofa. The rain drummed hard on the rooftops. She wasn't going anywhere, and yet... She could still catch a tram across town to where Anneliese used to live in Kurfürstendamm: she might still be there. Gunther had once warned her to leave that woman alone. The last known lesbian in Berlin had long since been arrested, probably to be sent away with those others, like the feeble-minded, to Hadamar or Grafenek where death certificates were made out in advance. Could Anneliese still be in Berlin, alive?

She had no other friends to speak of. Gunther had been all she'd needed. All men wrapped into one, she'd once heard somebody say. The names she'd jotted down in her address book had no faces anymore. All the parties they had gone to blurred and the attendees shaken in a dice cup by the war and dumped out – men into the military, women left behind to wait.

She had the radio on low, tuned to the Reich Broadcasting station. In the window the rain began to let up a little. A burst of the late, low sun flooded in. Shadows chased it back, then it rose and dimmed again like the houselights in a theatre. She thought suddenly she'd hurry and get into something warm, find her umbrella and go out. By the time she got to Anneliese's, the storm could be over. She might pay another visit to OKA. Yes, she'd do that. She hadn't tried hard enough last time. This time give that rude *Frauenwerks* bruiser a piece of her mind, if she got her again. Demand to see her superior and refuse to leave until she did. Bluff or no bluff, you didn't want to fool with the legitimate spouse of General Gunther Straub.

She went over to the radio and was about to turn it off when the sound of rapping on the door caused her to jump. She shut off the radio, hurried to the door and was pulling back the bolt when she glanced down at her bare feet showing white on the

20

rug, but it was too late. The rapping came again. She opened the door.

The scarecrow of a man in uniform stood looking at her anxiously, hugging a large package wrapped in brown paper. His cap sat low on his ears. He grinned through rotten teeth. "I have a package for you, ma'am."

The bundle he was holding looked heavy.

"Who are you?" Geli said.

"Corporal Obermeyer, ma'am. This comes from Captain Stumpff." He peeked over her shoulder. "Where do you want me to put it?"

Stepping aside, Geli pointed at the sofa. "Right there will be fine. No message from the captain?"

"He's right behind me, ma'am."

Obermeyer stepped in, staring hesitantly at the cushions where she'd left a rumpled blanket. She yanked it aside, he lowered the package and stood back, rubbing his hands together.

Cold air came in behind him like he was the iceman.

"Warm yourself a moment if you'd care to, Corporal."

Just then Stumpff stormed through the open doorway, cap pulled low on his forehead, coat buttoned up to his neck. "What are you doing, Obermeyer? Didn't I tell you to go down to the car and wait?"

"Yes, sir. I've only just got here. She said I could -"

Stumpff raised his palm, strutted over to the bundle on the sofa and touched it with the tips of his gloved fingers. "A little something for your larder, Madame." He glanced back at Obermeyer. "What are you waiting for, Obermeyer?"

"Sorry, sir. Just rubbing off the cold."

Geli suddenly felt sorry for the wretched creature, and said, "I don't mind him staying, Herr Stumpff. He does look awfully cold."

"He knows better than to jump up on your furniture like some stray cat. Don't you, Obermeyer? Now that you're all nice and toasty, why don't you start acting like a soldier?"

"Sir!" Obermeyer riveted to attention, started stiffly toward the open doorway.

"And shut that door!" Stumpff commanded.

Obermeyer did, so carefully there was no sound of the latch catching. Stumpff paced toward the window, hands clasped behind his back.

"That man is like a child sometimes. He tried to join up with a combat unit, but the Wehrmacht wouldn't have him. He tested very poorly on his aptitudes. Plus he's a hemophiliac. For him there's no such thing as getting wounded and living to tell about it." He turned suddenly, exhibiting a grin. "When they found a place for him with me, I tried to throw him back, but eventually I had to take him. Since then, actually, I've found his loyalty rather makes up for what he lacks in brains. You'd be surprised how well he does behind the wheel of a car."

"To tell you the truth," Geli said, "I didn't expect to see you again."

Hands still behind his back, Stumpff sauntered toward her. "Will you sit down a moment, Madame? I won't take much of your time."

Geli moved toward the sofa, sat close beside the bundle and threw her arm across it, thinking some kind of apology was coming for the other night, and she was ready to tell him there was no need for that when he said, "I took the liberty of making some inquiries about your husband."

She searched his eyes that blinked as solemnly as a sheet being turned back from a face in the morgue. "Oh God, he's dead!"

"No. Not that we know of. I asked a friend of mine to do

some digging for me. He came up with some quite interesting information."

"Yes?"

"Do you remember sailing on a freighter from Rhodes to Bremerhaven in 1938? It was detained in Karpathos for suspected smuggling. Your name appeared on the manifest as Geli Straub. No Gunther aboard, however, just you."

Footsteps climbed a gangplank in her mind, she saw herself in the salt air on the lido deck, looking out at the streaks of twilight on the sea. The twinkling from the masts of fishing boats as they bore toward the steadier lights that sketched the harbor of Karpathos, and the sounds of the sea washed up on a song spun into the night from the bar – 'C'est l'amour qui fait qu'on s'aime.'

She said, "Yes. I had to sail back to Germany without him. We'd been on our honeymoon when he got orders to report to Athens. What about it?"

"General and Frau Straub appears on the manifest, even though one ticket was not used. I'd call this fairly persuasive proof of your marriage."

"But how am I to prove I was the woman who used my half of the passage?"

He looked down at her hand draped over the side of the package. "You might try putting on your wedding ring the next time you pay a visit to OKA."

She heard the gentle scolding in his tone, brought up her unadorned left hand. "Yes, if I hadn't had to pawn it."

He raised his eyebrows, swung his face away with a long slow-motion blink. "You may be interested in a couple of other items that my friend came up with. Probably nothing to worry about, since it all took place so long ago, when you were young and fancy-free."

He levelled a bemused look on her, and she saw herself in those heady days when she sang three nights a week for Max de Groof's dance band. There in the chorus line, fourth from the right – but if you weren't half naked, why be a Tiller Girl at all, the best show in Berlin? Out late with almost anybody who wanted her, a regular at the Rezidenz Casino where she could watch the sun come up while her escort's eyes beside her couldn't stay open long enough to get what he had paid for.

With a cocky lilt she drove fear out of her voice. "We all lived in a very different world back then, Herr Stumpff."

"How well I remember. Long enough ago to be forgiven by your marriage to a dashing General." He came around and sat beside her on the sofa, brushing her arm with his sleeve.

She didn't try to move away.

"Since we last spoke I've been wondering if you might consider doing a certain - well, let's say a little job for me." He held a cheery grin on her.

This was it, she thought.

The package sat there like it might contain a flimsy lace nightie.

Say yes and it would be all over.

He was saying, "It would entail your coming out of retirement for a time."

She gave him a long look, began to shake her head. "You don't mean -"

He clasped his hands across his belly. "Don't get excited. Nothing to involve the Abwehr. Merely a little arrangement, strictly between you and me."

"No, I'm sorry. I'm through with all that."

He sat back, gazing at the ceiling dreamily. "You haven't heard me out. Try to think of me as a man off the street, looking to hire a private detective. My organization, perforce, will remain in the dark."

"You're not serious. When I was in Cairo I had the Abwehr and my husband to back me up if anything went wrong."

"Or hang you out to dry."

"It's been too long, Herr Stumpff. I'm rusty, and -"

He brushed a rutting once-over from her legs up to her face, eyes like X-rays, empty of desire, scanning horseflesh. "I don't believe you've lost your touch. There's no substitute for the kind of talent that kept you from being shot in Cairo." He snuggled forward, wriggling over his elbows on his knees. "You wouldn't have to go away, need not ever leave Berlin. Simply assume your old identity – if those papers are still good."

"They're due to expire a year from now."

"How good of the Abwehr. Well then?"

She saw him, safe now from the harmless little dance he'd backed away from, and her throat filled with the kind of fear you can't tell from excitement as a cloud of Cairo like a dust storm bore down on her little life that she had grown so used to.

He plucked at the tips of his gloves.

She'd never seen his bare hands. They must be plump and pink, like strings of sausages ready to be dropped into boiling water. The bribe sat in the package beside her, now it was her turn. She said, "I don't know, Herr Stumpff. What would I be getting into?"

"To begin with I must warn you. Everything I tell you henceforth must be kept in strictest confidence."

"Yes, all right, but -"

He cleared his throat with a loud hack into his fist. "It wouldn't be unlike your Cairo job, except this man won't be so easy."

She threw a blistering look his way.

He went on as if he hadn't noticed. "I met this man before the war. He'd been arrested and imprisoned at Welzheim Concentration Camp for distributing seditious pamphlets protesting the absorption of Church youth groups into the Hitler Youth. I was a brash up-and-coming lieutenant, assigned to review his case. In his cell I found him to be near suicide – a man of celebrated successes as a Youth Group leader in the Church, going to utter waste. He wasn't ready to recant, but I decided not to turn away and let him rot. I took a different tack. God knows he wanted to get out, but how? It came to me that the very zeal with which he clung to his religious ideals made him an ideal prospect of our organization, so I put that to him. Agree to join up with the SS and I will speak in your behalf. It didn't hurt, either, that his father was a noted magistrate at Neuruppin.

"At first he balked, but didn't hold out long. My argument won over the review board, who saw things my way – much to the satisfaction of his father, I might add. He was assigned to train in Holland for our Hygiene Service, after which we went our separate ways. Till this day we've never so much as had a beer together, in fact I haven't seen him personally at all, since the day I bade farewell to him in Stuttgart. My fond memories of him went beyond the feather he was in my cap I had every reason to believe he would pan out as the model SS officer he seemed to have the makings of. You might say he became, from being my protégé, something of a son to me. The son I never had and never will."

He stopped a moment to watch her. "I'm in no hurry to do him harm. He's definitely on our side, for all intents and purposes. However, something recently has happened to cast doubts on the ideals I dressed him up in. I will *not* hand it over to the Gestapo and their clubfooted methods. I could be wrong, yet I cannot afford to leave a stone unturned. The Gestapo would plow up a whole field and eat everything in sight. That's where you come in."

"How do you think you'll get away with this?"

"With the utmost discretion between you and me."

"To what end?"

He took a deep breath, blew it out through puckered lips. "Gain his confidence. In a word, seduce him. You're French. As such you'll harbor anti-Nazi sentiments. Appeal to the religious side that may still lurk in him. In time he will begin to tell you things. He's married, but he and his wife live apart because of the nature of his work and for her safety. Your job will be to get him to talk about his work, pro or con. Get close enough to him and he'll open up."

"What kind of work would that be?"

"I'm not at liberty to say just now. You'll find out, or you won't. Anybody who talks about it will be shot."

"Then if he talks to me, his doom is sealed."

"Only if it gets repeated."

She looked at him, but he just stared back. She began to knead her fingers in her lap. "How long could I be left to run around with information that could get *me* shot?"

"Who's going to shoot a General's wife?"

"Unless that General is dead."

"All you have to do is play your part as if you really *were* Mlle Miroux, and you won't get hurt."

"So you say. How much time would I have?"

"I won't lie to you, he'll be a tough nut to crack. You might not even like him. When it's over, you'll resume your life as if the whole thing never happened."

She looked over at Gunther staring sternly back. "I don't like it," she said. "I don't feel up to -"

"What did you know about your subaltern in Cairo before you started in on him?"

Her eyes came up ablaze. "I'm not exactly proud of that, Herr Stumpff."

He clucked, waving a dismissive hand. "I'm sure you've got a lot more in you than you think, both inside and out. Age has only made you prettier. If I were in his shoes -"

"You wouldn't be trying to blackmail me, would you?"

"How am I doing?" he said merrily, eyes slipping past her onto the package she was sitting up against.

"I still don't quite understand why you don't put the Gestapo on this man."

"Because I don't want to be wrong. I brought this boy along. He was my piece of work, and I'm not out to get him. Understand? So what do you say?"

"Will you let me think about it, Herr Stumpff?"

He grunted, pushing off the cushions to get up laboriously. His tone was brusque. "I don't have a lot of time. Do me the courtesy of keeping our discussion to yourself." He stared down at her as he fitted on his cap, tugging down the bill to just above his scant eyebrows. "I'd better get down to the car before Obermeyer turns into an iceberg. Stay where you are, I'll let myself out."

He started briskly toward the door, and as she watched him she wanted to say something else, but didn't know what. Then it was too late. He opened it, went through and eased it shut behind him, soundlessly.

Geli looked down at the package, then began to tear it open. A bottle of wine rolled out, wedged itself between two cushions. She dumped out all the other goodies onto the sofa: several packs of cigarettes, a string of sausages, blocks of Grueyere and Munster. She picked up a cigarette pack, tore into it and tapped out a clutch of three from which she took one, regaling in the fragrance of tobacco. She plucked the top off her King Tut humidor, dumped out a few and lined them up, picked up the matchbook, tore one out and struck it. Holding the flame under the tip she took a drag, swooning as she leaned back. A little raw, she thought, but you didn't have to count it out because the bluebloods wouldn't touch one. She waved out the match and took another long, voluptuous drag. Not Melachrino Number Twos by any means, but not bad. Not bad at all. She looked over at Gunther still accusing her of something on the piano. "What about it, darling? Shall I do it? What if something awful happened to me? What if I had to sleep with a man I might catch something from? Would you hate me more than that time when _"

His unyielding stare told her she was wasting her breath. She thought she heard him saying, like old times, *"Sorry, dear, you're on your own. You never wanted to be loved for what I loved you for."*

The goodies lay strewn around like Christmas, and she sat there with a semblance of herself, so quickly was he gone, and her heart kept beating in its soundproof room. She slumped down a little and dragged again on the cigarette, and Cairo seemed to close in, the camels' dung and the heat in the dust outside, shimmering in the distance past the window and the sun that brought it down into the cooling breezes off the Nile. Would it be anything like that? Cairo all over again? The adventure!

The date palms and the stucco rooftops loomed, the paddle-wheel churned up the sultry smell of the green Nile under the long hollow honk of a smokestack. The waterfront bustled with white-clad boys. Should she put away her parasol to set foot on this land where Cleopatra watched from the books that she had gone to live in forever?

His name was Reggie, he said. Hadn't been here but three weeks, and you? 'Oh, I'm teaching French to officers like you. It's so awfully hot all the time, isn't it? So much worse here than in Tunis.' There on the terrace voices floated over the rattan chairs and the highballs, and it became their favorite table after that, and what she'd do with liking him so much she didn't know. Where they were – my God! It was as if the war was a million miles away. It raged out there like the long-gone agonies of the slaves that left the Pyramids for them to grasp, but couldn't. And she would look at him the same way, with no right to make him hers. He wouldn't stay, as if she'd never cried out 'I love you!' to a boy that young. Tomorrow he'd be on his way across the desert. Then he would come back to her. Others would die, but not him. He was the only one of them she loved.

She still had him like a ghost whispering, 'I need you.'

'The Jerries don't know what they're in for, Love. We'll get them good and proper.' And she could hear him loving her, and see his face in the dark when being jolly wasn't him at all. So she would think of him, years ahead, when the paddle-fan above their naked bodies stopped, and there across the sands where he must die he would tell her to shut up about such things, it was bad luck. Do you feel it? she'd say, and gesture into the cool breeze coming in from the verandah, her Pimm's Cup waiting on the table, and he'd lean over whispering you don't know how damned sexy you look all in a sweat like that, and she would have to tell him stop it, now, they'll think I work here. What's so bad about that? But she knew it was just for him, nobody else, how what was there for ogling eyes to take was his, and that was why he said it. And she loved him for it; how he could excite her so soon, then upstairs, as if the incense burning somewhere wrapped them up into that nether world that lasted like the life of butterflies – like that was where they burned and burned and for that night the Nile came

down silently along their naked bodies and they could fall asleep far from the bugle that would one day blow the charge into the impossibility that he could die.

She went over to the phone, looked down at it and dialed his door number, 3-0-8. The bell rang twice.

"Yes?" Stumpff's voice groaned sleepily.

"All right, Herr Stumpff," she said. "I'll do it. You forgot to tell me something."

"What?"

"His name."

"Not on the phone. We'll meet tomorrow morning. Breakfast, shall we say, across the street. Seven o'clock. We'll iron out the details, then we can go from there."

"All right. In the morning, then. Goodnight, sir."

"Goodnight, Madame."

3

The ticket agent said, "The converter station at Baumeister has been destroyed. The tunnel's collapsed at Innsbrucker Strasse and Bayerischer Platz."

"I want to go as far as Bulowstrasse," Geli said.

"That line is open up to Falkenberger Strasse, for now. You can expect delays. From there you'll have to walk unless the trams are running."

"All right, I'll take my chances." She went ahead and bought her ticket.

She took the underground as far as Falkenberger.

Night was coming on, storm clouds had begun to gather and she set off walking with directions from a passerby, hurrying to beat the dying light. Three blocks later she turned where she'd been told, and hadn't far to walk before she found the two-story building, labelled 47 in tarnished brass above the entryway, undamaged while a few doors down the skeleton of a wall gaped with its blown-out windows and the floors collapsed into a mound of timbers, splintered furniture and bricks. She climbed a flight of stairs into a dim corridor, turned right and with a few steps came to number 12, fourth door on the left.

Behind the door a radio blared: the tinny voice of a news commentator, not German. She hesitated to knock. But she was here, she raised her fist, then held back, listening. The voice was British.

"Reports from Stalingrad are sketchy, but communiques leave little doubt that the circle is closing in around the German Sixth Army, and only a matter of time remains before General Paulus will be forced to surrender and the Russians will emerge victorious."

Geli rapped, hard. She heard the screeching of a chair, the volume of the radio quieted, then clumping and the door swung open and a tall, good-looking man in uniform stood there, tunic open at the collar, lank blond hair falling carelessly across his forehead.

Behind the brilliance of his cobalt blue eyes, there was a sort of pain that humbled his good looks. A streak of something tired, or tender, that scratched itself across the hard surface like the scar that cut through his right eyebrow. He said brusquely, "Yes, what is it?"

"I'm sorry. I'm looking for Marlene Spilde. Is she at home?"

"There's no Marlene Spilde here. You've come to the wrong door."

"Oh!" Geli held her ground as the tinny British voice behind him weaved in and out of crackling airwaves: *"German losses have already mounted to staggering proportions..."*

He glanced back at the radio, then quickly back at her.

Before he could speak she said, "Would you happen to know of a Frau Spilde living in this building, sir?"

"No." He began to shut the door.

"Oh, dear," she said fretfully. "Somebody really steered me wrong."

He held back on the door. "I'm not acquainted with any of the other tenants here. I'm rarely home. Have you tried any of the other doors?"

"This was the one I was directed to. Frau Spilde has no telephone."

Behind them on the stove a teakettle began to shriek, piercing the voice on the radio. He marched back toward the kitchen, paused in passing the radio to switch it off. At the stove he turned the burner off. The teakettle sighed. Now he was coming back and she clutched at her turned-up coat collar, giving off a little shiver.

"Well, I'll be on my way. So sorry I bothered you, sir. May I just -"

"Yes?" he said irritably.

"Well, I was going to say I thought I'd seen you someplace. But that was so long ago, it couldn't be. Besides," she gestured with one hand, "the uniform -"

He stared at her through the narrowed space of the doorway. "What about it?" he said.

"Oh, nothing. These days everyone is wearing one. Back then the man - well, somebody would have to strap him down to put one on."

"I see. Before the war?"

"Yes."

"I have absolutely no recollection of you."

"You wouldn't. We never met - that is, the man you resemble."

"What was his name?"

"I'm sure I've got off on the wrong foot here, sir. Now before I make a nuisance of myself -"

She was turning as he pulled the door open a little wider.

"You're shivering."

She shoved both hands into her coat pockets. "Forgot my mittens again! Will I never learn?"

He spoke bluntly, unsmiling. "Step in for a moment if you'd care to."

She looked up at him, searching his face. "Oh, I've been bother enough already."

"Come in," he said, "if you're not fond of freezing."

She made her faint smile look reluctant. "Well, just for a moment. Thank you."

He stood aside as she slipped past him.

As soon as he shut the door she turned to say, "Sorry, I'm Simone Miroux." She held out her hand.

He took it gently, barely squeezing. "French?"

"Yes, I'm afraid I got stuck here with some friends after the war broke out. Those of us who tried to go back were detained. Even if they'd let me go, I didn't think I'd be that much better off in Paris, you know, what with the occupation. I scrape along now, teaching French. Frau Spilde was my latest prospect."

"Who was this man you knew before the war?"

"Oh, as I've said, I never really got to know him. Just admired him from afar. Young enough to get a girl's crush on him besides." She blinked at him, pursing a coy smile, then suddenly switched to a wistful, solemn look. "That all came to a rather fearful end one night. But I got over him, in time."

He folded his arms across his chest, shifted his feet around and cleared his throat. "What end?"

She frowned and hooked a finger on her lower lip. "Good Lord, I almost said if only you had been there! Ah, well."

He watched her as she let the lines drilled into her by Stumpff come back as if what happened long ago, borne on a lifeless curiosity, shook loose, and she could tell it all by heart, but she was there again as if she had been.

"This was in '36, at the Municipal theatre in Hagen. A play we had no business going to, my girlfriend and I, it was so *dreadfully* anti-Christian. I remember the title of it on the billboard: Wittekind. The author, Edmund Kiss, was signing programs in the foyer. We turned our noses up and passed him by as snootily as girls can. When we saw the Brownshirts stationed at all the exits, we almost turned around and left. But Hilda said let's go on down to hiss and boo, if nothing else. It might be fun, after what we'd read in the *Zeitung* about all the arrests they'd made the night before, and tonight they were expecting trouble. We were in, so we just found our seats down near the front and looked around at all the people, wondering which ones could be upstarts, like us. Then they all got quiet when the lights went down and the curtain rose. The actors came out like a cast of Molière freaks. Here was this skinny priest on his last legs, a big Nordic bully treating him like dirt for drinking wine out of a silver chalice. Pretty soon we saw where it was going, getting worse and worse, but we held off until Act III, afraid to be the only ones to howl a catcall, when this disgusting actor spouted a line so dreadful, so disgusting - well, you could hear a lot of people gasp when a man down in the front row suddenly leaped up and shouted something like, 'This is unheard of! We won't allow our faith to be publicly mocked!' No sooner did that bring a big hush down across the audience than the Brownshirts jumped him. Two or three at first, then a whole pack piled on and dragged him out into the aisle where they began to kick him and I thought my God, they're going to kill him! I made a move to help, but Hilda grabbed me by the arm and we were in the stampede in the aisle and everything was pandemonium! Hilda

36

dragged me to a side door and we got out, just in the nick of time."

He was looking at her and she saw him now behind some glass.

She pressed her face to it and blinked.

He said, "Quite some story. That could get you into a lot of trouble in Berlin."

She lifted her eyes saucily. "I haven't told it to a single soul till now."

"How do you know I'm not in the arresting business?"

She shrugged and made coy eyes at him as he stood there, looking down at her. "I guess I don't. Maybe I was hoping you could be that man I couldn't make myself forget in all these years. Any chance of it?"

"Your memory serves you a lot better than mine does, I'm afraid."

She pulled a smile to one side, making it look sad. "Well then, I'd better go out knocking on a few more doors. Some of the nicest things happen accidentally, *n'est-ce pas?*"

His tone suddenly took on an on edge, he eyed her more intently. "Odd that you never knew his name," he said.

"I might have if I'd read the *Zeitung* the next day. By then I was so discouraged, and afraid. Most of the Catholics from the audience had been rounded up."

He stared down at her, lips parting as if he wanted to say something.

He didn't, and she said, "Well, thanks for putting up with me, sir." She thrust her hand out stiffly. "Goodbye, then."

He took her hand mechanically with a faintly dazed look, saying nothing.

She turned toward the door.

He stepped around her quickly, turned the knob and pulled.

She hesitated in the open doorway. "*Au revoir,* Monsieur. If I should ever find myself over this way again, and chance to knock on your door, for whom should I ask?"

He gave her a long look before he said, "I'm rarely home, but Kurt will do. Kurt Langsdorff."

"Doesn't ring a bell," she said. "So it's as if I've never ever seen you in my life."

"So it is. Good luck finding Frau Spilde."

She said goodbye again, using 'Herr Langsdorff' this time, swung into the corridor and walked briskly toward the landing.

Nearing the head of the stairway she glanced back to see if he was there, the way a man will watch a woman's body from behind. He'd gone in. She was halfway down the stairs when she caught herself smiling. It hadn't been that hard. He did have the cobalt blue eyes Stumpff had said to look for, marred only by a scar some Brownshirt gave him to remember him by. Frau Spilde waited somewhere, pacing the floor.

Stepping off into the vestibule she started across, then stopped there beside the mail slots to catch her breath, feeling suddenly elated. She pushed out into the air full of that glow of twilight when you can feel rain gathering, and farther on, under a darkened lamplight, the air-raid warden standing just outside the entrance to the underground saluted as she passed. A drop of rain struck her face, making her blink.

A woman passed her walking at a headlong pace, glumly staring at the pavement. No smile on a night like this.

She looked up and saw the tram ahead, just coming to a stop, and she began to run.

4

Geli woke up to the cold nipping her face. That girlish happiness she'd come home with had worn off, and she lay there, trying to get it back. She'd got her foot in the door. Had that to tell Herr Stumpff. Not much, but he wouldn't be expecting much, this soon.

She threw the covers off, opened the curtains to a bright day. She felt like making herself look pretty, for nobody in particular. On her way into the bathroom she turned on the radio and left it while she dabbed on makeup and fixed her hair with a beret, snipped off a few grey strands. Strains of Wagner broke through the crackling airwaves, then a silence fell. There was a drum roll. She stopped patting on her rouge and turned her head to listen. It was a voice she knew, and it was solemn. She'd seen him once across the room at Missie Vassilchikov's when she'd been working at the Propaganda Ministry. The tone of a dirge was given to Herr Goering to declare:

'*The battle of Stalingrad has ended. True to their oath to fight to the last breath, the Sixth Army under the leadership of Field*

Marshall Paulus has been overcome by the enemy, and by the unfavorable circumstances confronting our forces. The Führer has proclaimed four days of national mourning. All theatres, movies and variety halls are to remain closed until it is over.'

Static washed again across another pause, then gave way to the crash of what she knew to be the second movement of Beethoven's Fifth Symphony.

A shock-wave seemed to buzz her body for a place to land, but it was all in shambles, burning. The war had come for Gunther, and if he hadn't died near Minsk she saw him being marched away to Siberia, doomed to fall by the wayside in that wasteland where his being a General wouldn't save him.

She got dressed hurriedly, went out and down into the sunshine and across the street.

The bell above the door tinkled behind her. The butcher was talking to a young woman, wrapping something. The girl turned, saw her and smiled just as the butcher asked what she wanted, and Geli said a pound of Bratwurst.

The girl glanced at her again, as if she wanted to say something. Geli said it for her. "Don't you live across the street?"

"Yes, ma'am."

"We've seen each other on the stairway. You may not remember."

"Oh no, ma'am. I do remember you."

The butcher handed Geli a package and she paid him.

The girl lingered there while he finished up with her, but turned to go as she was handing him the coins.

Geli caught up to her in the doorway.

The door shut with a jingle and they stood out on the wet sidewalk steaming in the sun.

"You're Herr Stumpff's housekeeper, aren't you?" Geli said.

"Why, yes. How did you guess?"

"Herr Stumpff told me about you."

The girl stared, letting a simper linger on her full, young lips. "Yes, you're that lady, aren't you?"

"I'm Geli."

The girl took her hand firmly. "Hanne."

"Shall we get out of this cold? Come up and we'll have some cake and coffee."

"I could only stay a minute."

Geli smiled at her, they hurried across behind the passing of a milk truck, and the girl was so lithe beside her, climbing the stairs.

She was the prettiest thing, so fresh and supple like she'd been an athlete, so bright in her eyes without the slightest need of makeup.

Geli couldn't help but wonder how long she would keep that glow about her, living with the likes of Stumpff.

The flat was warm as Geli had left it, and Hanne admired the surroundings as she got out of her coat, saying, "Oh, what a lovely place, ma'am! Don't I wish I had *this* to take care of instead of - oh, well. It's a job."

"Please sit down. I'll get the coffee."

When Geli came back with the coffee and some pound cake on a plate Hanne was admiring her camel's blanket on the wall. "My, but you've *been* places, ma'am!"

"Not for some time. The war shrank the world for us, I'm afraid. Brought it down to wondering when the British will start bombing us again."

"Any day now, Herr Stumpff says. The farthest away I've been from Germany was Paris, when I was very little. I don't remember much. A lot of glass in a shop somewhere. We were on a bridge once, and there was a sailboat down on the river. I think I remember I was happy."

"Will you take a little sugar in your coffee?"

"Yes, please. One lump."

They sat together on the sofa.

Hanne bit into her cake and smiled, as though apologetically, showing some crumbs on her teeth. "Such tasty cake, ma'am."

"I'm glad you like it."

"I don't bake for Herr Stumpff anymore. He hated my pancakes. He's such a grouch about some things. He likes to say I'm lazy, just because he sometimes catches me reading on his bed. Talk about lazy. He wouldn't pour a little cream in Trude's dish to save his soul."

"Trude?"

"Our cat. Well, mine. He blames me for all the hair stuck to his coat. The way I try to share my *Blutwurst* with the poor little thing. He wants me to throw her into the street, but I won't. It's impossible to stand up to him. I've never known a man like that. You've seen him, ma'am. All scrubbed and shiny like a - and you can shut your eyes till you go blind, but he's still there. You can smell him, clean as he is, but you see I thought I'd better offer him my body, or he'd dismiss me for not making the silver shine. Well, forgive me, but one time he found me in there cuddled up and waiting in his bed, and what was the first thing out of his mouth? 'Have you had your bath?' Like I'd defiled the sheets with a corpse or something! 'No,' I said, 'but I'm not dirty.' Oh, did he fly into a rage! All of a sudden Trude was a scourge, and I began to wonder if he was well, you know - all there." She picked up her coffee, held it poised under her lips.

"You mean crazy?" Geli said.

The cup clanked on Hanne's saucer, she shook her head determinedly. "He doesn't look like much, does he? But one night he came home and slammed the door so hard I almost dropped a plate. I'd got the table set so nice, but how does he treat that? Flings down his gloves and the knives and forks go flying. Then nothing but this awful, hateful red mask looking for something else to cleave. He does that - stares me down without a word and I know what it means. Something happens to him at his work, and when am I going to say what's the matter, Willy? Like a ritual. I felt sorry for him, really, right when I was so mad at him I wanted to walk right out of there and never come back. Imagine that."

"I didn't realize he could get so violent," Geli said.

Hanne reached down and fiddled with her cup in the saucer, twisting it this way and that. Finally, she left it there and said, "He's kicked me out, you know."

"What?"

"I've got till day after tomorrow. He wants me to be gone when he comes back from wherever he goes. I'm sorry, ma'am, but it all started when you came along."

"Me? But Hanne, I don't - what makes you think -?"

Hanne snickered, turning her head aside. She reached for her cup. "No, it's all right, ma'am. You're different. You're sure to do much better with him than I did." She took a sip of coffee, swallowed and a breath caught in her throat. She looked up, smiling.

Geli said, "Oh, but I -" Then stopped herself, and lowering her head she said quietly, "I'm sorry, Hanne."

Hanne lowered her cup carefully onto the saucer. "Oh, don't be, ma'am. It's not your fault. That's just the way he is."

"Yes," Geli said. Then she looked up. "What way?"

Hanne shrugged. "I don't know. Strange. I'll miss the work, but I'll do better without him."

"You mean -?"

"I don't know, ma'am. I just did what he wanted, and, well, begging your pardon, but if he wasn't - why would he prefer you?"

"No, no, Hanne. Really, it's not that way."

Hanne hunched her shoulders again. "Like I said, ma'am, it's all right."

Geli looked at her. The girl's fear sidled up to her and took its shape with hers, and she said, "Have you ever seen that driver of his?"

"Him? You know that awful thing's got eyes for me. It's like some snake got loose in the house when I come around a corner and it's right there looking at me."

"You're very pretty, Hanne," Geli said.

"Not for the likes of that one, thank you very much!" She tossed her head, then looking across the room she said wistfully. "I could have been Queen of the May at one time, if it wasn't for my lowly circumstances."

"Don't think of it that way. Nothing's going to stop you from finding somebody to make you happy one day."

She frowned at her hands in her lap. "Sometimes I think Herr Stumpff will never really let me go - alive."

"It's just the war. Once that's over -"

"Did you read about the awful end that's on the way to Stalingrad? First Moscow, now this? What's going to happen as soon as we get beat? He's done some terrible things in Poland that he bragged about. I'm scared of him."

"What things?"

"I daren't say. Something about the Jews. He wasn't some stupid little watchmaker, he said, some farmer spreading chicken manure. Don't let the 'Captain' fool you, he said. It's really *Obersturmbannführer*, Captain for short. That's why he's got the privileges: a car, a driver of his own. One night he blamed me for not knowing. He had big responsibilities! These people were our enemies. The Führer had a plan, and he was part of it. He wasn't going to be left out. When he was in Warsaw in the early days, he said, all they needed was to find so little as a pen-knife on somebody, they'd arrest him. They'd never be heard from again. They'd go up a chimney. That's where they end up anyway, he said, not nearly fast enough to please Herr Himmler. I started to cry and he got mad and ordered me to stop." Suddenly a gasp escaped her, then a sob she tried to swallow back.

"Oh, Hanne." Geli wanted to take the girl in her arms, but she was snuffing back her tears and with her fingers smearing them across her cheek. Geli reached for her shoulder.

Hanne looked up. "He comes to see you sometimes, doesn't he?"

"I met him on the landing, once. I've asked him to help me find my husband who's gone missing on the Russian front."

"Pardon, ma'am, but I wouldn't ask for too much help from the likes of him. You might end up like me."

"I'll be careful," Geli said. "Now, listen. Do you have any place to go?"

"I've got some people, distant relatives, in Leipzig. I used to play with Inga when we were little." Her eyes suddenly grew wide, groping. "You won't tell him I was here, will you? You don't know a thing about me, where I've gone. All right?"

"Oh no, of course, if that's the way you want it."

"You'll inherit him," she said with a broken little giggle. "One thing about him, though."

"What's that?"

"I sometimes wonder if he's really a man. I should know. I guess he is, but just be careful. That type, they'll kill you if you ever dare to call them out."

"What type?"

Hanne smiled sympathetically.

"Don't worry, ma'am. I didn't have the - you know, what it takes to handle him. Anyway, I never wanted to. I just did it. Maybe I'll miss the work, but not him. I should be grateful there's a reason to get out, now. I hate to say this, ma'am, but you can have him."

Geli made herself laugh. "If he was never man enough for you, Hanne, what chance d'you think I'd have *if* I wanted it?"

"You'd be better at it, ma'am. My temper's quick. I get scared easy, too. Bare knuckles, you know, the way us folks are with so little breeding."

"Breeding couldn't improve you one bit, Hanne."

"No, not where I'm going." Hanne held up a defiant smile. "You be careful, ma'am. Be very careful, won't you?"

"I will," Geli said. "Would you like some more coffee?"

Hanne looked into her empty cup. "Yes, ma'am, I think I would, if I'm not keeping you."

"You're not."

"Well then, thank you very much. You make the nicest tea I've had in ages."

"You mean coffee," Geli said.

"Oh, goodness! What's the matter with me?"

"Nothing. I wish I were you, so don't change a hair. Not one."

Hanne reared back, laughing, as Geli reached for her cup with a smile on her face she couldn't contain.

5

Days passed, and Stumpff had not come back. She'd never gone up to his door, and was not about to start. He'd come for her when he was ready. Night began to fall and Geli went to the window and stood there, looking down until the last car passed, the last of the lights across the street went out, and she drew the curtain like everybody else, and the city fell into blackness.

She made up her mind. She'd go back out on her own. If that meant breaking ranks, well, why shouldn't he reward her for initiative? She set out the next day at 4 o'clock, guessing she'd arrive near 6. There were the usual delays and it was getting dark when she began to climb the musty stairway, seeing in her mind his handsome face there in the doorway: what did she want, now? What's this woman up to? She'd have a big smile ready, cut off his suspicions with being glad to find him home.

She stopped a moment in the corridor, got out her lipstick, put some on. At the door she took a breath and braced herself to face the man whose eyes she hoped and prayed would light up at the sight of that woman who, way back in 1936, had got a girlish crush on him at a theatre in Hagen.

The door swung open.

A stocky old woman with a leathery face stood there in a thick woolen coat, unsmiling. Her skin down to her neck had the texture of an eroded hillside that ran into a ravine. "Yes?"

Geli stared at her, a nervous spasm almost made her look back down the empty corridor when she said, "Kurt?"

"No, dear, he's away. I'm the housekeeper, Leokadia Hintz. What do you want?"

"That's all right. I'll come back another time."

"Just a minute, dear. Who are you?"

Geli let out a breathy, nervous laugh. "Really, I'll come back some other time."

"What is your name, dear?"

"Simone."

"A friend of Kurt's?"

"Well, not exactly. We just met the other day when I came to the wrong door."

"This door?"

"Yes."

"I see. But now you're back because -"

"We had a chat," Geli said. "I thought I'd just come back to say hello."

The old woman frisked her with shrewd eyes. A not unkindly squint, tinged with a smile. "I'd say you could use a little warming up. Come in a moment."

"Oh, I really -"

"Do as I say before you turn into an icicle, dear." The old woman stepped back pulling the door with her.

Geli hesitated, eyes taking in Frau Hintz's heavy coat

buttoned at the collar. "I see you're going. I don't want to keep you."

"Keep me from my flat with no hot water and no radio to listen to? Goodness, you'll be doing me a favor."

"Well, thank you. I can only stay a moment." Geli stepped into the warm room, keeping her own coat on.

Frau Hintz started on her way back toward the stove. She lit a fire under the teakettle, got two cups down from the cupboard and came back and set them on the wooden table, bare except for an empty vase and a folded newspaper. She pulled out one chair and then another for herself. "What did you say your name was, dear?"

"Simone Miroux."

"What a pretty name. French."

"I was born in Italy," Geli said.

"Italy! My goodness! Take a load off, dear." Frau Hintz pointed. "Sit there in the master's chair. He'll never know."

Geli pulled out the worn wooden chair at the head of the small table.

Frau Hintz stood where she was and said, "He's kept you secret, dear."

"Oh, there's no secret to keep about me, ma'am. I mean, we had a little chat but that was all."

"Enough to bring you back, though." Frau Hintz pulled up the chair to Geli's left and sat on her bulky coattails.

"Yes, I couldn't help but think he looked like a man I'd known before the war. Except I found it hard to believe it could be him."

"Why not?" Frau Hintz smiled benignantly.

"Well, this might sound simple, but his uniform."

Frau Hintz reached for the empty vase and pulled it toward her, tipped it slightly, turning it, then righted it. "You mean SS."

"Well, yes."

Frau Hintz rocked the vase some more, let go of it. "I've grown used to that. It isn't him. A uniform's a uniform."

"Of course. Who's not wearing one these days?"

"But I can tell you one thing. He gave *me* a start once, too. Bowled me over. Sometime, perhaps, I'll tell you the story of how he saved my bacon."

"Why don't you tell me now?" Geli said.

"You'll have to promise not to repeat it to a soul, especially him. I'd never hear the end of it if he found out I bragged on him behind his back."

"I promise," Geli said.

Frau Hintz traced a circle with her nail on the table. Her eyes followed the movement wistfully. At last she said, "I'd been very happy working for a Jewish family in Steglitz for some time. They paid me quite handsomely, and I loved them all. One day the SS came for them and took them all away. The children, every one of them. I tried to find them afterwards, but the authorities told me I'd better go find work elsewhere. I landed a job, of all places, mopping floors and taking out the trash for the SS Hygiene Office, right here in Berlin. It was convenient, and they treated me all right until, one evening, these three young officers in the day room, loitering after hours - they wouldn't leave when I came in to mop. One of them, by the name of Baab, he'd needled me before, but this time with these others there to show off to, he took a notion to have some fun with the old lady, you know. 'Come right on in, Hintz! Let's see how good you got at cleaning up after those messy kikes.' Well, I got scared, but I went about my business, hoping they'd get up and go before I had to mop under the table. They didn't. So I went ahead and gently shoved my mop around their boots. The only one that didn't move was Baab. He shoved his

50

boots right out and made me slosh them, then sprang up so fast his chair fell over, calling me a clumsy cow. He ordered me to get down on my hands and knees and *spit* on his boot. 'Use your nice clean apron there to shine it up,' he said. Well, I was shaking with such fright, but I said 'No, sir, I won't spit on anybody's boot.' He flew into a rage. 'Not ladylike, is it!' That was when Kurt happened to walk in. He asked what the trouble was. Baab wasted no time bawling how this clumsy Jew lover had spoiled his shine, then refused to obey orders. I thought I was done for. I didn't know that Kurt was senior to these other three. My Lord, did he light into Baab! Told him he was going on report for disrespecting his elders, plus breaking the laws of the Teutonia! Baab turned so red you'd think flames would come out next, then he stormed out. Kurt helped me up. He apologized for Baab's behavior, then told me if I ever wanted to quit this place, he was in need of a housekeeper. I've been here with him now for two years. The happiest two years of my life."

Something in Geli stirred, and it was rough and dangerous like a squall at sea. She took a chance and said, "But it does make you wonder, doesn't it, Frau Hintz, what a man like him is doing in the SS."

Frau Hintz gave her a look before she shrugged. "Oh, I don't know. There's a war on, dear. You go where you're needed, and he's quite good at what he does." Frau Hintz looked up at the clock. "Goodness, I'd better be off or I'll miss my tram."

"Me, too," Geli said. "I don't like getting home in the dark."

"How far did you say you have to go?"

"Lichterfelde."

"I hope we don't get caught up in the rioting out there."

"Rioting?"

"Right under our noses. All because the government won't

51

release the names of our prisoners taken at Tunis. If all you listen to is Herr Goebbels' soap box, it's not even happening."

The teakettle began to whistle.

Frau Hintz got up, walked over to the stove and turned the flame off. "I'm afraid we've missed our tea," she said. "Perhaps some other time. Shall I tell Kurt you were here?"

Geli pushed her chair back and got up. "Oh, I don't know. Maybe not."

"But you've come all this way. He'll want to know."

"It might be better if you didn't."

"Why?"

"He might get the wrong idea."

"What's so wrong about it, dear?"

Geli shrugged. "The chances are he's married, *n'est-ce pas?*"

Frau Hintz placed a finger on her lower lip, spoke with a tinge of distaste, "Yes, he is, but you'd never know it. She's a pastor's daughter. I've never met her and he rarely speaks of her. She's being kept in Tübingen, for safety's sake."

"Oh." Geli started for the door, feeling a gush of hot blood in her face. "It was so nice of you to have me in, Frau Hintz. Thank you."

Frau Hintz was right behind her.

They met at the door.

Frau Hintz tucked in her chin a little to say, "No need to be a stranger, dear. A man needs all the friends he can get. I'm old enough to know I don't quite fill the bill."

Ten minutes later Geli was thinking about that, hearing it again as she climbed up onto the tram, and dropped her coin into the slot, and found her way back past people seated snugly, none of them with a smile as they glanced up, and she saw that she was going to have to stand.

6

The sunrise cast a thin gray light through the slowly lifting fog in Pilsudski Square. Corporal Obermeyer pulled the car around onto the wet, deserted boulevard. From the back seat, sunken in his overcoat, Captain Stumpff stared out at the passing remnants of the broken city: the charred façade of the Roen Hotel, its windows blasted and the lobby stuffed with shards of glass and splintered timbers, barely changed in three years, like a man found grotesquely frozen to the long-past moment of his death, or a chalk diagram where the body of a murder victim had fallen.

He looked out at the darkened lamp-posts, still dripping soot, the iron brackets curled under empty sockets like once dainty fingers from which teacups had dropped during the terrors of the Stuka bombing. It seemed to him so long ago, a dream whose startling final scenes had jolted him awake and he would never be able to go back to that September day when Warsaw cracked, and its radio replaced their polonaise with, most appropriately, a funeral dirge, and the German infantry, led by mounted officers, held their victory parade here in this very square.

Obermeyer wrenched the wheel leftward and squealed around the corner, tossing Stumpff against the armrest.

Sitting up, Stumpff gripped the top of the front seat with one plump, gloved hand. "Take it slower, Obermeyer. We're in no rush."

"Sorry, sir. I didn't want us to be late."

"No chance of that. They're not expecting us today."

"What I meant was for the train, sir."

"Pay attention to the road, Obermeyer. That's all you need to do right now."

Obermeyer went silent.

Stumpff looked at the back of his pink, raw-shaven neck, the stalks of his tendons moving as he pulled back on the gearshift. He'd known from the beginning that Obermeyer was going to be a problem. Rejected by the Wehrmacht as a bleeder, they had no place to put him. He wanted to serve, they'd said, insisting he was smart enough to drive. He could be company on these long trips, but he wasn't smart enough to know his place. Loyal as a bird dog, but then what did that make Captain Willy Stumpff? Did they ever pass out idiots to majors? Colonels? To the back of Obermeyer's neck he said in his mind, 'Just do the driving. Keep your nose out of things that don't concern you.'

Rivulets broke from the mist collecting on the windshield, and Obermeyer reached forward to turn on the wipers.

Stumpff slumped down in the seat. "I'm going to have a nap, now, Obermeyer. Wake me in about an hour."

"By then we should be there, sir."

Stumpff shut his eyes. The wipers swished and clunked. The tires hummed and Stumpff drew up his knees, snuggling against the armrest. Soon he was fast asleep.

Forty minutes later he opened his eyes to the sight of the

bleak arms of ash trees reaching for the car. The crippled black and rusting hulk of a Polish tank bristled with frost in the ditch.

"Where are we, Obermeyer?"

"Just clear of Lublin, sir."

"Lublin? How much farther on to Lvov?"

"No, sir, remember? Lvov would be too far."

"Yes, of course." Stumpff settled back, taking Obermeyer's impertinent word for it. His puffy eyes began to water as he looked out the window to his left.

There, far across the fallow field, a long string of boxcars crawled behind a locomotive belching smoke.

"Look there, Obermeyer. That's got to be our train from Lemberg."

Obermeyer looked, then suddenly tromped on the accelerator and the car surged forward.

"What are you doing, Obermeyer?"

"Don't worry, sir! I'll get us to the crossing first! They'll stall us for God knows how long if I don't!"

Stumpff felt vaguely annoyed by Obermeyer's taking matters into his own hands. All the more because he was probably right. A blast of steam shrieked from the locomotive and Stumpff looked harder for faces in the small, wired apertures. He thought those looked like children, peering out. That wonderful etching of Daumier's came to mind, *The Third-Class Carriage,* which he had once sold to a woman in his shop, giving her the discount he'd known she was holding out for.

Obermeyer gripped the wheel, bending forward. The needle on the speedometer crept past 60 as the train closed from the left toward where the tracks made a V with the road at the crossing.

Suddenly the car rose as if it would take off, bounced over the embedded tracks as Obermeyer kept his foot to the floorboard and the car jumped onto a rise and Stumpff saw in the distance the stark, tall chimney, the barbed-wire corridors enclosing simple, raw-planked shacks and the railroad siding that ran along the outer gate. Atop the farthest building back the Star of David perched like a tuning fork to catch the pitch of the wind that swept across the Great Mazovian Plain.

Obermeyer eased back on the accelerator, the car slowed to a comfortably cruising 45. A putrid smell began to seep in through Obermeyer's partly open window, and Stumpff reached for his handkerchief as the car slowed and the stench grew stronger with a sharp turn leftward onto the rutted road that ran parallel with the railroad siding.

In the middle of the yard behind a high fence strung tight with barbed wire, a rawboned, disheveled-looking officer gripped a riding crop as he stood reeling like a dour sea-captain trying to steady himself on a rolling quarter-deck.

He's been drinking again, Stumpff thought.

One of the two guards at the gate held up his palm as Obermeyer stopped to roll his window down.

The guard leaned in, glanced at Stumpff and then stood back saluting as the other guard pulled back the gate.

Obermeyer drove through. He swung the car around to a stop beside the officer, and Stumpff looked out at the pinched yellow face of the man he despised. He grasped the door handle as if his glove was a protective rag, pressed and got out.

The officer came toward him with a few more swats against his jodhpurs with the riding crop. "Well, well! To what do we owe the pleasure? We missed you yesterday, Stumpff."

"Sorry, Wirth. I was unavoidably detained." Stumpff tugged on the cuffs of his gloves, making fists as if to wring them out.

Voices across the yard caught his attention. He looked and there were a group of soldiers milling about three canvas-covered trucks parked in a semi-circle. One man threw down a cigarette and stepped on it.

"Just as well," Wirth said. "Yesterday's delivery didn't make it."

"What? Not again. You can't be serious."

"Oh, yes. Deadly."

"You notified the railheads, of course."

Wirth shook his head. "Too late. We went ahead as usual, the old way. What's the difference, as long as the job gets done?"

Stumpff tried to shake off Wirth's insufferable aplomb.

They both held the same rank, but Wirth always had to be the big man. The hunter, he once bragged, doing all the dirty work while others picked up their meat at the market. Big man, who wasn't too proud to order all his vodka from the commissary.

"You know how anxious Herr Himmler is to speed things up," Stumpff said. "You should know our new Zyklon works five times as fast as what you have been used to."

"So I've heard," Wirth said.

Stumpff grunted, turning up his collar as he looked out across the yard. He raised his arm, waggling a finger at the trucks. "Today's delivery, I take it?"

Wirth gave his pants a quick slap with the riding crop. "Today we've got a little problem on our hands."

Stumpff stared at him incredulously. "What kind of a problem?"

"A number of the containers were found to be contaminated, and had to be disposed of."

"Disposed of?"

"Yes. Buried, as a matter of fact."

Stumpff's bulging eyes stung with keeping them on Wirth's steady leer. "Who was the officer in charge of this shipment?"

"Why, he's still here. Right over there. Lieutenant Langsdorff."

Stumpff felt the name like a blow out of nowhere. He said, "Surely there are enough containers to go through with today's operation."

"I'm afraid not."

"Impossible. What am I supposed to tell Berlin?" he fretted.

"Don't get too exercised," Wirth said. "We'll proceed as usual. In the end it's all the same."

"No! I want an explanation, Wirth." He turned his head to look across the yard again.

The tall young officer came around the front of the lead truck, lifted one boot up onto the running board and spoke to the other men. The left sleeve of his tunic had been torn away at the shoulder.

Wirth blared across the yard, "Hold up there a minute, Lieutenant! A word before you go!"

"No, no!" Stumpff bleated. "Just tell me -"

"You want an explanation? Why not get it from the horse's mouth?"

The young officer, now up in the cab, stared over his elbow through the open window. The door swung open and he climbed down. As he began to march this way Stumpff watched him, and the haze of time stirred in his mind around the height of him, the blond hair under his cap, the strangeness of his swinging one clothed and one bare arm; cobalt blue eyes and the scar that cut through his right brow closing like a short-cut from the past. Pulling up breathlessly the young man said, "Yes, sir?"

"The Captain here would like to know what happened to your sleeve."

"It's perfectly all right, sir. No harm done."

"*I* know that," Wirth said, "but why don't you go ahead and tell the captain how it happened?"

The young officer started hesitantly, as if he wasn't sure which man to address, and as his eyes came over onto Stumpff, something in him jumped. "Well, sir, it started at the supply depot in Kolin when we were being loaded up, and the foreman mentioned to me, by way of a reminder, that they had been directed to use up their oldest supplies first. That being the case, it occurred to me that an inspection was in order, but rather than hold things up there in the warehouse -"

"Inspection why?" Wirth cut in peremptorily.

"Yes, sir. You see, the crystalline form of potassium cyanide tends to become unstable with age: the older, the more dangerous. So I waited until we were several kilometers out on the road before I stopped the convoy. After inspecting seven or eight of the containers I found exactly what I'd been afraid of."

"Which was?" Wirth prompted.

"That we were carrying material which had reached a dangerous state of deterioration."

"There you are!" Wirth brayed. "He saved our asses, and in the process splashed some of the acid on his sleeve and had to tear it off. He could have unloaded all those bad containers on us, but no, he ordered his men to bury them right there on the spot. Good goddamn thinking, if you ask me. We can thank our lucky stars he wasn't some ignoramus who just wanted to get things over with and breathe easy."

The same thing reported by the commandant at Sobibor, Stumpff reflected, in connection with the name, Langsdorff. He looked at Wirth. "Do you mean to say that every last one of the containers were buried?"

"Ask him." Wirth flipped his riding crop at the lieutenant.

"No. But the seven or eight we did bury convinced me that

most if not all of the others had to be bad. It was a matter of degree, depending on the dates on the containers. We held some out to be used up as disinfectant."

Stumpff watched the lieutenant's eyes. They were hard. Too hard, he thought, to be the man he used to know. He said haltingly, "So that means this delivery, on top of yesterday's, leaves us too short for today's procedure."

"Listen, Stumpff." Wirth moved up close to Stumpff's face, "Imagine if we'd broken into any of those bad drums. Some of us could have been killed. I won't write up a man for breach of conduct when he spared us the surprise of choking on the goddamn stuff that really wasn't meant for us, now was it?"

Stumpff backed away from the fetid vodka breath, saying in a weak voice, "This isn't going to cut much ice with Berlin."

"Never mind Berlin," Wirth said. "Who's the expert on toxic gasses around here – if you're thinking of contradicting my report commending the lieutenant for his initiative?"

Stumpff stood up straighter pulling back his shoulders. He felt the young man's eyes on him, watching from two places: there so close he could reach out and touch him, the other from the distant murky nightmare of a prison cell, waiting to be claimed. He said crustily to Wirth, "My own report, as you well know, must be confined to the efficiency with which you have been carrying out Herr Himmler's orders."

Wirth sighed heavily, rolling his eyes. He looked down at his watch. "We're running short on time for our tour. Stick around, Lieutenant. I'll dig out one of my spare tunics for you to wear on your way back to Kolin."

"Thank you, sir, but I've been told to get the trucks back to the warehouse before dark."

Wirth looked up from under baleful eyes. "Let that foreman bite his nails. You'll get back when you get back. We're all in this together, you know. Go on and tell your men, then catch up to us. Clear enough?"

"Yes, sir." The lieutenant turned and took off at a quick-step, then broke into a jog across the yard.

Three men pacing around the trucks sucked on their cigarettes and let them drop.

Stumpff watched him talking to the men. Something was getting away from him. What were the odds? He felt glad, for a change, that he had gained a lot more weight than rank in these past years. He said to Wirth, "How well do you know that man?"

"Langsdorff? He's one of Colonel Fritch's darlings. Recently promoted to Head of Technical Disinfection. Heard of him?"

Stumpff let a stare at Wirth break off the sight of him. A voice came to him from long ago when he had saved a boy from rotting in a prison cell forever, knowing he could make him almost from the bottom up like one of Arno Breker's sculptures. From the wet clay of the Church to the sentinel at the *Ordensburg Vogelsang*. This didn't seem to fit – that jarring unexpected air of hardness, some almost ruthless undertone. Nothing like the desperate man of God he'd saved from martyrdom. Which one of them was he, now?

"I did know a Langsdorff once, before the war," he said.

Suddenly a clanking sound came from a troop-truck backed against the concrete building several yards beyond the shacks. A burly sergeant was draped over the fender, half-buried in the chassis.

"What's going on up there?" Stumpff said.

"Ah, that's Heckenholt, our mechanic. We'd be lost without him. Berlin does nothing but ignore our requests for spare parts."

"Spare parts? Surely you've given up on that since Himmler's orders came down."

Wirth didn't answer. He wheeled and began to move away

in the direction of the truck, saying, "Just a moment, Stumpff. I'll be right back."

Stumpff watched him striding purposefully away, switching his riding crop like a tail to keep flies off.

All at once a voice beside him said, "All squared away, sir." Langsdorff stood there stoically, tugging down his cap.

"Ah, yes. Wirth's gone up there," he pointed, "to have a word with the mechanic."

Langsdorff stared at him for a moment, then said breathlessly, "I'm very sorry, sir, I didn't recognize you before."

A strange wind swept in across Stumpff's heart, stirring up the past.

They were alone. It was his turn to apologize.

There was a troubled smile on the young man's face. "Don't you remember me, sir? Kurt Langsdorff. Welzheim Concentration camp, 1938."

Stumpff let his face split open suddenly, feigning surprise. "By God, of course! It's been so long. And you in that uniform. It just didn't register. I thought I'd seen the last of you - what has it been? Five years, now?"

Stumpff thrust out his gloved hand, Langsdorff took it and they shook lustily. "I must say you look splendid, splendid. I've often thought of you, you know, with every confidence in the outcome of your plans. Of course I never knew, because we parted ways. Who'd have thought, back in that dreary prison - I can tell you, *I* knew from the start you had it in you to become *somebody*. And look at you! I should have tried to look you up, but you know how it is, the war, and, well, by not hearing anything I knew damn well you must have made good, somehow or other."

Stumpff noticed a pained look coming into Langsdorff's eyes.

He changed his tone and said, "Did you ever marry that girl you were engaged to, Kurt? The pastor's daughter?"

"Yes, sir, the year after I got out of Welzheim."

"Well, that's - any children?"

"No sir, not yet."

Stumpff shook a finger at him. "Better not let any grass grow under. You're still living in -?"

"Tübingen, sir. Not me, my wife is there. I've got a flat in Berlin. Elfriede will remain in Tübingen for her safety."

"Ah, yes, Elfriede. How could I forget that day -"

Wirth's voice across the yard brayed, "Good man, Heckenholt!"

Just then in the distance a train's whistle shrieked.

"Do me a favor, Kurt," Stumpff said.

"Yes, sir?"

"Wirth doesn't need to know about our past acquaintance. So not a word about that if you don't mind, all right?"

"Of course, sir."

There was a crunch on gravel to their left.

Wirth came up to them, shaking his head. "That Heckenholt. A miracle worker if there ever was one. All right, gentlemen, we haven't got much time. Follow me."

Wirth made a wide arc with his riding crop as he set off toward the idle row of shacks, enclosed by wire, and Stumpff, motioning Langsdorff to go ahead, fell in behind and they caught up to Wirth just as he reached the entry to the wire corridor, behind which signs identified the row of shacks one after another like store-front shingles: VALUABLES, CLOAK ROOM, HAIR DRESSER. A sign strapped to the wire read: TO THE BATHS AND INHALATION ROOMS. Over the door to the final, larger building Stumpff made out the words: HECKENHOLT FOUNDATION. Wirth stopped and swept his hand out with the flourish of a swelling Italian tenor. "We call this the bank. They're told to turn in all valuable items at this wicket – jewelry, watches, currency – to be returned of course after they've stood under the showers."

Stumpff looked in at the rain and dust spattered wicket. With a glance back at the few men milling aimlessly around the trucks he was about to speak when jets of steam came into hearing from the train, and he hurried on, slick leather soles slipping on the frozen pebbles.

Abreast of the shack called the Cloak Room, Wirth turned to say, "This is where we make them take their clothes off. We tell them we'll be sending their things to the laundry, and they'll get them back as soon as they've had their baths. So they come out of here, and then..."

Wirth leaned around into the hand in his pocket and the arm under which his riding crop was pinned, strolled on a few more yards. "...from here the men are herded on, but the women are detained to file into this room quite naked, except for their hair, and we take that from them, too. You'll be amazed at what we do with this hair. We stack it in bales and ship it out of here. It's finally converted into industrial felt. That's right! Woven into slippers for our U-boat crews! Nothing goes to waste! They have no idea how much they're helping our war effort. What do you suppose our U-boat men would think if they knew they were walking on the tresses of Jewish bitches!"

With a twisted smirk Wirth waited for a response, got none and then moved on until he stopped again a few feet from a dented, tin-plated door on a large concrete building with no windows.

"If you'll excuse me," Wirth said, "I'll only be a moment." He walked around the corner and strode up to Heckenholt, who slid off the fender of the troop truck, holding a wrench, nodded at some words Wirth spoke, took a pat on the shoulder and climbed up into the cab on the driver's side.

Wirth turned and, planting his boots widely apart, swatted the side of his trousers with the riding crop. The tin-plated door opened and a tall, barrel-chested sergeant stepped out, snapped to a salute. Wirth's arm rose languidly, he smacked the palm of his free hand with the thick of his riding crop.

Stumpff watched the sergeant's sooty, well-fed face for some fulsome expression, but just then Wirth turned to come back, haughtily lifting a thin, cold smile. In a loud voice he said, "Who needs Berlin when we've got Heckenholt, that's what I say!"

Stumpff pointed at the top of the building where the barrel-chested sergeant stood. "That sign," he said. "It's ridiculous. You really ought to take it down."

"What are you talking about?" Wirth snarled. "Do you know where this place would be without Heckenholt? The sign stays."

"I wouldn't insist on that, Wirth."

Langsdorff started to speak, but his mouth became a soundless cavern in the sudden deafening screech of iron wheels on tracks.

Steam sprayed the cold with more steam, the couplings slammed and strained, the locomotive backed a little, settling into a long echo of iron across the stillness of the fields. The train jolted once more, then stopped. Ukrainians, pouring out of a barrack, came running toward the boxcars, knocked out bolts, pulled back the heavy carriage doors. Faces packed the frames of sudden air and light. The Ukrainians shouted orders, men and women began to jump down. On the ground they held their arms up to the elderly and the smaller children. Some women handed infants down. The Ukrainians laid about them with their whips. A bearded old man stood apart, picking bits of straw from his hat. A Ukrainian jabbed him with the thick end of his whip. The old man stumbled and in his eyes there was a groveling for dignity as if it were a pair of spectacles he couldn't see without. A little boy wandered this way and that among them, handing out bits of string.

Among the heaps of dead left in the boxcars, some of the bodies were small. A little girl, her tangled hair pinned with a bow, lay on top of a woman.

One of the Ukrainians climbed into the boxcar. He whipped at several corpses. When none of them moved, he picked up the arm of a slender young man who was dressed as if for some occasion. His shoes were missing and one side of his boiled collar had sprung away from its attachment to the shirt. The Ukrainian dragged the corpse to the edge, gave it a shove with his boot. It made no sound as it hit the ice-hard ground.

The Ukrainians were barking orders: "Hurry, now! It's cold out! We'll get you into a warm place! Your valuables will be returned to you!"

From the far end of the Cloak Room people were already stepping out, naked, onto the frozen gravel walk that led to the Hairdresser's. Women hugged themselves. The barrel-chested sergeant beckoned them on toward the building containing the baths and inhalation rooms, where the three officers stood outside the wire, watching. The sergeant spoke in his dulcet, priestly voice, "All the way up here! Don't be afraid! You'll have a bath for disinfection! You've been a long time on that train! Come along, nothing will happen to you! Breathe deeply! It's good for the lungs!"

"My God," Stumpff said, "naked in winter. They'll catch their death."

Wirth rolled his shoulders, saying, "That's what they're here for, isn't it?"

The line began to pack together between the Hairdresser's

and the Bath House, where the tall sergeant waited. A little girl dropped a pearl necklace. She tried to pick it up but was shoved on and she began to cry. Another child asked his mother for a drink of water. She bent down and told him softly that he would have to wait. There might be some after their shower. A man was speaking to a boy of about ten. The boy began to cry and the man pulled him close, pointing at the sky. Suddenly from the Hairdresser's a beautiful young woman stepped into the cold.

Stumpff's eyes dropped from her lovely dark face down the length of her body, along her tawny legs to a pair of delicate ankles, in which he saw the tendons flex as she stepped on the gravel, and the drizzle glistened on her shoulders where, just over the left collarbone, a dark mole dotted the smooth waxen slope to her breast. He hauled in his glance, then held his eyes on her face. A face that now stared back at him with hatred. She made no attempt to cover her breasts, or to wipe away her tears. The crowd behind her shoved. She stumbled on ahead. Stumpff saw her prettiness drawn up into hiding from the light of a piano lesson, a girl long ago where he'd been visiting, and he walked in on her but hung back, waiting for that smile at the sight of him, 'Come over here, Willy, I'll show you how.' The ugly needn't wait. She'd made fun of him out by the pond. Somehow he'd make her cry. Like this girl now where in his mind she lay on a pillow in the dark, looking at dreams into which her father would soon whisper, unheard, 'Good-night.'

All at once the girl's blazing eyes found Langsdorff. She laid her finger on her chest between her breasts, stabbed the finger into her bare skin and cried bitterly, "19!"

Stumpff swallowed. A voice so close it startled him like thunder moaned, "Jesus!"

He looked at Langsdorff's ashen face beside him, at his shoulders trembling, eyes fixed on the girl. Only natural, he thought like a plunger on revulsion. Pick out the handsome one, for all the good that would do her. Grief could wait till after they were dead, and there was nothing you could do about it anymore.

"There's a fetching one," Wirth bleated. "She fancies you, Langsdorff. Why don't I pull her out? I could give you, say - half an hour with her?"

"For God's sake, Wirth!" Stumpff snapped. "Lieutenant Langsdorff is a married man!" Then realized in horror that that he was not supposed to know.

Wirth cackled. "If I was married, she could make me wish I wasn't!"

Langsdorff stood there stoically erect, saying nothing. The girl now had been pushed on, lost in the crush ahead.

The dulcet voice of the sergeant standing beside the open tin-plated door droned, "Come along now, everybody. Don't push. It's warm inside. You're going to be disinfected. Remember now, breathe deeply."

Men and women pressed against each other in the line with shuffling steps.

Stumpff couldn't see the girl anymore. She'd looked at him but passed him by. He wouldn't make himself remember her. Remembrance claimed too many dead for one to matter. From the numbing enormity of death the trivialities came forth: steam from a waiting train, the grey light rushing frost and dirt, moles and scars at the slow circling of a morning that would return westward, like the train, empty. In his mind he saw Langsdorff on a camp bed with the girl. He heard a pounding on the door when time was up.

White feet mussed the gravel. The sergeant sometimes reached for a shoulder with a gentle gesture. He stepped in front of a little boy whose mother quickly drew him back by the shoulders.

"That will be all for now!" The sergeant bellowed. He rammed the door shut, drew the iron bolt. Looking at Wirth, he nodded. "Like a well-run laundry, sir! We'll have them all brand spanking clean in no time! Heavy on the starch!" The sergeant beamed as he caught sight of the little boy staring wonderingly up at him. He laid his hand on the little bald head and gently patted his cheek. "Just look at where we've got ourselves, my boy. Head of the column. You're the commander of the troops!"

The little boy stared upward from his big brown eyes. His mother pressed him back under her breasts. Her eyes glistened with hate.

The sergeant looked again at Wirth, indicating the corner around which Heckenholt sat waiting in the truck.

Suddenly a pretty, strapping girl bolted from the line and began to claw her way along the wire.

One of the Ukrainians unfurled his whip and drove her back.

She slipped and sprawled onto the gravel.

A man who could have been her father broke from the crush of people, shouting "Ewelina!"

Wirth drew his pistol.

Two guards charged in from the yard. The one who got to the man first drove the butt of his rifle into his face. The man staggered backwards with blood pouring from his crushed nose. In the line a teenage boy shook sobs into his hands. An old woman screamed something in Hebrew. The baby in her arms began to cry.

"Take that girl to D-Barrack!" Wirth bawled. "Tell the hags to put some clothes on her! If that bastard there is still alive, put him back in with the others!"

Stumpff thought, he wants her for himself, the filthy lout. Then it came to him again, how wrong it all was. What was the use of Heckenholt, if...

Heckenholt sat waiting in the truck.

Wirth motioned to him, and Heckenholt reached forward, pressed on the starter and the motor whinnied.

Stumpff felt a flushing from his brain, all going down to nowhere. He tried to gird himself. He wanted to stop everything, but it was too late. Before he could think he opened his mouth, but nothing came out.

Wirth had been watching him. His face contorted with a deadly scowl. "For Christ's sake, Stumpff. Pull yourself together."

Heckenholt's boot knocked on the floorboard. The throttle clicked. A smell of diesel fuel laced the breeze. Heckenholt climbed out of the truck. He lifted the bonnet, reached in muttering to himself. He rammed the bonnet shut, climbed back up into the cab.

Wirth said, "Don't worry, gentlemen. Heckenholt's the best spare part we've ever had," and he roared laughing as the sound of weeping broke out in the building.

Stumpff gulped down a wave of nausea, brought his chin up sharply feeling the lumpy skin stretch out of his collar.

There was a movement to his left. In Langsdorff's hand a stopwatch ticked.

"What are you doing, Kurt?"

"For your report, sir," Langsdorff said. His voice was thick and tremulous, squeezed off by some encroaching gag.

Suddenly the truck fired up. The motor coughed a few times, then Heckenholt goosed it to a steady, throbbing roar.

From the fainter sounds of weeping in the gas chamber a piercing shriek arose. A man wandered from the other naked people waiting in the cold. He held out trembling hands in a supplicating gesture. "Will no one give us water to wash the dead?"

A guard shoved the man stumbling back into line. "Stop babbling about the dead! Nobody's dead!"

Stumpff felt himself reeling. His mind began to whirl. They were witnessing a debacle. He felt guilty of letting them get by with it. He'd never once lied to Berlin, yet now in order not to contradict Wirth's commendation he must falsify a report to spare the man who was to blame. The very man he'd been so proud of once, now delivered unto the velvet hands of a spy. How had it ever come to this? Why did it have to be *him*?

A mother held a freezing child close as she leaned against the shivering flesh of a stranger.

Heckenholt let off on the accelerator, the motor throbbed, then idled unevenly. In the cab he leaned back, lighting a cigarette.

A group of Ukrainians, carrying hammers and pliers, ran toward the rear of the building.

The big sergeant waiting near the tin-plated door looked down at the little boy shivering against his mother's legs. "You haven't been crying, have you, commander? That's not the way to do it. The commander never cries. He's the strong one. He's the one who gives the orders."

7

There across the room from his perch on the piano Gunther stared as if being dead was his excuse for hating her.

She marched toward him, picked up the frame and slammed it face-down on the polished wood. On her way into the bedroom she turned out the light and felt her way along the familiar path to bed. She pulled the covers up to her chin. Just then she thought she heard a rapping on the door. She waited a moment. There it was again. She flung the covers off, threw on her dressing gown and flopped out in her muff mules to the door. She pulled it open.

Stumpff stood there, looking tired in his rumpled uniform. He pulled off his cap and looked her up and down. "My apologies, Madame. I know it's late."

Geli became aware of being out of breath. "Yes, I was in bed."

There was a sooty look about his face. He stared at her through bloodshot eyes, beneath which dark crescents hung like shadows.

"Come in," she said, swinging the door open.

He plodded in, brushing a faint putrescent smell past her, made straight for the sofa and sprawled onto it. "Aahh!" He lifted one dusty boot, examined it, then let it fall back with a thud. "Forgive me, Madame, I know I'm a sight."

"I can see you're awfully tired."

"If you think *I* look tired, you should see Obermeyer. Those roads in Poland - some of them goat paths at best. Next time I'll take the train." He sat up a little, gloves still snugly on.

"I've seen Langsdorff," she said.

He pushed himself more upright, patted the cushion beside him. "Excellent. Come over here and tell me about it."

She went over and sat beside him, crossed her legs and let the silk slip back behind her knee.

"All right, then, what've you got?" Stumpff said.

"Not a great deal, yet. He seemed to like me, but these things take time, if you know what I mean."

"I do indeed," Stumpff said softly, his voice tinged with wonderment as he let a smoldering leer come out from under his heavy lids. "How did your story go over, the one we rehearsed?"

"I'm pretty sure he bought it. I played it straight, threw in a little shivering and he asked me to come in."

"You had your looks to keep you warm."

She pursed her lips to toss that off. "There was one moment," she said.

He was watching her narrowly, mouth slackly open. "Yes?"

"When he cornered me about the oddity of being a French woman living in Berlin. I made it sound like French instructors were in demand."

"Pretty ones." He grinned.

"One thing," she said, "I caught him listening to the BBC. He had the volume turned up quite loud."

"How loud?"

"Loud enough for anybody to hear out in the corridor or the next flat."

Stumpff flung one hand out carelessly. "One of our privileges forbidden to the average citizen. I tune in to those lies myself when I get bored. How do you think he'll feel about your going back?"

"I have already."

"Oh!"

"This time he wasn't there. His housekeeper, Frau Hintz, invited me in and we had quite a nice, long chat. She told me the story of how Langsdorff came to her defense one time when she was treated badly by some rude young officer."

"Ah, yes. That would have been Lieutenant Baab. Apparently the churl had it coming. Kurt *is* one officer you don't want to rub the wrong way." He gave her a sidelong look, then moved slightly and didn't seem to know that, pressing up so close against her, his arm touched her breast.

She let it be.

He said, "Getting chummy with the housekeeper won't hurt, but I wouldn't overdo it."

"It wasn't hard to like her," Geli said.

He put his hand out just above her knee, then took it back and buried it with the other hand between his legs. "You seem to be off to a good start, Madame. Keep it up, but you're going to have to go one better."

"What do you mean?"

"I want you to pay close attention to his deportment – moments of distraction, sullenness, perhaps, distress you can't see any cause for at the time."

"Well, I've already -"

"No, things have come to light since I last saw you. Quite

74

disturbing things I will be counting on you to tap into. Understood?"

"Yes, of course. You were right about one thing. He'll be a tough nut to crack. I don't know whether -"

"Do you want out, Madame?" he said with a flash of annoyance.

"No, I'm only saying I sometimes don't know where I am. Feeling around in the dark. It would help if -"

"We've been over this. Don't ask me to say things for which I could be shot."

"Saving a bullet for me, too, besides the cheese and cigarettes."

"Bullets are no laughing matter, Madame."

"No laugh intended, sir."

He held up a gloved palm. "Listen to me, now. I have some information about your husband."

Geli clutched at her dressing gown. "What kind of information?"

"My friend dug up some items that could have a bearing on his whereabouts. Or his fate. This happened in June of '41, at the height of Guderian's drive to Moscow. Some of it made the newspapers, but not ours. Guderian was rushing ahead in his armored command vehicle when he came upon a roadblock some 60 kilometers south of Minsk. He got behind a machine gun and personally fired on a Russian tank. Quite a reckless thing to do, but that's Guderian for you. The tank fired back, killing two other generals by his side. The Russians hurried to print this incident in their newspapers, stating that Guderian was killed. This proved to be untrue, but my informant's attempt to learn the identity of the actual victims came to nothing. The incident was suppressed. You can see why. The assault on Moscow had begun to stall. Hitler's orders to divert to the

Ukraine was proving costly. We didn't need any more bad news from Russia. Especially not of an embarrassing sort for Guderian. The truth kept under wraps is no sin in light of the judicious manner, for the sake of morale, with which Herr Goebbels keeps us in the dark. Now you say your husband went to Russia as a part of Guderian's staff."

"Yes. Then are you saying Gunther could have been one of those generals killed?"

"Not with any certainty. No names have been released. One could say that things add up. The time of your last letter from your husband, the runaround you get from OKA, your stipends cut off. They can't afford to acknowledge the existence of a casualty not approved by the Minister of Propaganda."

She understood, and suddenly felt empty in this raw light on the selfishness with which she'd done away with Gunther in so many other ways than the bullets he had no defense against. "You're telling me he's dead, then, aren't you?"

"No. There is every chance of it, but not necessarily."

She turned toward the piano and saw that Gunther wasn't there, as if his ghost had blown him over.

Stumpff's head turned at the same time, following her gaze. "Looks like your photograph fell over, there, Madame."

"Oh! I was dusting. Stupid me." She got up and hurried over to the piano, picked up the frame and used a reverent touch to pull the prop back out and stand it up. She came back to him and sat down, this time not so close.

Stumpff's crooked finger came up under her chin, lifting to get her into his line of sight. "You mustn't do a lot of worrying, Madame. Leave the worrying to me." He got up laboriously. "You've done well, so far. I'm going to be away again for upwards of another week. I've instructed Obermeyer to keep the car at your disposal in my absence."

"I can do without that kind of transportation, thank you."

"Don't be silly. Make it easy on yourself."

"I'd rather walk than -"

"Now, now. Throw the poor man a bone. He's going to have his feelings hurt."

She emptied a groan into a whimper. "What about my feelings?"

"I'm only saying if you need a ride, he'll be at your disposal."

"Going off again to Poland?" she made innocent eyes at him, hearing Hanne in her mind again.

He levelled a dark look on her, letting it linger. "It goes without saying you're never to mention my name. Not to this Frau Hintz. Nobody. If Langsdorff should ever make mention of me, in any context, you're to report that to me at once."

"Of course," she said.

"We do travel together occasionally. The fact is, he's about a day behind me in Warsaw. Make it easy on yourself and try to cooperate with Obermeyer. Why should you stand for hours on the underground?" He reached for his cap, ran his fingers around the sweat band.

"Don't expect me to be taking any joyrides with that creature," she said. Then in a caressing voice, "By the way, Willy. I'm running rather short of cigarettes. Could you do anything about that?" She fingered his sleeve.

He stared down at her hand as if it were some stain that had escaped his notice. "I'll get Obermeyer to bring some around for you."

"Why couldn't *you*, before you leave?"

"Give Obermeyer a break. That's what he's for."

She shrugged and stuck out her lower lip. "Cigarettes are coming at a higher price these days, Willy."

He tossed off a wooden smile. "Be nice to Obermeyer and he'll be nice to you."

"Maybe I'll just go without till you get back."

He blew a snicker through his nose. "Suit yourself. Goodnight, then. Obermeyer is quite harmless, really."

"You might remind him of that before you leave."

He stared at her hopelessly, then chortling drily turned for the door, flung it open breezily and went out.

8

Geli barely made the last tram running from Dennewitzplatz and it was pitch dark in the street when she got out.

A raid was due at nine o'clock.

From the corner where the watch repair shop had been boarded up she ran three blocks before the siren started. She stopped and looked up at the sky. A misty slice of moon shone through the high grey clouds. There was a distant thrum of the B-17s. The first bombs hit far away, their flashes spurting low, lighting up the clouds.

She'd given it another day, hoping Stumpff was right and Langsdorff would be home. She counted on it as she bounded up the stairway.

Just as she raised her fist to knock she heard Frau Hintz's voice inside. She held back, listening. Somebody else was in there, a man's voice, unintelligible. She went ahead and rapped hard on the door. Shoes inside clumped toward it, the latch clunked and it swung open widely. There in the doorway Frau Hintz had a bright grin spread across her broad, leathery face.

Behind her in a shroud of cigarette smoke hovering over the kitchen table two pairs of curious eyes stared at Geli like dim shapes at sea. She saw some papers spread out on the table under a lamp. A bottle stood there, three small empty tumblers.

"Oh, it's you, dear!"

"I'm so sorry" Geli said. "I see you have visitors. Is Kurt -?"

"Due any minute now. Come in and wait." She gestured toward the two men at the table. "You've only got two gentlemen ahead of you, but they won't bite." She shook her finger at the men sitting in the cloud smoke, hands fingering the stems of wine glasses.

A chair screeched and the shorter man with spikes of red hair stood up, clearing his throat. "We're just over from Lembeck, ma'am. Old friends of Kurt's, catching up on lost time." He spoke in a nervous voice that went with his spiked red hair like electricity with wires.

The other man, blond with a pinched face and canny eyes that gave his scowl the look of a mask that would be too much trouble to take off, stubbed out his cigarette as he began to get up. "Three years it's been," he said with a slightly haughty air as he came around the table. "All that water gone under the bridges we were going to build. Big plans. The three of us were going to set the world on fire. Then the world caught fire all by itself."

"With a little help from Herr Hitler," the shorter man said, watching Geli.

The other man stepped toward her. "Call me Ubbink, ma'am. This fellow here is my Svengali, better known as Henk de Vos. The three of us – that is, we two and Kurt – all trained together at Lembeck. That's where we learned how to be bad boys in spite of graduating with honors."

The mask seemed to want to smile. But the eyes looking through it had other ideas.

The shorter man clicked his heels together, taking a bow. "At your service, ma'am."

"Simone Miroux," she said. "Please forgive my intrusion."

"Not at all. Not at *all*. I take it you're a friend of Kurt's?"

"Newly made," she said.

"Ah."

Just then there was a rattling at the door, it flew open and in the doorway Langsdorff was bent over, picking up his grip.

Frau Hintz stepped toward him with open arms. "There you are, dear! Surprise! Good friends here to see you, mein Führer!"

Partly stooped over, Langsdorff scanned everybody with tired, blazing eyes. They fell on Geli. "Back so soon, Mlle Miroux?" The blistering rebuke in his voice stung her.

"We're all getting acquainted, dear," Frau Hintz said brightly. "Here, let me take your coat."

He backed away. "No, I'll keep it on a while longer."

"But we've got a fire going, dear. Get out of that thing. It's damp."

Langsdorff broke over toward the two men, shook hands with them in turn.

"You look all worn out, Kurt," Ubbink said solemnly. He laid a hand on Langsdorff's shoulder. "Long trip from -"

Langsdorff turned aside. "How was yours?"

"Ah, the usual holdups at the border. Of course they perked up right quick when we showed them our papers." He turned to Geli. "People like us are in short supply in Germany. We've practically got a free pass coming across to look for work."

"People like -?"

"We're engineers, ma'am." Ubbink took a slight bow.

"How interesting," Geli said, "I didn't realize -"

"Not too many people do," Ubbink said in a tone that made her do a double-take on him.

De Vos clapped Langsdorff on the shoulder, squeezed and gave it a shake. "Come on over here, Kurt. I think you could use a nice tall glass of Dunkelfelder."

"Where did that come from?" Langsdorff said.

"We brought it with us," De Vos exulted.

"Hold on a moment, gentlemen." Frau Hintz stepped around behind Langsdorff, grabbing the shoulders of his coat. "This wet old thing is coming off, no arguments." She pulled on the padded shoulders.

"Stop now, Hintzchen!" Langsdorff growled.

But the coat came off in Frau Hintz' thick hands. She marched with it toward the coat rack, saying, "Oh for goodness sakes, dear! Why don't you say hello to Mlle Miroux. She's come all the way from Lichterfelde to see you again."

"Yes, I can see that," Langsdorff said, then glanced at Geli as if startled by his own crabby voice. A sudden kindness in his eyes rose from a restless slumber. "Sorry, Mlle Miroux. I've been standing on a train most of the night. Any luck locating Marlene Spilde?"

Geli sighed. "I finally had to give up on her. One of those things."

He levelled a smile on her, so unexpected it went through her like a warm wind. Thank God, she thought, he hadn't made a big thing out of just how strange it was for her to be here.

He loosened up a little, saying, "My French could use some brushing up, but I'm afraid I couldn't afford you."

"Who said I'd charge you anything?" she said.

In the middle of the room Frau Hintz brought her fists down on her hips. "Mlle Miroux teaches French, gentlemen. We Germans could take a few lessons from the French these days, *n'est-ce pas?*"

Both Ubbink and De Vos snickered.

Frau Hintz stepped up to Langsdorff. Her hands trembled a little as she fingered the buttons on the front of his shirt.

"I'm going now, mein Führer, before the bombs get in my way." She smiled up at him, making a kind of private affair out of it.

He took her by the shoulders. "I wouldn't go out into that -"

"Now don't start trying to baby me. I won't be in for a couple of days. You'll have to do your own dishes. D'you think you can handle that?"

"What's the occasion?"

"Do I have to tell you all my secrets?"

He looked down at her solemnly. "When you get back I'd better hear you've gone to the doctor."

"Look who's talking. You going around on the verge of a diabetic fit."

"I've got an excuse, Hintzchen. You don't."

"Oh, I see. Men get all the excuses."

Ubbink spoke up, "Perhaps we'd better meet you at St. Anne's later on, Kurt. Say in the morning. Pastor Mochalsky has been kind enough to put us up tonight."

Geli slid one foot toward Ubbink. "Don't go on my account, gentlemen. I won't be staying."

"Why not, dear?" Frau Hintz said. "Hot water's on the stove." She minced a scowl at Langsdorff. "You remember how to make tea, don't you?"

"It's coming back to me," Langsdorff said.

Frau Hintz grunted. "Keep up the good work, mein Führer."

"Better stop calling him that," De Vos said with a grin. "It might go to his head."

"Why shouldn't it, with that lovely uniform he's got on?" De Vos put in.

Frau Hintz clumped toward the coat rack, lifted her heavy coat off the hook and shrugged into it.

Langsdorff called after her as she was making for the door, "I want a full report from Doctor Roenne when I get back!"

Frau Hintz ignored him marching toward the door and going out, then from the corridor twiddled fingers through the narrowing gap of the doorway. "Goodnight, all!"

As soon as the door shut Geli said, "What's the matter with Frau Hintz?"

"Bad heart," Langsdorff said.

"You'd never know it by the way she hops around here like a heifer," De Vos said.

Ubbink looked at him. In a guarded tone he said, "Got a minute, Kurt, before we leave?"

There was something suddenly in the air.

They didn't want her here and Geli knew it, thinking it was time to go. Then it was him, Ubbink's obvious dislike of her that held her back.

She gestured toward the door that stood slightly ajar at the far end of the kitchen. "Kurt, would you mind if I ducked into your... ?"

He hurried to say, "Ah yes, of course. You'll find the light switch just around the corner to your left as you go in."

"Thank you."

She walked across the room and, dogged by a gaping silence, stepped into the cramped little water closet. Inside, she didn't touch the light. She swung the door to just within a crack of being shut. The dark she stood in now would be to them a closed door.

Voices mingled out there in low tones, heatedly, in grating whispers.

One she recognized as Ubbink's hissed, "Who *is* she?"

"I hardly know her." That was Kurt, as if his voice was being lowered on his own radio.

"Can you afford to know her?"

"I'm not worried."

There was a silence. Glass clinked on glass, a faint sound of gurgling, in her mind she saw wine being poured.

The voice she knew to be De Vos's said, "We'd better finish this at the church tonight, Kurt, or let's say in the morning. The only thing... "

The rest of it got drowned out by the sound of a chair that screeched like a sagging bedspring.

It felt like they had all turned to look her way, thinking she'd been in here too long; no flushing sound, no water running. The darkness in the slit she'd left ajar would make them wonder why the light was out. She couldn't risk turning it on, now. She'd better flush the toilet, run some water in the bowl.

"...Mochalsky said that Van der Hooft was dead. He didn't know if Karski's message would get through in time before... "

She reached for the toilet chain, but didn't pull. Sometimes, in the rasping low tones they were using, she could not tell one voice from another.

"... the problem is, the Finns are still too nervous about Russia, they think they can't do without German protection. They'll need convincing."

"... contact in Helsinki is a Jew himself. Can't you go sooner?"

She pulled the chain. The gush of water went down loud enough for them to hear it in the pipes. No time to wash her hands. She pulled open the door and stepped out jauntily.

De Vos was getting into his coat.

Ubbink, she remembered, had never taken his off. She had something, now. The whispering, Helsinki, those few snatches that could mean anything, but Stumpff would pounce on that. Start something she couldn't stop. She'd swallowed something that she wanted to spit out.

They were at the door with Kurt as she called out, "A pleasure meeting you, gentlemen!"

De Vos stood where he was.

Ubbink strolled back a few steps, toward Geli, saying, *"D'où êtes-vous en France?"*

She shrugged, answering with a smile, *"Je suis juste une fille simple, née aux agriculteurs en Provence."*

"And now?"

"Most of my business has dried up because of the war, but I scrape along."

"I'm sure you do. Forgive our curiosity. How did you meet Kurt?"

"Accident. I came to the wrong door, looking for a client."

"Interesting. It might just as well have been the right door, now that you've come back."

With a sweet smile Geli said, *"C'est la vie."*

The contours of a smile etched Ubbink's mouth like the illusion of good will from a well-fed crocodile.

From the open doorway De Vos said, "Come on Ubbink, before those bombs catch us with our pants down! Remember, we're hoofing it."

"Goodnight, Mlle Miroux," Ubbink said acidly.

He doesn't like me, this one, Geli thought. She could feel it like a knife being twisted in her gut.

"Goodnight!" she said pleasantly.

From the corridor both men turned to wave, Ubbink calling out, "See you in the morning at St. Anne's, Kurt! Tell Frau Hintz to hurry up and get well now, won't you?" He swung the door shut.

Langsdorff came back into the room and, sighing heavily, sat on the sofa.

Geli walked over and sat down beside him. "Sorry, Kurt, I feel I've chased them away. Bad timing. I should have turned right around and gone home."

"No. They couldn't stay long anyway."

"Ubbink doesn't like me."

"He's never had much use for women."

"Even so, I'm sorry I barged in on you the way I have."

"You don't need to say that anymore."

He didn't say *I'm glad you're here*, she thought, and got the feeling that maybe it was not just kindness, but curiosity that kept him from turning her away: give his friends the chance to look her over. Later on they'd tell him what they thought. *Be careful of that woman, Kurt. She could be poison.*

She said, "Do you think Frau Hintz is going to be all right?"

"I don't know. She's let it go too long."

"What?"

"Angina, so the doctors say. She's a tough old bird, but -" He shook his head, swallowing, and looked out across the silence in the room. "She seems to be quite fond of you."

"Think so? So she told you I'd been here."

He nodded, something in his eyes forgiving Frau Hintz for her impudence. "She thought your coming all the way from Lichterfelde was quite some feat."

"And you?" She cocked her head at him saucily.

He shrugged. "She's always looking out for me."

Geli lowered her eyes. "She quite adores you," she said.

"Well, I'm lucky to have her," he stated.

"Brags on you, too. She told me all about how you once – well, the way she put it – saved her bacon."

"Ah, that. Anybody would have done the same."

"Not the way she tells it."

"I might have handled that situation somewhat differently if I hadn't borne a grudge against the officer in question. They gave me a talking-to, then let me off with a warning. I didn't tell them what I'd held against Lieutenant Baab. They would have frowned on the complaint. When it was his turn, he came out of our superior's office grinning."

"What did you hold against him?" Geli said.

"He used to work at a place where the so-called insane and feeble-minded were committed. Baab liked to brag about what happened to them, which he took part in proudly, so one day I asked him if he'd ever heard of a Bertha Ebeling."

Staring at him, Geli saw Anneliese stumbling into the hands of a policeman, shrieking for help. "Bertha was -?"

"My sister-in-law. Baab asked what she was to me, but I said I'd just heard a rumor. He took pleasure in telling me that none of them lived long enough to prove they weren't mad. Pneumonia saved them the trouble. Then up the chimney, making room for more. I might have killed him that day, but then what would have happened to Frau Hintz?"

She reached for his hand and he looked at her, not pulling away, just leaving his hand under hers and she almost squeezed to stop up his weakness through which she could pick him clean. The dead and dried-up longing she had left somewhere in Cairo, that old clipping telling of Halfaya Pass in Reggie's blood, burned in her heart. Langsdorff was staring at her.

"What is it, Kurt?"

He slipped his hand out from under hers. "Why did you tell Ubbink you came from Alsace Lorraine?"

She kept her eyes on him.

Needles pierced her face.

"Did I?"

"You told Frau Hintz that you were born in Italy."

"That's true. We came down to Alsace when I was very young, not three years old. My father bought a farm, ran goats and sheep. I'm a French citizen, Italian blood." She felt anger rising as she spoke. "Should I write it all out for Ubbink?"

He blanched a little.

A little anger wouldn't hurt right now, she thought. "Good thing I won't be seeing him again, to tell him what I think."

His face changed, ears pinned back on a sour expression as if he were chagrinned. "There's something else I want to ask you."

"Fire away."

"Since you're French, why haven't I scared you off?"

"D'you think you've missed your chance?"

"Most people go out of their way to avoid me. What keeps you in Berlin?"

"I've thought of getting out, except - oh, I don't know. It's too late. Funny how it is to feel safer in the land of the enemy."

"How safe do you feel telling me?"

"So far you haven't given me any reason not to," she said.

Watching her he made a halting sound like disused laughter trying to start on a dead battery. Suddenly his face darkened. He looked around at the wine bottle on the table. "I think I need a drink of that."

"I'll get it," she said, and scooted forward, but didn't get up. "What's the matter, Kurt? Worried about Frau Hintz?"

"I'm annoyed at her for trying to prove that she's too tough to die."

"Well, aren't we all afraid of finding out what we don't want to know?"

"I wish I didn't have to go away right now."

"Oh? You're going -?"

"Finland. Routine inspections, but I'm afraid she won't be here when I get back. I mean alive."

"Don't say that. We'll pray for her. I'll pray with you."

"Yes."

Just then a faint shuddering in the walls accompanied the distant sound of an explosion. Cups clanked in their saucers in the breakfront. The shriek of falling bombs cut through the rising note of a siren nearer by.

Geli looked up at the swaying chandelier that cast a shadowy spoked wheel on the ceiling. "Kurt, I'd better go."

"Out into that?"

"Oh, but -"

"They shut the trams down when the bombing starts."

She looked down at her fingers in her lap. "Just when I feel I'm getting to know you."

"You might not like it if you got to know me," he said.

She steadied a gaze on him. "Are you asking me, or telling me?"

He blinked as if he hadn't been listening. "You must know by now that I'm married."

"Yes. What of it?"

He looked at her incredulously. "Well -"

"Can't a woman be your friend? Or is that just one more of our many shortcomings?"

"No. I -"

"Don't bother tearing yourself down. I'm not scared of you, and won't be if you should suddenly sprout the well-known Nazi fangs. Otherwise I wouldn't have so freely told you I was French, *n'est-ce pas?*"

For a moment he looked at a loss, then said at last, "It's not safe out there. You might not make it all the way to Lichterfelde.

You can have the bed that Frau Hintz sleeps in, when she stays over. It's not much, but -"

"Well, that's -" She almost said *I hope you know I didn't plan it this way*, and a kind of shiver scaled her heart. The grandfather clock against the wall struck nine, and something in her moved, as if Reggie was giving her another chance. *He spoke softly in the bed beside her, his boyish voice in the dark not long for this world. 'We've got a big show coming up, love. The Jerries will get it good and proper. Day after tomorrow, the worst place they can be, they'll find out quick enough. Halfaya Pass. We're taking them by surprise. It'll be a rout. You'll hear about it, love, before I get back.'*

"I don't know, Kurt. I'm sure I'd be in the way. I'd better go."

He shrugged. "You can leave as early as you like in the morning. Me, I'm going up to St. Anne's. Pastor Mochalsky has been kind enough to put up Ubbink and De Vos in the rectory. I'll say goodbye to them, then I've got that plane to catch. I'll try not to wake you in the morning."

"Unless I'm up and dressed before you."

He grasped his knees and got up abruptly. "Come along. I'll show you where you're going to sleep."

9

She heard a sudden movement in the other room. Her watch had stopped, but sunlight lit the hallway. There was a moan that sounded full of pain. She threw the covers off and made her way around the corner to his room. He lay there in a sweat, one arm thrown across his forehead. She took a few steps in. "Kurt, are you all right?"

The arm swept off his forehead. "What are you doing here?"

"Don't you remember? You wanted me to stay the night."

He sat up suddenly, bracing on his elbows. There was a wild look about his face, stricken there like some grimace he had no control of. "God, what time is it? I'm late."

"I thought you'd gone already, then I heard -" She stepped over closer to him. "Are you ill, Kurt?"

He waved one hand dismissively. "It'll pass." He made a move to swing one leg over the side of the bed, fell back. "Damn it!"

"Kurt, I think you're ill. Is this how your diabetes -?"

He waved his hand again. "If I don't make it to St. Anne's by half past nine, they'll go."

"Let me go and tell them that you're not feeling well."

He sat up suddenly. "No! All I need is - Frau Hintz left some muffins in the breadbox."

"Stay where you are, I'll get them."

He struggled to his feet and stood there, reeling.

She made a quick move toward him, caught him in her arms. "Lie back and rest, Kurt." She eased him onto the bed and he stared up at the closeness of her face as if he didn't know her. She said, "I'll be right back."

She found the muffins stacked in the breadbox, started some water boiling for coffee. She was getting down two cups from the cupboard when he came into the doorway. He was still sweating and his face looked ashen. She picked up the sugar bowl, saying, "How much?"

He shuffled toward her. "Make it two lumps."

She dropped the sugar in and held the cup out to him, pushed the plate of muffins on the table toward him.

He picked up one, bit into it, slurped greedily from his steaming cup and blew a sigh into the cold air. "Thank you. This usually does the trick."

"You've got to see a doctor. These episodes aren't going to stop."

He had his watch on now, and looked at it.

She knew what was coming next and said, "Listen, Kurt. This trip to Finland. Why not put it off until you feel up to going?"

"No, I've got a plane to meet and they won't leave until I'm on it."

She stared at him, holding her breath. "All right. I guess the war won't wait for the sick and the halt."

"That's what they tell me," he said caustically.

She swallowed, forcing a smile. "So you're off to St. Anne's? I've got a shoulder you could lean on if you like. Or would I slow you down?"

"No. I'm going now. If you would be so kind as to lock the door on your way out."

"I will. I have only to get dressed. When shall I see you again?"

He looked at her. "Why?"

"To check up on my patient, if you like."

He hesitated too long, and she went up to him. "Are you going to be all right?"

"Of course."

"Just a moment. Your top button." She reached up and fingered the undone topmost button on his tunic, fastened it and looked at him. "There."

The moment trembled like a vase that might or might not topple to the floor, and she went up on tiptoe, leaning toward him. "Hold still," she said, "while I kiss you for good luck."

She thought he was going to shy, but he didn't. She moved her face toward his. She laid her fingertips on the scar above his eye, slid them lightly down to the corner of his lips. She was afraid. He didn't pull away, and something made her want to cry.

10

The day outside was gloomy and the stairway dim. Geli trudged upward, thinking she would climb right into bed and sleep some more. Frau Hintz's lumpy bed had been little better than a cot. She'd grappled with the thought of hurriedly getting dressed and rushing in a taxi to St. Anne's, looking to pick Kurt up, but she could hear Ubbink snarling, 'Her again? What's *she* doing here?' Routine flight, Kurt had told her, on a Heinkel for Finland. He could be gone for up to a week.

She'd laid to rest the word Helsinki in her mind, some plot afoot with those two Dutchmen, but now she wondered whether she could keep it there, the next time she saw Stumpff's eyes on her expectantly. It was too soon. She didn't know enough, yet. Whetting Stumpff's appetite could only send him off half-cocked, then where would she be?

There was a clumping on the landing just above. Around the corner suddenly shambled Corporal Obermeyer.

She stopped dead in her tracks.

He lowered his foot onto the next step.

She tried to slip to the side of him just as he moved enough to block her way. "Keeping late hours, I see," he said.

"Please let me pass."

He didn't move, looking brand-spanking new in a black uniform of the sort the Storm Troopers used to wear. Sam Brown strapped across his chest, bright *Blutfahne* cinched around his left arm and a holster, too, containing a gun. She'd never seen him wearing a gun. A paper sack dangled from one hand.

"A lady shouldn't be out so late at night, all by herself. It's not safe. Of course I'm a night crawler myself. Herr Stumpff and me – the miles and miles we drive at night on our long trips to Poland. I always find ways to entertain myself while he sleeps like a baby in the back seat." He stopped and gave her a long, lascivious look, eyes shining. "He's gone to Poland on the train this time, you know. Should be back tomorrow, but in his absence he thought it best for me to place myself at your disposal with the car."

"I know that, Obermeyer. I told him I wouldn't be needing your services, or the car."

He toed the step, looking downward at his boot, kicked at the step in front of it. "I'm quite a good driver, you know. Herr Stumpff calls me a marvel, staying awake behind the wheel for all those miles across a land as dreary as any land you'll ever see. That's Poland for you – the Mazovian Plain. Have you ever been to Poland, ma'am?"

"No, I never have. I'm very tired, Obermeyer. Please let me pass."

"I shouldn't wonder, ma'am - your being tired, keeping such late hours."

She looked up and saw some secret being kept in his leering, gray wren's eyes. "That's really none of your business, Obermeyer."

He shambled aside, saying nonsensically, "Yes, ma'am," and she started up the few remaining steps to the landing.

She heard him coming up behind her.

"Just a moment, ma'am. I've got something for you here."

She stopped to look back down at him and the sack he gave a shake to at the end of his outstretched arm.

"What is it?"

He shook the sack at her again. "Here, open it."

"You shouldn't be giving me things, you know."

"Don't you want to know what it is?"

"Why don't you tell me?"

He thrust the sack at her. "Come, take a look. Herr Stumpff told me."

"I'm going in now, Obermeyer." She turned away, now she was on the landing and she hurried across to her door, with trembling fingers fishing the key out of her coat pocket.

"I wouldn't do that just yet, ma'am."

She was fumbling with the key, it flipped out of her hand and fell clattering on the floor. She stooped to pick it up, his boot came into view beside her hand.

"Here, let me get that for you, ma'am."

"No!" She snatched up the key, crowded the door as she stabbed it at the hole with shaking hands. The latch clunked, she turned the knob and heaved herself against the door and lunged inside.

She was just swinging it the other way when Obermeyer stepped across the threshold, forcing her back. "I need a word with you," he said, then quietly turned and shut them both into the room.

She'd left a lamp burning, but the air was ice-cold. Fear gripped her throat, her heart began to pound. She had to break his train of thought. "Why don't you leave that sack with me?

Here, let's see what's in it." She looked into the sack, seeing the cigarettes she'd half expected. She looked up, just managing to smile. "Tell me, Obermeyer, do you smoke?"

He eyed her, growing a frown between his eyes. "Cigarettes are very hard to come by, ma'am. My mother's saved some from before the war. She'll smoke one halfway down so she can have the rest some other time. You know she lives right around the corner. Same little house we've lived in all my life."

"Well, why don't you take a pack of these to her? Keep one for yourself."

He scowled at her as if she'd caught him in some lie. "I bought these with my own money, ma'am. If they weren't all for you, I wouldn't have."

"That's very thoughtful of you, Obermeyer. You did get permission from Herr Stumpff."

He cocked his head and squeezed a puzzled look into a squint. "Yes, but I used my own money to buy these." She smiled at him the way a teacher would chide a boy for bringing her a big bouquet of roses. "But Herr Stumpff gave you the money."

"Oh, no! No. I knew how much you liked to smoke."

"But that's not your responsibility."

He shrugged. "A cigarette's a cigarette."

"But taking it upon yourself... "

A devilish grin broke out on his face. "Why should he have to know?"

"You wouldn't want to keep any secrets from him, would you?" She stumbled a little as her backward-moving heel caught on the rug.

"Herr Stumpff instructed me to look out for you while he's gone, ma'am. He told me to keep an eye on you."

"Did he? I'm quite capable of taking care of myself."

"That may be. But you see, I never disobey an order." He

stopped and let his eyes crawl around on her face, like ants bumping into things to nibble. "I waited for you last night for quite some time, but you never came out. I didn't how what I was going to tell Herr Stumpff."

"You waited for me where?"

"Outside that tenement on Bulowstrasse. Where you went in, but didn't come out. There weren't a lot of people going in and out at that hour. Except for two strange men. Strange because, in the first place, they weren't German." He suddenly thrust a finger in the air and shook it. "I may not be a world traveler, but I know a foreigner when I see one!"

"Just what foreigners are you talking about?"

"The ones I saw go in. Two of them." Obermeyer led with his stiff finger as he crowded her. "Then I began to worry, because these two looked shifty. Especially when they came back out and you were still in there. I followed them. I tailed them all the way to St. Anne's, thinking to myself, what were a couple of foreigners doing, going to church at *that* late hour of the night?"

"So you saw two men come out of the tenement. What are you getting at, Obermeyer?"

Obermeyer toed the floor. "Herr Stumpff will want to hear about it."

"Why?"

"I wouldn't feel right if I didn't tell him," he said doggedly.

"As right as telling him about the cigarettes?"

He ignored her. "Not with you still in there. Staying the whole night."

She stared at him incredulously. "Obermeyer, first you call these two men foreigners, then you think they've got something to do with me, without having the slightest idea which flat they went into, if any."

Obermeyer's grin twitched across his thin, uneven lips. "They were in there much too long to not go into one."

"Perhaps, but you couldn't possibly know which one."

"I told you I followed them to St. Anne's."

"So what?"

"Do you know who the pastor is in there? My mother does. Thanks to her, that man is being watched."

"A man of the cloth? Did she say *you* should watch him?"

"Oh, no! You don't make fun of my mother. If you knew what that priest is suspected of, you'd know why I got on those two men's tail – all on my own, ma'am. No, I take that back. Under orders."

"I don't believe you, Obermeyer."

Obermeyer frowned. "That's not at all nice of you, ma'am. You wouldn't ride with me, so Herr Stumpff *told* me to keep an eye on you. He wouldn't, unless -"

Suddenly a few packs of cigarettes tumbled out of the sack onto the floor.

She stooped for them, but Obermeyer was quicker. He handed over two packs, kept the last one and began to peel it open.

"Just take it with you, Obermeyer," Geli said.

He tapped out a cigarette, held the pack out to her.

"Please go now, Obermeyer. I'm in no mood to smoke right now."

"Go ahead, ma'am. Let me light one for you like a gentleman."

Her fingers trembled as she took the cigarette and heard the snick of a lighter.

She leaned toward the flame, feeling idiotic as he took her through the motions, snuffed out the flame and gave the pack an underhanded toss onto the sofa behind her, saying lazily, "I could change my mind, you know. Maybe I don't need to tell Herr Stumpff anything about your staying the whole night with that man on Bulowstrasse. I could forget about those two foreigners, too. After all, they only looked suspicious. My mother tells me all the time I let my imagination run away with me."

She looked at the door behind him. She couldn't remember if he'd locked it.

He said in a breathy confidential tone, "It'll be our secret."

She looked down at the burning cigarette as the trembling of her hand shook ash off the end and it fell onto the rug with sparks enough to step on, which she did. "You've been very kind, Obermeyer, but I think you'd better go, now."

"A couple of extra minutes wouldn't hurt, now would it?"

"Minutes for -"

"Nobody will know, ma'am, if you decided to be nice to me."

She looked at him. "How nice, Obermeyer?"

He blinked at her as if in hopes that her mind was as thick as his. "You know my first name is Klaus, ma'am." A hideous grin broke across his rawboned, sallow face.

"What good would a little kiss do, Obermeyer, if you knew I didn't mean it? What would your mother say?"

His face darkened. The grin shrank. "You're mocking me! You're going to be sorry you didn't let me drive you, like Herr Stumpff wanted me to do, to keep you out of trouble!"

"But if you tell on me, Obermeyer, then I might have to tell on you."

His head listed toward his shoulder as he looked at her. "You'll be sorry, ma'am, that's all I've got to say!" He stood there rigidly, as if the sight of her sickened him, then spun around, jerked open the door and stormed out, leaving it wide open.

She stood there as another plug of ash fell from the cigarette. They were a nasty Turkish brand. Or was that just the taste of

Obermeyer on the kiss he'd wanted her to plant on the slit of his repulsive, fetid lips. The little kiss he'd use to haul the rest of her into his clutches, fumbling with her limpness like she'd fainted dead away to keep from fighting him.

He'd left the door wide open. He'd be a fool to say anything to Stumpff. But then fools say all kinds of things, thinking they're not. A fool with a gun now, too. Make him a big man and you might not get away with telling him watch out, Obermeyer, that thing might go off.

11

Stumpff was due back any day now. Obermeyer plagued her mind, stuck like a leech to every waking thought of some escape. You couldn't count him out for being dumb. That kind of dumb got smart when survival was at stake.

She got her coat, hurried out and didn't care what time it was or where the underground was stalled or, when a tram broke down, how much farther on she'd have to walk. She got there on a blur of will and suddenly she was standing in his doorway.

She found him in a foul mood.

"What do you want?"

"I'm so glad you're here, Kurt," she said breathlessly. "How was your trip? Did you just get back?"

"Frau Hintz died in the hospital while I was away," he said.

"Oh, God, no! I'm so sorry." Her hand flew out to touch him, fell short of his sleeve.

He didn't move. "Her body has been sent to Bornichen where she'll be laid to rest tomorrow. I'm leaving in the morning."

She hardly thought before she said, "Take me with you."

He looked at her. "No, I'm afraid not."

"But I was so fond of Frau Hintz. Besides, I -"

"You barely knew her."

"But I promise I'll stay out of the way."

"No, that won't do."

She felt angry, suddenly. Now was no time to falter. So he was trying to shore up his grief, but the iron was hot.

"All right! Remind me of how little I knew of her. Maybe I just thought you might not want to be alone at such a time."

He stood back with a sigh, began to shake his head. "I haven't thanked you for the other morning. You were kind."

She let herself relent a little. "You forgot to promise me you'd see a doctor."

He gave her a long look. "Some people at the funeral are sure to look askance at you."

"I couldn't be that bad, being with you."

He got off a careless smile. "It's quite a long trip. The train pulls out in the morning, early."

"I'll be there," she said. "What time?"

12

She met him at the station the next day, where they caught the early train to Dresden, due to arrive in time to rush to another track for the 11:15 to Bornichen. Most of the way he sat beside her silently and somber, preoccupied, and she didn't try to break through his mood to cheer him up. His grief was his. He didn't need her trying to get in on it.

She looked at the disheveled top of a woman's head in the next seat. The rhythmic clackety-clack of the wheels on the tracks ran along her nerves. Her eyelids began to get heavy, then she couldn't keep them open anymore and they came down like shades on the cold glow of a moon, fitted like a skullcap on some forbidden face.

She awoke with a start, as if there'd been a jolt. She looked to her left. Kurt wasn't there. The pneumatic door came open at the end of the car, letting in a racket from the coupling space as the conductor came through, taking tickets. She saw Kurt, then, a short way up the aisle, talking to a large man leaning back against the iron balustrade under the window, smoking a cigarette. He was bundled in a black topcoat, a grey fedora perched on his head. Distinguished-looking, she thought. The conductor came abreast of them, fanning tickets. Geli heard the big man say, "Any chance of a seat farther down?"

The conductor shook his head. "Nothing but the laps of Colonels and Majors, I'm afraid."

"What about the baggage car? I'd gladly stretch out on a mail sack."

"I've got a party of General staff officers down there, now. Perhaps -" The conductor looked the big man over. One of those looks that contemplates some reward for making an exception. "Why don't I take you down there, sir? We can't have all those generals' laps going to their heads."

"Oh! Very kind of you." The big man turned to Kurt, felt for his hand and, grasping it firmly, held on as he said something earnestly that Geli couldn't hear.

The conductor was waiting.

The big man broke away and Geli shut her eyes. She could feel Kurt brushing past her knees. She opened her eyes. "Oh, Kurt. Sorry, I dozed off. Where are we?"

He got settled in his seat, not looking at her as he said, "Not far to Dresden, now. We'll be there in plenty of time to catch our train to Bornichen." His voice sounded husky.

"Where were you?" she said.

"Ah, there was a man was up there," his hand jumped off his leg to point up toward where he'd been standing, "I saw him trying to light a cigarette. The flint was bad or something. I had some matches, so I went up and offered him a light."

"Oh, how good of you. Anybody interesting?"

He turned to face her. His eyes were blood red. Tired? If she didn't know any better...

"Yes, a diplomat from Sweden. Secretary to the Swedish Legation in Berlin. We chatted for a while, he stood there out of courtesy, but it wasn't hard to see that he was getting nervous. Me in this uniform, you know – provocateurs are everywhere. I couldn't blame him if he thought I could be one of them."

"So what happened?"

"He thanked me for the light. That was about all."

"Mmm. That's funny. Seems like your uniform alone should not have scared him off, unless -"

"Unless what?"

Unless you told him something he didn't want to hear, she thought. "Oh, I don't know. Forget it. Did you try to make him know you wouldn't bite?"

"No use. I couldn't have convinced him if I'd tried. I let it go."

"Yes, of course. Well, he got his cigarette lit, anyway."

"Yes. I gave him the matches."

She looked at him again.

His thin smile was wan.

"Are you all right, Kurt?"

"Yes. Why?"

She wasn't going to say, "Have you been crying?"

He would deny it. He'd get angry.

She could see that he was already heating up.

"Oh, I just thought, maybe the diabetes had come back on you."

No." He gave her a sharp dissatisfied look, swung his face toward the window.

She'd opened up the gap again, and didn't want to wallow in it. She slumped down in the seat and shut her eyes, trying to dive deep beneath the light along her lids to where she could forget. Down there with all the good intentions of this French woman in his life, knowing there was no forgetting, any more than what could have driven him to tears would empty out into the fields that he was watching go by.

13

They caught a taxi to the cemetery. A scattering of people stood around the gravesite. Frau Hintz's sister, Amelia Wulf, and her husband, Oskar, kept glancing furtively at her, whispering, until Kurt presented her as a 'friend'. Their faces seemed to bloat with all they'd have to ask him later on: how much does your dear wife know about this friend?

A long white limousine pulled up and a tall, heavy-set man got out. Kurt told her he was Superintendent Dr. Otto Dibelius, head of the Confessional Church, an old friend. He had consented to come all this way from Uppsala to deliver the eulogy.

A gust of wind swept against the white soutane of the large man as he read the service, stirring the pine branches laid around the open grave.

Kurt took a stalwart stance beside her, while on the other side of the casket Amelia Wulf wept and snuffed into her handkerchief. Kurt stood there rigidly, stoic and dry-eyed. Then she saw that he was trembling slightly, once or twice there was a shuddering about his head, and she traced back in her mind that almost always austere presence about him, like some dam building pressure whose cracks you couldn't see. He must have felt her eyes on him, but he kept looking straight ahead across the casket toward the morning sunshine glistening in the glades of the surrounding mountains, flashing in the spectacles of the man who now turned from the grave, closing his Bible on the passages with which he had committed the soul of Leokadia Hintz unto God. Kurt met him halfway as he came over, they clasped each other's hands.

All at once Dibelius took on a hurried air. "God bless you, Kurt, I must be off! I have to speak in Württemberg tonight. A lot of people counting on me."

Kurt led Dibelius out of earshot where the wind blew into what they were saying and Dibelius listened nervously, making halting movements while Kurt kept talking, lips moving, saying things she couldn't hear.

Then the wind changed and she heard, "No, it was no use. The Nuncio threw me out."

Dibelius took a fretful stance in the white sand. His voice carried on another lull in the wind, "... not easy, Kurt. The Bishop of Württemberg sent a letter to Hitler himself in favor of the privileged non-Aryans."

Kurt raised his voice as he stepped closer to the big man. "Mere courage, Otto. Try to pretend for just a moment that Frau Hintz was a Jew! Would you have found some excuse to get out of coming all this way to bury her?"

Dibelius lifted his chin haughtily. "... Wurm's protests get repeated abroad, he'll be a dead man. You want that for me, too? Now I must go, Kurt. Come see me in Berlin!" The large imposing man wheeled and quickly strode across the grass, kicking his soutane, toward his waiting car.

A voice from the shadow of a large sheltering pine called out, "Will you come back to the house with us, Kurt?" It was Amelia Wulf, dogged by her husband, coming toward them.

"Perhaps not right away," Kurt said.

By then Amelia Wulf was reaching her arms around him. She pulled him close. "God be with you, Kurt. I know you loved my sister dearly."

Oskar Wulf put on his hat, emerging into the sun from under a pine bough. "We'll have refreshments at the house. Do come and eat with us. We're counting on you. Ham and black bread, fresh baked."

"We'll try," Kurt said.

The Wulfs both smiled uneasily, eyes darting on and off the woman they would have to save for gossip at a later date, or at the wake.

Kurt took her hand, then, and they walked past the leaning headstones and the trees, and she let something of her feeling for him out into the sun where it could find him. He looked so handsome, the way he squinted to adjust his eyes to the light.

They walked clear to the edge of a wooded hillside, sat on a wooden bench and, looking back the way they'd come, she saw the Wulfs had gone. She knew Kurt couldn't leave all his sadness back at the grave, but here the dead had not so much to do with them, and she had him to herself. Something was pent up in him.

She took a chance and said, "I missed you."

He gave her a quizzical look as if she'd spoken out of turn.

She went on, "Oh, I know I shouldn't have worried, but I was afraid you might not come back from Finland. Silly of me, I suppose. Still, I hear those Heinkels make good targets."

He turned away moodily. "It's not over, yet."

"You have to go back?"

"No. My superiors want to see me first thing in the morning."

That he would tell her this at all moved her, unexpectedly, closer to him, where the road led to some abyss that smelled dangerously of the Nile, and the pomade on the empty pillow next to hers.

"Did something happen? I mean, did anything go wrong?"

He searched her face, giving her a look that made her feel uneasy. "I'll be told tomorrow morning if they think it did."

In her mind the two Dutchmen, skittish about her presence, left the room as if it wasn't her that made them go. She knew it was. They'd finish what they had to say about Helsinki at St. Anne's.

Kurt was watching her. He looked away, sniffed in a breath and looked out across the tranquil land of the dead. At last he said with a sigh, "The Wulfs will be expecting us. I suppose we should put in an appearance. Of course they'll want to put me up for the night."

"And I'll just find my way back to a train."

He looked at her and she could see he would be hard put to it to beg off the Wulfs's invitation.

She didn't feel like being polite, or hear what she saw brewing in his eyes, and be the poor little girl left out. She said decisively, "Or else that leaves me with some other place to stay the night. Know of any cheap little inns around here?"

He stared at her. "The Wulfs won't miss me that much if I don't show up."

"Oh, they'll miss you, all right. Long enough for them to wonder how I've come into the picture. Where has he been hiding *that* one, they'll wonder."

"I doubt it. They've never met my wife."

She glanced at him, trying to see how near or far his wife was in his eyes.

He looked away from her to say, "What do you suppose she'd make of my being here with you?"

"I won't be telling her," he said.

She turned a scathing look on him. "I could catch the late train back tonight."

"Or we'll ask around about that cheap little inn," he said with a kind of wanton smile.

She took him up on that. "There's no other kind as far as I'm concerned," she said.

He was silent for a moment, then, squinting a little as he blinked out at the shadows slanting from the headstones, pines and alders in the waning light. At last he said, "You know they put me up at the Savoy in Helsinki?"

She raised her face to him, feeling a strange fresh breeze flow in across her heart. "You must be pretty tired of hotels," she said.

"I wouldn't want to pay good money for another long, hard seat on a train. Not tonight."

She wasn't sure it was him, talking, or some nonesuch voice in a crazy reverie she'd once put words to. She felt better now, being with him. That was all she knew. "So you're not sending me back?"

"Let's sit here a while, then take a walk."

Something told her not to ask where to, and they sat there together, as if they were in love, and it was strange to wonder if they were. If there was something to get out of him, tonight was the night.

They came upon an inn not far from the cemetery, a quaint two-story stucco with leaded windows in the shade of several birches and one soaring, stately pine.

"That's it," he said, as if he'd known the way by heart.

She didn't act surprised, and suddenly it felt good to be away from the city, far from the bombing. Far from the bonds she'd slipped as if she'd never have to go back, and she was here only because he wanted her to be.

A stone walk led through a rose garden to the front door. They registered on the unspoken appearance of being man and wife, and Kurt asked for a bottle of wine to be brought up.

The room smelled of fresh roses in a fluted glass vase on one night-table.

They didn't wait long before the concierge knocked lightly and came in with a Château Boyd-Cantenac, 1937, two glasses and a corkscrew, a plate of bread and cheese.

Kurt used the corkscrew on the wine, poured into the glasses on the table. She picked up hers and, strolling over toward the window, parted the curtain and stood there looking down at the rose petals scattered like the remains of a wedding in the dirt. She turned to see Kurt catching sight of a radio under the unlit lamp on the other night table.

"Look at this." He reached for the knob.

"It looks so old," she said, "I'll bet it doesn't work."

"Let's give it a try."

He twisted the knob. Static came in, airwaves squealed as he fiddled with the dial. Faint strains of music came through what sounded like the crackling of a distant storm. He turned the knob some more until a voice broke in, speaking in French: *'The old colonial city has unfurled her tricolors and plunged into festivity. Her jubilant population, doubled by refugees from the fighting and a horde of exultant, victorious allied soldiers who at last were out of the harsh North African deserts and mountains, is giving itself over to wine, song and dance. Young women smother marching British and Free French troops with kisses, and shower the victors' tanks and trucks with roses, lilacs and poppies. The Hotel Majestic, where Axis officers resided only two days ago, now accommodates Allied officers. At the same moment this revelry is going on in North Africa, we have received reports of rioting in Berlin. Families of Panzer Army Afrika soldiers have taken to the streets of the German capital after being denied news of their men in Tunisia. In a further report from a suburb of Tunis, we hear of German soldiers willingly walking into prison compounds. A German infantry band was said to be serenading arriving captives with strains of Viennese Lieder.'*

In the background you could hear the trumpets, trombones and a tuba playing the *Lieder*.

Kurt switched the sound off, came back over to the sofa where she sat, holding her glass. "Imagine that," he said.

"Yes, all those captured soldiers. What a shame," she said.

"For them the war is over."

"Do you think the end is near, Kurt? Will there ever be an end?"

He raised his glass and took a long, deep drink. There was a kind of reckless thickness in his voice. "Frau Hintz used to say she couldn't wait see every last one of Hitler's gang of thugs paraded in front of the old Chancellery in chains."

"Taking a big chance saying that, wasn't she?"

He looked at her, clutching his empty glass. "She always spoke her mind, no matter what I thought."

"Well then, shall we risk drinking to victory in Tunis for Frau Hintz?" She held up her glass.

He looked into the emptiness of his. "Wait a minute." He wheeled toward the table, grabbed the bottle and filled up his glass.

As he was coming back she patted the cushion next to her thigh. "Come sit beside me, Kurt. You're too far away."

He sank into the cushion, raised his glass and bellowed, "Frau Hintz!"

They both drank and then he blinked at their reflection in the window, looking strangely dazed and disoriented.

She laid her hand on his. "I hardly ever see you smile, Kurt. Why don't you ever smile?"

He raked his fingers across his forehead, examining his half-empty glass. "I'm not used to this. I think I'm getting tight."

She threw her head back with a breathy laugh. "So what? You deserve it. You know you're such an easy man to like, but - no, I take that back. I was going to use that old cliché, hard to love, but that's not true. Not true at all."

He didn't answer. He was looking at her now as if he couldn't place her. As if he wasn't seeing her at all. The wine was going to her head already, too, and she wanted him to lean on her, and want her more than Gunther ever had before he started hating her.

"What's the matter, Kurt?"

He kept on looking at her as if he hadn't heard. "I shouldn't have brought you here, Simone. Forgive me."

"Forgive you for -? Oh, I see. Why me when it could be your wife?"

"No, that's not it."

"Then what? You think it'll get around? Some French lady who could be a partisan or something, showing up at a funeral with you?"

The glass jerked in his hand, he raised it to his lips and drained it. "You're being seen with me. I hadn't thought it out."

She pretended not to remember what the wind had let her overhear.

"Kurt, what troubles you so much about tomorrow? Ever since you came back from Helsinki -"

His eyes flicked onto her and stuck. "I'll take care of that."

"You're scaring me."

He shrugged. A cloudy look came into his wandering eyes. "Remember this. If you lose track of me, don't try to find me."

"Stop it, now. If Frau Hintz could hear you."

"You don't know who I am, Simone," he said.

There was something in his voice that made her press her hand down onto his. She held on tight. "I couldn't love you any better if I did," she said, watching his face to see if his belief could tell her that she meant it.

He looked down at her hand as if to keep from falling. "I've seen things for which we were once told, don't talk about it if you want to go on living. One day they'll get around to me."

Shock swung at her heart. She put her fingers on his lips. "Then be quiet. I don't know. They can't get anything out of me that I don't know."

He looked away from her. There was a trembling around his lips, like words were clawing from inside. The light caught tears pooling in his eyes. She felt she'd gone too far. Rejected him and put on blinders to protect herself. He'd found his way inside and there was nothing but his voice, now, taking her like a weight into a well with no bottom as she held onto his hand and he began to tell her where he was.

She thought it was the wine at first.

Then with no preliminaries he began to speak in a sepulchral, unearthly voice; how desolate a place it was to die, he said, but they were made to think they would be put to work, after a nice, warm shower. Whips flailed among them as they spilled out of boxcars, clutching children, searching for the hand of God that came only for their clothes, and then their hair and drove them on, stark naked, toward what they were told would be a nice, warm shower in a gas chamber.

"I stood there beside the commandant, watching. To wish any hope for them was a ghastly fairy tale. The stench of dead flesh in the air told them what their fate was going to be. The eyes of a beautiful young girl, hugging herself against the cold, found me through the wire. She pointed at her bare chest and said, 'Nineteen'. The age at which her life would cease. I couldn't take the others in. There was only room enough for her, because she hated me and I knew why. Now every time I shut my eyes she's there. I sleep in a coffin I should be in with her and all the others. Too many thousands to remember. I'd thought of breaking through the wire and disappearing with them in the death house. But death struck me as the useless, stupid way out. The easy way. Only by living could I try to stop it, get word to the Allies, anything that stood the ghost of a chance of getting past deaf ears. That's who I am, Simone. Just as you thought, the man I couldn't be."

She'd lost her breath. She was so deep in hell it felt like she was trying to fly above a snake pit. She reached for his hands clenched in his lap like stumps. "What are you going to do?" she cried. "Why were you there?"

"I was the officer in charge of delivering the substance meant to kill these people more efficiently than the diesel exhaust system being used until then. Back along the road I'd stopped a convoy carrying the poison, found a dangerous state of instability in more than half of the containers and ordered my men to bury them. Those remaining were safe enough to be used up as disinfectant. The commandant accepted this. The other officer disagreed."

"What other officer?"

"Why?"

She stared at him for a long moment.

"Nothing. I don't know."

He looked past her left ear, eyes drifting. "Strangely enough I'd liked that man once. He did me a favor. But for him I would have died in prison. He'd been thinner, then."

Helsinki came to her in those hushed tones among the Dutchmen. That gentleman whose cigarette he'd lit... She didn't think before she said, "That man on the train -"

"I tried to tell him all I knew. He seemed to care. I don't know whether he'll get through."

Clothed as if in the rags of death she tried to feel what he felt, fear what he feared.

All at once he threw his face into his hands. His back began to heave. "Christ, I can't go on! I can't go on!"

She clutched his hands. It fell at her feet like a dead bouquet at the curtain call. Stumpff would let Obermeyer, who liked to play with guns, handle her reward. It was all the fault of Mlle Miroux, who'd played her role too well.

What was supposed to be, now was.

"Be quiet, now," she said, and saw the drowning of his eyes again as she drew near and, kissing him, caught fire inside, and took him by the hand and led him toward the bed and they fell on it together and she could feel him wanting her, and that was all there was, the darkness as she turned the lamp out and brought her lips down onto his and, tasting his tears, kissed him with all the heart she'd left for dead. But for now she'd give it to him with the longing in her body writhing down into those things he could no longer keep from her when darkness let in only light enough for them to feel.

14

Major Joachim Fritsch sat forward at his desk, silhouetted by the ashen morning light behind him in the window. A dun brown widow's peak lowered his hairline to an escarpment on which hoary brows bristled like dead shrubs.

In the chair across the room, Stumpff sat looking uncomfortable with his short legs crossed. The door behind him swung open. Twisting around and with a merry smile he started to speak when Fritsch said, "Come in, Lieutenant. Have a chair."

Langsdorff took the few steps toward Fritsch's desk, stopped and raised a slack salute. He moved one leg aside and thrust his hands behind his back. "I'd rather stand, sir, if you don't mind. You know how long those chairs take to get out of."

Fritsch looked up. One eyebrow climbed the escarpment. "As you wish, Lieutenant. This shouldn't take too long."

Stumpff leaned a smile out over his fat knees. "Those bucket seats that Kurt came home in leave something to be desired, Joachim."

Fritsch kept his attention riveted on Langsdorff. "You've been back from Helsinki now for how many days, Lieutenant?"

"Two, sir. Not counting today."

"I don't have your report, yet."

"Something unavoidable came up as soon as I got home."

"Unavoidable?"

"My housekeeper, Frau Hintz, died while I was away. I was able to come home one day early from Finland, having completed all my duties. I saw the opportunity to attend her funeral."

"I see. Opportunity without informing me."

"Yes, well -"

"You took the liberty of regarding this one day as being yours to use as you saw fit."

"I may have acted hastily, sir, but I wouldn't have gone if I hadn't come back early from Helsinki."

Fritsch sat back, picked up a pencil and jabbed a few dots into his blotter. "Hintz," he mused. "That name rings a bell."

"She worked for us at one time, sir. Janitorial chores, until -"

"Ah yes, that old woman who caused some friction between you and Lieutenant Baab. I trust the two of you have patched things up."

"In a manner of speaking, sir."

Fritsch cleared his throat. "About this funeral. Where did it take place, and who went with you?"

Langsdorff stared at Fritsch, who kept his eyes lazily averted. "Frau Hintz was laid to rest in Bornichen, sir. Her wish was to be buried there, where she was born and grew up. I went alone."

"Did you?" Fritsch looked up. "I should think you would have asked your wife to join you there."

"No, sir. She wasn't personally acquainted with Frau Hintz."

"But this could have been your chance to see her."

"There was no time for her to travel all the way from Tübingen on such short notice. Nor was it for me to take the liberty of asking her."

"But you did take the liberty of going."

"I may have acted somewhat hastily, sir, under the circumstances."

"Yes. But now, how do we justify this extra day of yours, at a time when my impression was that you were still attending to your duties in Helsinki?"

"I finished up early, sir, unexpectedly."

"With no time to leave a word with me."

"I didn't think, since -"

"Let's hope you didn't hurry things along. Your duties, I mean."

"No, sir. Nothing was left undone. I didn't learn about Frau Hintz's death until my return."

Fritsch began to probe his chin with the eraser end of his pencil. "Who else besides your wife can vouch for your presence at this funeral?"

Langsdorff looked at him, searching for the trick buried in a lapse of memory. "I beg your pardon, sir?"

Fritsch raised his voice. "I don't like repeating things, Lieutenant."

Stumpff's chair creaked under him as he leaned forward. "What I believe the Colonel wishes to establish, Kurt, is the identity of witnesses to your presence in Bornichen. Anybody would do. Isn't that right, Joachim?"

Fritsch shot a sharp glance at Stumpff before his eyes jumped back onto Langsdorff. "Well, Lieutenant? Names?"

"Other than assorted mourners, sir, there was no one that I

really knew, except Frau Hintz's sister. As I've said, my wife was not there with me. In fact, she knew nothing about the funeral."

"Yes, yes. Still I find it rather hard to believe that you were the odd man out at your own housekeeper's funeral." With a steady smirk Fritsch drummed his pencil against his open hand.

Langsdorff sucked air through his nose and drew himself up haughtily.

The hiss brought Fritsch's eyes up. "Yes, Lieutenant?"

"Forgive me, sir. Am I to understand you doubt my word?"

Fritsch reddened, then looking downward spread aside some papers on his desk, wrinkling the top one. He smacked them with his open hand as if they'd tried to move. "All right, then. Let's turn a page, here, shall we? Your membership in the Party. The last time you applied for reinstatement was in 1942. Tell me what steps you've taken to remedy that neglected situation."

Stumpff cleared his throat, sat forward noisily. "Allow me to shed some light on that for you, Joachim. Kurt's status in the Party, while never to be taken lightly, has had no effect whatsoever on his exemplary performance here since he began with you in 1941 - of which of course you needn't be reminded of."

Fritsch raised his head slightly, aiming a scowl at Stumpff. "Why don't you let Lieutenant Langsdorff do his own bragging?"

"I'm merely trying to point out, sir, that Party membership, while desirable, need have but little bearing on the performance of a man's duties."

"I see. You may be forgetting that such membership is mandatory. Not to be taken lightly. How is *your* memory, Lieutenant?" Fritsch hung wide eyes from the ledge of his bushy brows.

"I've always kept in mind the great pains my father took to get me reinstated, with no success. After that I thought -"

"You thought why bother, as long as you became too busy to get back into the Party like the rest of us."

Langsdorff brought his hands back around from behind him, clasped them across his belt. "I can't deny, sir, there've been times when I allowed my duties to take precedence over my standing in the Party."

"Don't get me wrong, Lieutenant. I'm well aware that your father is a magistrate at Neuruppin. Be that as it may, we have this matter of your report from Finland. It's overdue. Have it on my desk by no later than tomorrow morning."

"Yes, sir. Will that be all?"

Fritsch glanced up at him skeptically before he began to muss through some papers on his desk, then pushed the stack aside. "There is one other thing. Simply out of curiosity, how did you enjoy your stay at the Savoy this time around?" Fritsch stretched the rictus of a smile across his beaming face.

"I could have done with humbler billets, sir."

Fritsch began to shake his head, ruefully. "Modesty was not the better part of *my* stay there in '41, before the Winter War. I remember once in the dining room a waiter introduced me to Marshall Mannerheim's favorite dish: *Vorschmack.* The old soldier knew his food, all right. You didn't happen to catch sight of that illustrious old swine while you were there?"

"Mannerheim? Oh no, sir. I'd certainly know it if I had."

"Yes, I wonder if that dining room is still the same. Such a hubbub you could plot somebody's murder like you were discussing what's on the menu."

"There's still quite a din in there, sir, with all the - well, we've got so many of our people in Helsinki, now, you could say there's no better watering hole for us in all of Finland."

Fritsch doodled on his blotter, connecting two squares with lines to make a box. "Yes. I don't suppose you heard what happened while you were there." Fritsch turned aside, dropped a torn-open envelope and watched it float into his wastebasket.

"Happened, sir?"

"Yes. Any rumors floating around? Furtive whisperings, that sort of thing?"

"No, sir, I can't say that I did."

Fritsch propped his elbows on the desk, squashed a woebegone grin into his hands. "It wasn't splashed all over the newspapers. Nobody heard it on the radio. But did you know, Lieutenant, that at the very moment you were sitting down to enjoy your meal in the dining room - or how do I know? Maybe you were strolling along the Esplanade or driving past Parliament House or the National Museum. People right there under your nose might have been cupping their hands over it - Marshall Mannerheim's refusal to turn over his Jews to us. Hardly able to contain their glee when they couldn't wait to run out and start dancing in the streets."

Langsdorff heard again the babel of voices, a clank of silverware on plates. The fat German officer at the next table laughed. His cause for delight pouted on the pretty red lips of the busty blonde who sat across from him, sipping her champagne. Feverish eyes broke through a blind with the rustle of a wounded animal. Fritsch was saying, "Imagine what you would have thought if you had known what was going on right there under your nose while all those people were laughing it up, stuffing their faces and snickering up their asses at us Germans. Just think. Mannerheim put one over on us. But you might just as well go on ahead and finish your champagne. Right?"

Langsdorff shifted his weight onto the other foot. "I'm afraid, if anything like that -"

Fritsch sprang to his feet, sending his chair back with a wobbly crash into the wall. "We had them in the bag, you know! Then suddenly that pompous bastard Mannerheim says no! If it were up to me, I'd have that whole frozen little postage stamp bombed right off the face of the globe! I'd turn Helsinki into a rock pile! I'd go in there and take hostages until they coughed up every last kike! Somebody warned them! I've long suspected those goddamn Swedes. The Finns and the Swedes! For how many years have they been scratching each other's backs?" Fritsch flung his chair aside and stomped over to the window. He stood there breathing hard as he squinted out at the bleak, grey light in which barren trees were cheerlessly assembled out across the dead snow-speckled grass to the deserted street.

Langsdorff stood still.

Behind him Stumpff made choking noises in his throat.

He sat alone in the soft glow from the chandeliers, the candles on the tables lit under the breath and drafts that made them flutter. The pretty girl passed him a furtive smile, turned toward her date.

'I've never heard of it,' she said gaily. 'What's it like?'

'Pure heaven.'

The girl raised her eyebrows. 'Heaven's none too good for me.'

The fat officer clapped his menu shut. The gaunt man in a pinstripe suit pulled out a chair saying, 'I hear the Vorschmack here is highly recommended.'

Ubbink had said he was a Jew himself, the Finance Minister. Don't say his name until you're sure. Pay attention to the sequence. First, the Vorschmack, then he'll be Eliel Aalto.

The fat German officer leaned a grave expression toward his date as if suffering from too much light on the pleasure he took in her, saying, 'Everybody should have a hobby. Mine is working for the Third Reich.' They both roared laughing.

A voice blared inches from his face. "What do you think of that, Lieutenant?"

Langsdorff looked at Fritsch's blazing eyes. Spittle clung to the corners of his twisted mouth. A rough hand smeared it off. A face he could feel sorry for.

A voice inside him prompted him to say, "Why that's unheard of, sir! Absolutely deplorable!"

"Deplorable? Too bad you didn't hear it on the radio. You could have grabbed the nearest Jew and thrown him out the window, head first."

Langsdorff shook his head woefully. The man they knew him for was him. The lie in his mind was the only truth there was. "I can't imagine, sir. I'm sure something will be done about it."

Walking stiff-legged, Fritsch was on the way back to his desk. "You're goddamned right. If Mannerheim doesn't get stripped down to a private, there's no justice. We'll hear about it when the Führer puts his foot down!"

"Hear! Hear!" Stumpff bleated, clapping patacakes with his plump hands.

Fritsch glared at him. "All right, then. That's all, Lieutenant. You're dismissed. Stumpff, I'll want a word."

"Of course, sir," Stumpff said with a little bow.

Langsdorff saluted smartly, turned and strode toward the door. The door shut with a faint clunk and his shadow in the pebbled glass moved off.

Outside in the pale light and the cool blustery air he slumped back against the wall and lit a cigarette. The pose which bore him always, without feeling, toward the hardness that upheld his reputation was no longer just a mantle but a growth, and he felt the tentacles winding round and round, protecting him as he tried to shake it off. When danger squeezed, he almost even loved the pain that stood him back beyond the tears of others, and he could strike at a man like Baab as if at Hadamar he'd killed Bertha with his own hands.

"Ah, there you are!" Stumpff was pushing on the door against the wind. A gust slapped his cheek with his coat-collar. He rubbed his hands together, took out his platinum cigarette case, fumbled out a cigarette and turned his back to the wind to light it.

Langsdorff said, "Is everything all right, sir?"

"Ah, he didn't appreciate my interruptions. I couldn't help it. I had to set him straight. Sorry he was so rough on you in there. It's not *you*, you know. He takes it all too personally. That business with the Finnish Jews."

"Thanks for sticking up for me, sir."

"Not a bit of it, my boy! You're not the only one. I got on his bad side, too." Scissoring his cigarette between two fingers, Stumpff puffed on it. "I suppose he dug into the files to refresh his memory on my role in getting you signed up right out of a seminary, as it were. Pardon me, a jail cell."

Stumpff paused a moment, chuckling. "He just gave *me* a piece of his mind, too. Hell, I wasn't going to argue with him. You saw it. Spoiling for a fight. This Helsinki situation's got him tearing his hair out. Plus I don't think he ever forgave you for how you dealt with Baab. Flouting the laws of the Teutonia, for Christ's sake! So your report from Helsinki was late. No big deal, but suddenly it's all news to him – your standing in the Party. I didn't appreciate it, when it was me who set you on the path to where you are today. Where's the respect?" Stumpff puffed nervously on his cigarette.

Langsdorff took a long pull on his own, flipped it out into the dead flower bed behind the walk. "The reason I went to

Bornichen the way I did, sir, was that I knew Fritsch wouldn't let me if I'd asked permission."

"Of course! Right on the money, Kurt. He's spit and polish all the way. Still, in the future, better do things by the book."

"To tell the truth, I wish my wife *had* been there."

"Yes, but then you'd have a problem, wouldn't you? You couldn't lie about it." Stumpff took a step toward him, reached for his arm but fell short of touching it. "Give Fritsch a day or two, he'll cool off. So Mannerheim wins one. It's no skin off our teeth. How many Jews slipped through our fingers? A lousy handful. We'll make it up. If I were you I'd get that report on his desk tonight."

Langsdorff smiled at the cold protruding eyes bathed in benevolence, in which sincerity made almost likeable the man he knew he should hate.

Stumpff dropped his cigarette and stepped on it. "Goodbye, Kurt. You keep your chin up, now."

"Goodbye, sir." Langsdorff was careful not to squeeze the plump, gloved hand too hard.

He watched until Stumpff disappeared around the corner onto the walkway to the street, then leaned back, lit another cigarette and took a long, deep drag.

She was there in the clearing smoke. French, they say, as if he'd hired her to hold his hand until the shovels gagged Frau Hintz forever. He could feel her body down along the length of his, that moment he had loved her, trampling on Elfriede.

She lay asleep beside him, and he looked at her, a child almost, the curly wisps of golden hair that fringed her temples and her forehead. He remembered the narcotic of her closeness to him as she stroked his face and ran her hand through his hair and then began to kiss him, and her body burned life into the years of his strength propped in a vain and rotting fastness, and he saw no conquest sleeping with her, no sin drawn from him; it was as if the spasm of life burst on the crypt in his soul and the dead, for just that instant, stopped shuffling through. Yet he felt the unfurling of those years now suddenly emptied into a violent encounter with what seemed hardly more than an apology of love, an announcement of its presence commanded elsewhere. She had done him a kindness, but it was just the relief that pierced his conscience, and peace eluded him again. A sound shook through the sudden selfishness of their repose. The hum of bombers far away, trombone notes held in menacing harmony, on their way to the munition dumps, the oil fields and the bridges. A darker, slighter body flopped to the frozen ground in his mind. He wondered why he so recklessly wanted Simone to know. Why he wanted a margin of shame to surround her Frankish advantages that spared her from the gas chambers. He didn't know what good there was in goodness, if only he profited. If God could blame him for continuing to fail, why then didn't He in His infinite power intercede? If Kurt Langsdorff, in his littleness, was to blame, how did God in his immensity get off? Simone had whispered, 'There, there, I'm here.' But she could no more deny the futility struggling for his soul than a sense of laurels could recover the feeling he longed for. He could see it marching on him now, that such understanding as he had craved from her would capture him, and he would be down to only a confession, his last few shots. But hadn't he meant, all along, to keep one of the bullets for himself?

15

Obermeyer pulled over along the curb and stopped.

In the back seat Stumpff reached for the door handle that gleamed faintly as the overhead light came on and the door swung open. "Don't bother getting out, Obermeyer."

Obermeyer hadn't tried. He sat there staring straight ahead out at the darkened street.

"Come back for me a little later in the morning. Say ten."

The motor idled softly, rocking Obermeyer slightly. He roused himself, turning his head. "I'm sorry, sir -?"

"I said pick me up tomorrow morning at ten o'clock, not eight as usual."

"Yes, sir. I'll be here."

Stumpff grunted as he swung his other leg around. At the edge of the seat he stopped scooting out. "What's the matter with you, Obermeyer? Your mother still down with the vapors?"

"Oh no, sir. She's feeling better. No troubles there." Then Obermeyer went back to looking through the windshield into the darkness glowing faintly with the sweep of searchlights overhead.

Stumpff got out laboriously. From the curb he leaned in, clutching the open door. "Don't forget now, come for me at ten o'clock sharp. Got that straight?"

Obermeyer said nothing. His hands were on the wheel. Exhaust fumes drifted up over the top of the car.

Stumpff thought he'd seen him faintly nod. Promises with that man meant very little, anyway. God only knew what route obedience took through that thick skull. He gave the door a shove. "All right, Obermeyer. Goodnight, then."

The door slammed behind him as he started for the iron gate. He trudged up the stairs. Something seemed vaguely amiss in the corridor as he passed a few doors, some of them ajar. Well, that was their business. As he was turning for the next flight up he glanced at 211, saw no light under Frau Straub's door. Asleep, he thought. Leave her be until morning. He kicked something that clattered across the landing. He went over and stooped to pick up the fountain pen that looked expensive. He thought about saving it to ask around. No, the alabaster finish must be imitation. The other things that looked like refuse scattered around were just as worthless, a scuffed and wrinkled pair of shoes outside a door. He was too tired to care, and tossed the pen under the stairwell. Going upward now, his legs felt heavy, clumping step by step. He was panting by the time he reached the top.

He came into his cold and darkened flat, threaded his way through the kitchen to his chair and turned on the lamp. Strands of Trude's hair flew into the light as he sat on his coattails. He looked across into the half-dark where Hanne had so often got his dinner. There was no Hanne now. No cat. The cream in the icebox had gone sour. She hadn't left the steam heater on. Selfish bitch, he thought.

A wave of hatred came up into his heart like nausea, a wave of hating her for being gone. He got up and trudged to the cupboard and took down the cognac bottle and a snifter, carried them over to the table and sat in the sturdiest chair he'd designated as his own. He felt a presence lurking in the stillness of the hollow where she'd been, and twisted around as if a hand had touched him uninvited. He thought he heard her giggling back there in the bedroom: *Surprise! I'm staying, Willy! Now take off that coat and let me warm you up!* In the darkened doorway, through which he could make out the bedstead, green eyes glowed on their haunches: the ghost of Trude left behind to get her share of pilfered sausage. He choked back a laugh and, reaching for the bottle, poured up to the brim, raised the glass and the cognac went down burning.

He'd never had Frau Straub up here, naturally, while Hanne was in the way. In his mind he saw that woman's cat-eyes fluttering, lips pouting, the way she moved that brushed him with desire. All she'd wanted was a little dance that night. But no, he had to wince and whine, 'It just isn't *me!*'

He grabbed his glass and slurped down another swallow of the tasty VVSOP, then slammed it back down the table. She was all right, he thought. He wasn't worried. The only thing…

In his mind Fritsch said, 'I'll want a word.' He wished he'd had the guts to say, *'If I appear to be too friendly with Lieutenant Langsdorff, that's because I am. Take it or leave it.'* He smiled as he saw himself raising a slack salute, muttering 'Heil Hitler,' then striding to the door and summarily going out. He spluttered with a laugh that broke into a cough. He washed it down with another slurp of cognac. Everybody knew *he* was a man. Just ask Hanne. And *her*, the stronger one. Those times she'd stood there in her nightie in the doorway, sleepy-eyed, bare legged. A woman with experience.

His mind began to roll like a heavy, unrelenting sea. A voice came to him from long ago when he had saved that boy from rotting in a prison cell forever, knowing he could make him almost from the bottom up like one of Arno Breker's sculptures. From the wet clay of the Church to the sentinel at the *Ordensburg Vogelsang*. It didn't seem to fit – that jarring unexpected air of hardness about him, some almost ruthless undertone. Nothing like the desperate man of God he'd known in those strangely happier times. Those days when...

Was Fritsch guessing, or did he know? He could see Frau Straub at the gravesite, looking every bit like she belonged there by Kurt's side. Who was she? People would wonder. Kurt's cousin from Provence? She'd beat a pastor's daughter any day. But then if *she* had been there, Kurt had lied. Kurt's wife was a decoy. The only other women in the picture...

There was a tapping at the door.

A timid voice passed through it like a ghost. "I beg your pardon, sir – it's me, Corporal Obermeyer."

"Christ almighty!" Stumpff growled. He lurched up onto shaky legs, suddenly felt lightheaded and stood there for a moment waiting it out, then reeled toward the door and jerked it open.

Obermeyer stood there, wide-eyed.

"What is it, Obermeyer? Why haven't you gone home?"

Obermeyer's eyes were open wide enough to load with shotgun shells. He pulled off his cap and kneaded it like bread dough. "Forgive me, sir. I should have spoken up in the car, but - it's about Frau Straub. The orders you left with me about her."

Stumpff blinked. "What are you talking about?"

"Your orders, sir, for me to keep an eye on her, and what to do if she refused to ride with me."

"Oh, for God's sake, Obermeyer, it's getting on toward midnight."

Obermeyer kneaded his cap some more. "Yes, sir, I know. The thing is, I forgot to tell you earlier. It was on my mind, but you see, she *did* refuse to ride with me, for no good reason. So I got to wondering and I followed her, according to your orders. Now I can report to you which I forgot to do downstairs."

"Did I leave you with any orders to follow her?"

"You did say keep an eye on her, sir, which I couldn't do unless I followed her, and would be disobeying orders if I didn't."

Stumpff vaguely felt a sort of animal intelligence barking at him like a dog expecting him to understand. His eyes fell upon the gun strapped to Obermeyer's side. "What are you doing with that gun?"

Obermeyer raised his arms to peer under one elbow. "I've had it on all day, sir. It's mine."

"I told you once you don't need to be carrying a gun around."

"Yes, sir. It's been in the glove box for some time."

"But now you've got it on."

"Well, you know how things are getting anxious in the city, all the commotion and the talk of where the Russians are, people packing up and -"

"Rumors, Obermeyer. I hope you're not intending to shoot somebody with that thing."

Obermeyer didn't smile. "Well, if I had to, sir -"

Stumpff looked at the stubborn glaze drawn across Obermeyer's eyes as if the gun had made him smarter. "All right, Obermeyer, what's all this business about Frau Straub?"

Obermeyer shifted his feet around, looked up through a

canny squint. "Has she spoken to you, sir, about the way she treated me?"

"You know as well as I do that I've had no chance to speak to her."

Obermeyer's body slumped with a sigh. "I don't believe you're going to like this, sir. She didn't state it, but there was a reason why she wouldn't let me drive her anywhere in comfort."

"Why shouldn't I like it?"

"Foreigners, sir." Obermeyer made a shuffling movement, chugging his arms as if to plant himself for some defensive maneuver.

"Now you've completely lost me, Obermeyer."

"Yes, but if I hadn't seen *them* coming out of the tenement while she stayed in there, perhaps I wouldn't have followed them clear out to St. Anne's Church."

"Followed whom from where?"

"The foreigners from the tenement on Bulowstrasse, to which I could have given her a ride, but then it came to me why she refused. As soon as I set eyes on these two men I knew that's what they were, and I had to ask myself, what business did *they* have walking all the way to church that late at night, when all the services were over and the doors locked up tight?"

"Let me get this straight. You followed a couple of men from Bulowstrasse to St. Anne's because they looked to you like foreigners?"

Obermeyer was already nodding. "That's right, sir. Furthermore, that pastor at St. Anne's, Mochalsky – my mother's got nothing good to say about him, man of God or no. The rumors are that he's a foreign agent. She put her foot down on attending any of his services anymore. Not only her. Before long he'll be preaching to empty pews."

"But Obermeyer, you're telling me these foreigners, as you

call them, came out of the tenement where Frau Straub had gone in. How could you know which flat they visited, if any, if you stayed out in the car, unless you didn't?"

Obermeyer began to shake his head. "To me there was as good a chance as any that Frau Straub was in the flat that they had just come out of."

"How do you figure? Chance covers quite a lot of territory, Obermeyer."

"But I've got an eye for foreigners, sir, thanks to my mother. She taught me." Obermeyer brightened. "So aren't you glad I followed them, sir?"

Stumpff stepped back, pulling the door with him. "Get in here, Obermeyer."

He obeyed, nodding like a horse being led in at a canter. Stumpff shut the door, took Obermeyer's arm and hustled him a few more steps into the room. "Now Obermeyer, it's fair to say that you were upset by the way Frau Straub treated you. But let's get down to brass tacks. Could you be trying to frame her because she slighted you?"

A tic started to jitter in Obermeyer's left eye. "*Lie* to you, sir? Goodness, no."

"Here's what we'll do. I'll have a word her, then we can clear the whole thing up."

Obermeyer's face flattened back as if he'd been hit by a shovel. "But I can get the *proof*, sir!"

Stumpff began to shake his head. Something made him want to laugh. "I've had a very long day, Corporal, and I'm tired. Run along, now. Get some sleep. You're dismissed."

Obermeyer hung his head, fitted on his rumpled cap and dragged a step back toward the door. Stumpff yanked it open, Obermeyer plodded through. Stumpff watched him for a moment shuffling slowly down the corridor toward the stairway, then shut the door and started back for his chair, feeling drained of all desire for another drink. It looked more like a dose of medicine for his nerves. Nerves writhing around like hydras, snapping at what wasn't there. Obermeyer seeing goblins in a couple of men his mother would pick out of a lineup blindfolded. And yet...

He tore back his cuff, read 11:49 on his watch. Past her bedtime, but she hadn't reported to him yet. She must be down there now. No, he couldn't. He was too drunk. He trudged back across the room, sank into the hard chair, making it clatter, and began to wonder now if he had cooked his own goose, sticking up for Kurt. He looked up at the picture of the Führer on the wall where he wished there was a window to look out of. A window Hanne used to grouse about, *'No sunlight ever, Willy? Why did you ever take this flat? With just a few more Reichsmarks -'*

He suddenly sat up rigidly, pushed off the table to his feet and hurried to the door, opened it and saw that Obermeyer was halfway down the corridor trotting like a pickpocket whose hands had been too light for him to feel. He thundered, "Obermeyer! Come back here!"

Obermeyer stopped so suddenly his back lurched forward, then he spun around and took long stumping strides until he pulled up in front of Stumpff's upheld hand.

"About that gun, Obermeyer?"

"Yes, sir? I know. I'll return it to the glove box."

"No. I want you to keep it on."

"On, sir?"

"Just in case. Those things you said about the foreigners –of course they could be harmless. But, do you know how to use that thing?"

"Oh, in training, sir, they said I was quite some shot!"

"Mmm. I'd like you to keep up with your surveillance for a few more nights."

"Surveillance of -?"

"Frau Straub's movements, of course. But keep an eye out for those foreigners, too. I don't have to tell you not to use the gun unless you absolutely have to. Show restraint."

"Are you serious, sir?"

"Well, of course I am. You're going to have to keep late hours."

"I've always been a night owl, sir."

"Be a man and keep a level head. No lynching command is going to chase *you* down and corner you in somebody's woodshed."

"Not on your life, sir!"

"And whatever you do, don't fall asleep in the car."

Obermeyer looked down at his gun, caressing the holster. "No chance of it, sir."

"All right, then. Off with you. Come back for me tomorrow morning, ten o'clock on the dot."

Obermeyer saluted. He turned around and marched through the door and out into the corridor on thudding heels.

Behind the closed door Stumpff let out a sigh. He walked back to the table and lowered himself slowly into his chair, looking at the empty snifter. Another drink? Yes, that might do it. He reached for the bottle, then thought better of it. Fortify yourself and wind up acting like a fool? Where could she go in the middle of the night? Could she be holding out on him? No, she wouldn't dare. Just who was the fool around here, anyway?

That woman crept around the edges of his life. Circling, like one of those Greek birds, and he thought back to happier days. Simpler days. Were there any? A strand of Trude's fur clung to the far edge of the table. He leaned over to blow it off, but then let his breath out slowly. He swung his hand around, grabbed the bottle and poured, watching the amber splash. He took a small sip, *comme il faut*. The French, he thought. Now *she* was French. Strange how he had given her life back to her. If I were a woman, he thought, I wouldn't want to ride alone with Obermeyer, either.

16

Kurt was gone when she woke up in the hotel. She had to catch a later train back to Berlin alone. He hadn't left a note, and that worried her. She hoped he'd read the one she'd left in plain sight on the chair where he had draped his tunic: her exact address in Lichterfelde, adding 'In case anything goes wrong...'

There were delays along the line and it was nightfall by the time the train pulled into Berlin, and through the window she could see the thin blue lights at the tunnel exits, the zinc sculptures standing their massive ground as they were left behind, and they wound past the sidings and the freight yards toward a shift onto the track that soon would straighten through the city toward the great domed hub of *Anhalter Bahnhof* and the walkways winding round the fountain in *Potsdamer Platz*, no longer spouting water.

The platform swarmed with people waiting for a train – any train, as long as it was going westward. She caught a tram to her Lichterfelde stop and hurried up the stairs. She didn't see the man bounding downward until he clipped her with his bag and kept on going. Dressed in mufti, now, whereas she'd seen him once in uniform, his long unbuttoned overcoat flying like limp wings behind him. The corridor was messy – scraps of paper, a rumpled tunic, empty bottles. Doors on both sides stood ajar and everything was quiet. Eerily quiet, as if everybody had gone except her. Stumpff's letterbox, she'd noticed in the vestibule, was empty. The Russians could be here within a week. Why should he stay behind? Why bother with her anymore, if everybody else was getting out?

Her flat smelled of damp wallpaper. She turned on the steam heater, lit one lamp. There was a flash against the curtains and she went over, parted them and looked down. Rain flittered in the headlight beams from a long black staff car. Behind it, the young man she'd passed on the stairway was cramming bags into the open trunk. Another car splashed past. She let the curtain fall. There was no use trying to sleep, she knew, and paced the floor from room to room, smoking up her cigarettes. She wouldn't go upstairs to see if Stumpff was gone. She couldn't face him now. Those bulging eyes of his would get her in their sights and she would crack, she knew. She was afraid that Kurt would come and Stumpff would catch them here, together. She'd been too full of love for him last night, too quick to pour it out into the note she'd left: 'If anything goes wrong. Second floor, number 211.' The only other thing to do was run, or watch the walls close in. Whenever they made up their minds it was time to come for her, Kurt would never know and she would disappear. One thing they didn't have and couldn't do without before they killed her: all she now knew about Kurt that they didn't. Gunther had once said, 'Under torture, everybody talks.'

The room was heating up. She flopped onto the sofa in her damp coat. Things here and there across the room gleamed in the faint light. The glass that Gunther kept looking through.

God couldn't make him see her. He should be happy where he was. She shut her eyes, feeling a sting under her lids. All that foul air on the train, the acrid smoke and brick dust from the bombing and the fires. The steam heater knocked and banged.

All at once she awoke with a start. The room felt hot; she had been sweating. She listened to the smacking of the rain down in the street, the rush of water in the gutter drains. She got up and went to the window, parted the curtain and looked down into the street – deserted except for one small car on the other side, shining mirror-like in the long slick of the rain under the streetlamp, dripping from its fenders. She was about to let the curtain go when something made her look again. She hadn't heard the car start up, but it was wobbling faintly now. Puffs of exhaust spurted out from under the rear bumper. A black shape behind the front window moved. She couldn't make out any features, only a shape hunched over the wheel. She stepped back quickly, letting the curtain go, hurried over toward the lamp to snap it off when suddenly the phone rang. She looked up at the clock on the mantle: 12:22. She let the bell ring four more times before it stopped. Cold gripped her heart. At any moment now the streetlights would go out, darkness would cloak the city, preparing for another British raid. That wraith behind the wheel could be from the Gestapo. She snicked off the lamp, went back over to the window, stood behind the curtains while she plucked back a view through the slit. The window on the driver's side was rolled down halfway. A face peered upward over the spattered glass. Henk de Vos! Was he alone? She couldn't see anybody in the back seat. If he'd brought Kurt along, why were they just sitting down there? Suddenly three sharp knocks hammered on the door and she stood stock still, barely breathing. Her heart thumped like a jungle drum. The knock gave it away. Too vicious to be Kurt. She heard a creaking near the door, pictured a gloved fist poised to hit again. No voice roared through the door. Just creaking, like somebody out there pacing. Then it seemed to move away, becoming footfalls, now dull thuds on the stairway, moving upward. Silence for a moment, then the muted slamming of a door. Her eyes fled toward the clock, its heedless, blithe tick-tock like sound given to the trick that now might not be time enough to get out before he came back.

She ran back to the bedroom closet getting out of her wet wool coat, dumped it onto the pile of soiled clothes and tore her trench coat off the hanger. She grabbed her handbag off the bed and hurried back out into the vestibule where she had left her shoes. There in the dark the doorknob faintly gleamed. Her heart caught in her throat. In the strip of light under the door she saw the scrap of paper lying there. She stooped for it, stayed on her haunches while she held it near the light and read: *Urgent I see you. Be thinking of Helsinki. S.*

She stood up letting the paper flitter to the rug, slipped into her shoes and flew out pulling on the door until the bolt clunked and she broke into a trot and took the stairs on tiptoe, swung open the inner door and then the iron gate and stepped out into the rain. The streetlamp still gleamed on the wet street and across the hood of the small car. She kept her eyes off the windows as she pulled up her collar and turned down the winding route toward nowhere. She would say St. Anne's if they came after her, thinking Ubbink could be hidden in the back seat, if not Kurt, they were so seldom apart. Still not looking at the car she crossed to their side, veering toward the same direction it was pointed. She walked briskly at first, waiting for their headlights to come on and light her up, but as she moved deeper into the murk and closer to the corner where she'd have to turn, she slowed to keep from sinking into the dark where they might lose her. Behind her suddenly headlights flashed on and found the scut of her coat before she made the dark again rounding the corner. She heard the rumble of a motor just as the streetlights went out, like a power failure in one neighborhood after another, and for a moment she was in pitch black. Then light from behind, moving up on her, spread onto the shapes ahead and all at once the car pulled along the curb beside her, tires splashing gutter water as brakes squealed and it stopped.

She stopped. There was no use running. Nobody got out. The car sat there idling in the rain, drops drumming on its hood. She felt a hand on her shoulder, clamping down, and as she twisted toward it the wet face, inches from hers, belonged to Ubbink. He must have got out way back there and followed her on foot. He gave her a shove toward the car. She lurched and stumbled as he pulled back on door, saying harshly, "Get in."

Nobody else but De Vos was in the car. She did as she was told and sat there, soaking wet, as the car began to move and Ubbink, with the wet pelt smell of a river rat beside her, rammed the door shut. Presently she said, "What do you want? Where's Kurt?"

"Shut up," Ubbink snarled. "We'll let you know."

She felt too afraid to speak, now, as if a word was all they'd need to tie a gag around her face. The streets, as De Vos careered around one corner after another, gunning the motor on straightaways, were deserted, and she kept expecting some air raid warden to step out of the dark and hold them up. So far the sirens were silent, but searchlights swept the low rain-soaked ceiling. Finally she flung her face at Ubbink and cried, "Where are you taking me?"

"You'll see," Ubbink said.

Her mind raced in the silence as De Vos drove on, taking corners as if he knew some route by which they could avoid being stopped. The next thing she knew they were pulling up to the narthex of St. Anne's, and the stately cypresses that rose above the pathways into a pale misty moonlight.

"This is where we get out," Ubbink said.

"Is Kurt here?" she said.

He didn't answer, but got out and held the door for her until she was out, too, rain pelting her head. De Vos drove the car around to the side where he doused the lights and shut the motor off. There was the slap of the door shutting.

Ubbink took her roughly by the arm and hustled her around to a side door. He gave her a shove and they followed her in. A draft swept in on the candles lit for the Virgin Mary, and shadows from the dancing flames pulled at her motionless serenity.

Pastor Mochalsky's voice fell fervently out across the mostly empty pews. "Behold, I have told you before. Wherefore if they shall say unto you, Behold, he is in a desert; go not forth, he is in the secret chambers; believe it or not. For as the lightning cometh out of the east, and shineth even unto the west; so shall also the coming of the Son of man be... "

Ubbink pushed her past the edges of the pews, unheeded by Mochalsky, then through a passageway to another door at the back. Outside the rain had stopped, except for an occasional drop. They shoved her along to the edge of a flight of stone steps and she stumbled once before they came down to a street and turned along a row of brick tenements, then crossed where the road began to slope from the edge of a ruined building toward a dip under a bridge, and she could barely make out the piers sunken in ink-black. She heard only their own footsteps, the breeze whistling past heaps of spired fragments of what had once been sturdy structures. They stopped her near the abutment under the bridge while Ubbink fumbled out a cigarette. He struck a match, it flared and he touched the flame to the tip, then held it up close to her face. The breeze blew out the flame. He looked back up the hill toward the faint glow in the colored windows of St. Anne's.

De Vos came down from the direction of the grass.

Ubbink hurried to say, shoving his face up close to Geli's, "Where did you think you were going?"

"I saw you from my window. I thought Kurt might be with you."

Ubbink shook his head. "Hoping he'd walk right into a beehive full of German officers?"

"No! They've cleared out – all but a few."

"Why did you leave him your address?"

"In case I wanted him to know."

"But didn't want to be there when he walked into your trap."

"You've got it all wrong. What do you want of me?"

De Vos stepped forward, speaking quietly. "Kurt asked us to come and get you."

Her heart soared.

Ubbink reached between two buttons of his coat and came out with revolver fitted with a silencer.

Geli sprang back, buckling in one knee as a dead branch rolled under her heel. Terror gripped her like a blindfold.

De Vos said, "Put that away, Ubbink. You know what we agreed."

Just then Geli heard the smack of footsteps. Something moved into the blackness near the abutment, then stepped away into the faint light from the other side of the bridge. She saw the cold lurid smear of a face under a slouch hat, a ghostly luminescence as it moved toward them, arms swinging in long sleeves. The slick of small thin lips quivered with the uncertainty of a grin. A lump drove up into her throat.

Suddenly nearby an air-raid siren wound up its ear-splitting high note.

Ubbink raised his gun, spoke in a loud commanding voice, "What do you want? Speak up! Who are you?"

The figure turned abruptly and began to hurry away into the fog.

Ubbink took aim, but suddenly there was nothing to aim at.

The air-raid siren cranked up, howling.

"I know that man!" Geli cried.

But the siren drowned out her voice, and the figure disappeared like all the other traces of light gone out across the city as the earth shook with the landing of the first bombs.

17

Between the crumps and the far-off flashes she could hear the thrum of the B-17's overhead. They were dragging her away, back up the hill into the shelter of a tree. One of them turned her around to face the trunk and held her by the shoulders from behind, then let go.

"What are you going to do?" she cried.

"Shut up." Ubbink came around her on the bed of wet decaying leaves until the gun was pointed at her belly.

She threw up her hands in front of her face. "I'm not Simone Miroux!"

"We didn't think you were," Ubbink said.

She thought now that maybe Obermeyer had spared her to be killed by them. She pointed out into the mist where he'd been swallowed up.

"That man came here to kill me! He would have killed you, too. His name is Obermeyer. A man I know was trying to be sure it was me, consorting with two men he suspects as being who you are – Dutch partisans meeting with Kurt to further his aims and theirs."

"I had a shot," Ubbink snarled. "You scared him off."

"Listen! This Obermeyer drives for a German officer living in my flat. Now that he's seen me with you, if you let me go I'll be dead within hours. So will the truth you'd better know before you -" She looked down at the gun and up at Ubbink again, filling her eyes with something he could do about her fear.

"Don't worry," Ubbink said, "we're not going to let you go." He dragged on his cigarette and lowered it, scribbling the dark across his face.

De Vos stepped between them. He lowered his hand onto Ubbink's gun arm. "Let her talk, Ubbink."

Ubbink gave him a sharp, shrewd look. "Get wise, Henk. Kurt will never know the difference."

Still buttressing himself between them, De Vos turned to Geli. "This German officer – is he still alive?"

"I don't know," Geli said. She suddenly felt like crying.

"When did you last see him in your tenement?"

"Not for several days. Most of the tenants have already fled. Tonight there was a note from him under my door. That makes me think he hasn't gone."

"Who are you?" De Vos said.

Geli stood up straighter, shaking inside. "My name is Geli Straub. My husband is Gunther Straub, a Wehrmacht officer now fighting in Russia – the last I knew. Whether he was killed or - I never found out why, but his stipends stopped coming. I had no money, so I seduced a lonely officer in my tenement: SS *Obersturmbannführer* Stumpff. The bait I offered didn't interest him. He had other ideas. In return for his gifts of food and cigarettes he wanted me to find out whether Kurt was loyal to him and the Reich's aims. I was to work on Kurt as if I'd known him years before the war, and was still as much an enemy of the Nazis as he'd been, then."

"What made Stumpff think you could do this for him?" Ubbink put in.

"I'd had experience in Cairo."

"Ah! Made to order. I should have known."

Geli ignored that. "I didn't want to do it. I'd had enough. But it was either that or starve."

Ubbink shook a smug sneer up and down. "You were good," he said, "because Kurt made it easy for you. I knew it from the moment I set eyes on you."

Geli felt his hatred feeling for her. She went on as if she hadn't. "I grew fond of him. I hadn't intended this to happen but it did, and I became afraid that, one day, he'd tell me things I didn't want to know. Snicker all you want, but I began to care for him. Everything changed. One night I thought he was beginning to have feelings for me, too. From then on -"

"From then on you could work your voodoo on him until you'd earned your keep. You begged him to let you go with him to a funeral."

"No. I wanted to go because Frau Hintz -"

"Frau Hintz was nothing to you but a way to him."

She wanted to hit him, but held onto her nerve. "That night in Bornichen he drank too much and told me things I didn't want to hear. Terrible things about the death camps. I tried to stop him, but it was no use."

"This note under your door," De Vos said. "What did it say?"

"He signed it S, for Stumpff. It said he wanted me to think about Helsinki. I knew he meant to flush me out."

"There you are, Henk!" Ubbink crowed.

"No!" Geli cried. "I'm not sure, but I think he'd somehow found out that I'd gone to Bornichen with Kurt."

Ubbink tucked in his chin to snigger. "More like he'd sent you, wouldn't you say?"

"No, I went on my own."

"Where you could tie up all the loose ends on Helsinki."

"I knew he'd gone, but I never asked him why, and he never told me."

"Tell us why we shouldn't think you've given Stumpff enough to send for the Gestapo."

"First, he wants nothing to do with the Gestapo. Second, if he'd got all he wanted out of me, he wouldn't need me anymore and I'd be dead."

Ubbink dropped his cigarette and clamped his hand down hard on Geli's arm. "After all you've done to Kurt, why shouldn't we save your Nazi friend the trouble?"

She saw the hell-bent murder in his eyes and wrenched out of his grip, stumbling backward. "You want to kill me so badly, Ubbink, go on then, pull the trigger!"

Ubbink fondled his gun, leering. "I've never shot a woman before."

De Vos cut in. "Kurt wanted us to find her, Ubbink. He didn't say anything about killing."

"God damn it, Henk!" Ubbink snapped. "You know goddamn well what we decided."

"What *you* decided."

"What the hell's got you?"

"We promised Kurt we'd bring her back if we found her. She could have gone on lying, but I don't think she has. What've you got to shoot her for?"

"We didn't find her. That's all Kurt has to know."

"Sorry, I won't back you up on that."

Ubbink spat into the leaves. "She's no good to Kurt. What we don't know is how bad she is."

De Vos stepped up to him, causing him to turn the gun aside. "If we go back without her, I won't lie for you. Either that or you can kill us both. Go on, then. Dust off your blood lust and pull the trigger. Just remember, Kurt will have to know."

Ubbink's face darkened to the same shade as the night. He swung the gun toward Geli. "You're bluffing, Henk."

Geli lunged up against the silencer, feeling the snout until it hurt. "How do I know it's not *you* that wants to do Kurt harm? Kill me as if I wouldn't talk. But don't pretend to love him if you don't know what I'd say. And if you don't, you won't get it out of me!"

Ubbink stared at her, then took a step back from the pressure of the gun against her belly.

"All I want to do is go with him!" Geli wailed, and heard her voice again out there banging against the night that seemed to take a breath before the next bomb hit, nearer than the last. A sickening gob of fear stuck in her throat. "The war will soon be over. The Russians are at the gates. One of you come with me to my flat and wait there while I pack. The other - right now all Kurt needs to know is - you'll be going westward, won't you? Toward Allied lines."

"We'll have to let Kurt off someplace before we turn back for Holland," De Vos said.

"The Allies are almost in Belgium. My French passport will help us once we get close to Allied lines. I'll be there to vouch for him. I'll back up every word he's got to say to the authorities."

De Vos said, "To be of any use, you know you'll have to fall on your sword."

"She hasn't got that in her," Ubbink muttered.

"Give me a chance!" Geli cried. "If you care about him, let me try! What can you lose?"

The gun in Ubbink's hand began to lower until it hung

limply at his side. "Once you're free of us, you could double cross him."

"And gain what? I'm telling you the war is almost over. My love for him is all I have to offer."

"Love," Ubbink sneered. "If it were up to me -"

She looked at the hate buried in his eyes, too shallow, and in her heart she faltered where she'd thought love was safe, and it turned restlessly. A shadow lurked and fled, cast by Reggie running for his life. But he was dead. Kurt was alive.

"Even if he doesn't love me, Ubbink, and I knew it, for God's sake take me with you. Think of him, not me."

Fog drifted across Ubbink's eyes. He raised his arm and bent his head over the luminous dials of his watch. "You're going to walk back to your flat. If you don't see one of us soon, make your own arrangements to get out."

"Promise me you won't tell Kurt about me. Please! Let me tell him when the time comes."

"You're in no position to be promised anything. One of us will come back for you tonight, or not. That will depend on Kurt. Now start walking."

Her mind jumped with another plea: Obermeyer. He could be out there, waiting, but her only chance was to keep quiet. She watched them walk away, then, until the mist fell in around them and they were gone. She started up the hill toward the narthex, but she would skirt it, not going in. Pastor Mochalsky's eyes might follow her all the way through the nave, clearing his conscience of the silence in which he had not really gone along with her murder for the good of God's better plan.

18

In the dark she felt around for the gun in the top drawer. A little light came through the doorway from the other room where de Vos waited. The cold, heavy steel came into her hand. She hurried with it back into the kitchen.

De Vos looked up from the table where a candle burned and he was chewing on some bread and cheese. She couldn't know what had moved Kurt to send him, but was glad he was the one elected. He stopped chewing.

Geli laid the gun on the table, near his hand. "You'd better keep this. My husband left it behind. It's loaded. I've never had to use it."

De Vos laid back a rumpled corner of the tablecloth. "No. I've got this."

She looked down at a large revolver fitted with a silencer. "Then -?"

"Leave it here." His eyes searched her quizzically. "You're packed?"

"Another couple of minutes."

"Hurry it up. Ubbink's due back soon. We don't want to keep him waiting."

"Just a few small things," she said, "of sentimental value." She went back and dragged her heavy suitcase from the bedroom into the sitting room, and stood there looking at the things she knew she'd never see again. She had salvaged her jewelry, what little money there was left. Not enough to get very far alone, she knew.

There were all these things she had once loved. They didn't seem to matter anymore. Some did. The dresses she'd worn when she had hoofed for the Haller Revue. The napkin signed by Richard Tauber. The Chocolate Kiddies poster she had once so coveted. Those photographs from Egypt. The rugs and tassled pillows, Cairo finally left behind. She went over to the Giorgione, said goodbye to it. Tears came into her eyes and smeared the tranquil nudes under the oak trees and that troubadour, plucking his mandolin. Tears for what? Another life when Gunther...

In the distant dark outside an air raid siren wailed. The bombs hit far away, but in the china cabinet glasses and dishes shifted, tinkling. Tram tracks were torn up everywhere, the underground a death trap. The ending of Berlin was paved with rubble, gaping craters, pictures still hanging in rooms blasted open like calling cards left behind by the obliteration of a family.

The sudden knocking sounded like a hammer trying to split the door. A chair clattered in the kitchen and De Vos exploded into the doorway.

"Who's that?"

"I don't know. Stay back there. I'll get rid of them."

He disappeared back into the gloom of the kitchen, dousing the candle, and she stood absolutely still. They might go away.

The knob rattled, she snapped off the light, then took one final chance on silence. Weight crunched the door and it flew open.

The dim light in the hallway silhouetted Obermeyer, draped in his civilian getup. He stood aside and Stumpff trotted in a grin and stood before her, shaking his head ruefully. "Why didn't you open the door for us, Madame? Is that so much to ask? You're not yourself. That must be it."

"You didn't give me time."

Obermeyer was fumbling for the chain under the abalone lamp. He found it and gave it a tug.

Stumpff's face lit up in red light. "Put that out, Obermeyer!"

There was a clank of the chain against the porcelain and dimness clutched the room again.

Geli smelled smoke. The candle that De Vos had blown out. She prayed they wouldn't look that way. Stumpff felt his way toward her, step by gingerly step. The other light still dimly on in the vestibule was not much to see by. Her eyes fell on her suitcase in his path. As he came on he kicked it, lurching forward. He reached down, feeling for the shape he'd tripped over, then straightened up. "Going somewhere, Madame?"

"No, I just haven't unpacked, yet."

"Come, now. Why would you need a suitcase for a little trip to St. Anne's?"

"I've been -" She stopped herself from saying Bornichen. She didn't know how much he knew, and stood looking back at his smugly leering, earthworm-pink lips. Fear ached in her neck and sucked on her breath. She tried to reach for the old mockery. The smell of smoke was stronger, now. She didn't dare look toward the kitchen. Obermeyer stood in the way of every lie she thought of, setting her adrift. She'd never paid much attention to the whiteness of his face. It was as if he'd lost a lot of blood, and like a vampire in dire need of a transfusion. De Vos was listening, she knew. He was waiting not for them to leave, because they wouldn't. The lies that used to light her path flickered in what little time there was to stall them. Under his soggy slouch hat Obermeyer licked his lips. She shrugged out of her coat and tossed it onto the sofa.

"You wouldn't have a cigarette on you, would you, Willy?"

He gaped at her. "Ah, how perfect. Let's all have a cigarette, shall we?"

"I wish you'd keep a tighter rein on Obermeyer," she said. "He followed me all the way to church, and when I spoke to him, he acted like he didn't know me."

"Ah yes, the church. We picked up Mochalsky, by the way. The cross didn't seem to suit him when words finally ran out. You're familiar with the good pastor, aren't you?"

"No."

Obermeyer fidgeted restlessly, shuffling his feet. "She's making fun of me, Herr Captain. Let me take care of her, now."

"Nobody's taking care of anybody. Put that lamp on again."

Obermeyer felt for the chain under the shade and red light slicked a boiled look across Stumpff's fat jowls.

"That's better," Stumpff said. He grinned at Geli. "Now I can see your face. I wouldn't advise trying to lie to me. I believe I told you not to go out, but you did. Why?"

"I was going crazy, all cooped up in here. There's no crime in going to church, is there?"

"Riding with a couple of men you once claimed not to know? Good church companions, were they? Devout believers? Or did you just need them to carry your suitcase?"

Obermeyer said heatedly, "They were the ones, sir, like I told you! The very ones! I was never wrong."

"Oh God, Willy. Don't you know he sees what he wants to

see? He's seen me naked, but I've never undressed for him. How can you take the word of the man who tried to rape me?"

"Rape you!" Obermeyer squealed. "I should -" His hand dropped onto his holster flap, clawing under the snap.

"Shut up, Obermeyer!" Stumpff thundered. "Get out of the way!"

Obermeyer's face seemed to peel back, pulled by his ears. "You mustn't let her talk that way about me, sir! I can't let that happen!"

"You'll stay out of this and keep your mouth shut!"

"Sir, I -"

Stumpff wheeled toward Geli with a kind of slithering aplomb. "Once and for all, Madame, I want to hear it from your lips. How easy was it, running out on me? Did you shed a tear for anybody but yourself?"

"Willy, can't you see it? Obermeyer's mad at me because I sent him on his way. I wouldn't let him touch me. He would have if I hadn't threatened to tell you. Tonight he tried to shut me up so you would never know. Willy, his stupid loyalty got to you, put you in a spell. The loyalty of a bird dog. Remember? Talk about a secret weapon! He's smarter than you think. Just smart enough to use his stupidity against you. Otherwise you'd ask him why he tried to get his way with me behind your back. Reduce the charge to insubordination, he'd go for that, but, now that he's got that gun he'll never tell you how I had to put him in his place while you were gone."

Stumpff shot a scowl at Obermeyer, who stared back in sheepish wonder. "What about it, Obermeyer?"

Obermeyer's mouth fell open, eyes draining of comprehension. "You couldn't take her word over mine, sir. She lives by lies. You can't believe a thing she says."

Stumpff grunted, as if kicking dirt over the sight of

Obermeyer. He turned to Geli. "You've been to other places in my absence, Madame. Small wonder you had no use for the car. It wouldn't do to ride all the way to Bornichen with Obermeyer, now would it?"

"Bornichen? Why should I -?"

"Don't lie to me, Madame."

"I'm not lying. You're guessing."

Stumpff raised an eyebrow, leering. "A little late for wordplay, Madame. I'm getting angry."

Geli settled the tempest in her mind with lazy aplomb. "All right. I wouldn't want you to get angry, Willy."

"Then you don't deny going to Bornichen with Langsdorff."

"No. The occasion was his housekeeper's funeral."

"When were you going to tell me?"

"How could I while you were away?"

"I'm here, now. So let's have it."

"What?"

"Don't play dumb with me. You stayed the night with him. What did he have to say about Helsinki?"

Geli began to shake her head. "Before he left he'd told me he was going, but never why, except - routine inspections, that was all."

"You left it at that?"

"I had no reason not to."

"And after his return?"

Geli blinked and squinted as she kept on slowly shaking her head. "No, he only said that all went well, but he was glad it was all over. His mind was on Frau Hintz."

He stared at her, veins bulging across his forehead. "All went off without a hitch, then, did it?"

She looked up. "Why, yes."

"Did you ask him what he meant by that?"

"Why?"

"I'm asking you."

"If there'd been some reason to, and it occurred to me to probe, at such a time I couldn't have or tip my hand."

"Yes. Being quite considerate of his grief, of course. I'd really hate to think that you're holding out on me."

"Willy, you're accusing me of doing something you wanted me to do," she pouted.

"Because I think you know more than you're letting on. You had a golden opportunity, and what did you do? I'm going to ask you one more time, then I may have to hand you over to Obermeyer, which I would also hate to do."

Obermeyer's eyes lit up. "I'll take her, sir! Let me have her!"

"Get away from me, Obermeyer! Just stand there and shut up."

Obermeyer slunk back, cowering. His eyelids flapped as if to put out his scowl.

"Now, Madame," Stumpff said, "Helsinki."

Geli sighed, gave him a steady, piercing look. "What about it?" she said.

Stumpff's face hardened like a startled death mask cast in lava. "You should ask. Because you haven't told me, yet."

"What good would it do, now, Willy?"

He stamped his foot. "What in God's name do you mean?"

"Everybody's busy getting out. Nobody's left to care. It's every man for himself."

"You, too? Don't be so quick to join the cowardly defeatists. We've stopped the enemy in the Ardennes. I'm still here, and so are you."

"All right, but you're not going to like it."

"Try me." Stumpff ran his tongue across a grin.

"I tried. I used every trick I could, but it was no use. I was afraid to tell you. He's a closed book, like you said. I don't see any point in going on."

He stared at her. "Say that again."

"I've had enough, Willy. I want out."

"*Do* you? Just like that. Shall I arrange things for your sendoff? Help you with your bags?"

"All right, I've failed. See if the Gestapo cares."

"And leave you high and dry? Like selling out that Tommy you were supposed to love in Cairo. Death does have a way of keeping love from getting out of hand."

"God killed Reggie, not me."

"Perhaps so. But then God's never around to defend Himself."

Obermeyer stepped forward, reaching for his gun. "Herr Captain, let me -"

"I told you to stay out of this, Obermeyer!"

Geli stepped between them. "Willy, I'm dying for a cigarette. Don't make me suffer."

"Cigarettes? I left a note for you. Why did you run out on me?" He put his face up close to hers. "Who were those men you were with at St. Anne's?"

"I was kidnapped. Obermeyer couldn't let that happen. He had to be the first to shut me up, then got scared off and left it to them."

"But here you are, alive."

"Would you rather have me dead? And never know why Obermeyer did away with me?"

"I don't know. When you're dead, you're dead."

Geli shook her head. "That's what you get for giving him a gun. A crazy little boy who can't be satisfied with shooting birds. But never mind. Add a gun to loyalty and you get the perfect killer."

"Those men who took you to St. Anne's – what were they to Langsdorff?"

"That's right, sir!" Obermeyer shouted. "Make the she-devil tell another lie!"

Stumpff scowled at Obermeyer hard enough to knock him over.

Geli reached around behind Stumpff's ear and twirled a little of his thin greasy hair around her finger. "You still love me, don't you, Willy? That's it, isn't it? You're jealous."

He slapped at her hand viciously. "How dare you! You think you've made a fool of me! Thrown me out and made a mockery of – of my boy. You protected him!" he screamed. "And you – you -" He choked back a sob. "Just because I've had feelings! Then you took him, too – my son! You tore him down piece by piece until there was nothing left but -"

"That was the deal, Willy. You knew there was no other way. I did what I had to do, the only way I knew how."

"She-devil!" Obermeyer spat. His coat swished and from the rush of movement his hand came up with a gun.

"Don't let her do this to you, sir! Let me take care of her. I'm not afraid!"

"Put that away, Obermeyer. You don't give the orders around here!"

Obermeyer kept the gun tight in his hand, eyes flaring insanely, swung it around until it pointed rigidly at Geli.

Stumpff stood stock still, watching them.

Obermeyer's eyes rolled sideways, then back.

Stumpff's hand crept onto his holster like a spider feeling for the snap. He tore at it, fumbled out the gun and had it up along his belt when it went off.

Obermeyer yelped as a bullet strummed a loud, sour chord in the piano, and Stumpff kept firing at Obermeyer's twisting figure until it jackknifed and crashed into the lamp, eyes locked in a dizzy, searching perplexity.

The smell of cordite laced the air.

Stumpff looked at the gun in his hand as if he didn't know how it got there, his face a plump white apoplectic mask. His eyes found Geli.

She started to say, "Drop the gun," when shoes thudded into the kitchen doorway. There was a sound like the quick swish of maracas.

Stumpff twitched and looked down at the hole in his sleeve. The hiss of another shot bucked in De Vos's hand, and buckling at the knees Stumpff began to crumple slowly, then pitched onto Geli's feet, clutching at her ankles. Slowly his hands began to loosen and he rolled over onto his back, and lay there, breathing thinly as he groped at the dark red blood seeping into his coat just above his belt and through his fingers. He struggled to get up, fell back onto his elbow, gasping for air. His eyes fixed on Geli. Blood ran from the side of his mouth, and formless words seemed to splash around, blowing little bubbles as he stared up at her, begging for something. Something she knew then that she had almost felt for him, swimming feebly toward her, going under.

"Tell me I was right about my boy. Tell me - I never, never wanted -" Gasping for air he blew more bubbles that drained into a red rivulet like a brushstroke down along his mump jowl.

De Vos stepped sharply to her side, pointing his gun downward. As he fired Stumpff jumped, then suddenly was still.

Geli looked down at the dying face still looking up at her and her hand clapped over her mouth, muffling the sob she knew should not be there. She dropped her hand and looked up and De Vos stood inches from her, glaring, eyes aflame, gun pointed at her gut. His eyes clenched as they met hers, and fear arched up out of her groin whipping like a live wire. "Now are you going to shoot me?"

De Vos let the gun drop loosely to his side.

She stared at him and felt the sting of tears behind her eyes.

"It's not for me to do what Kurt might regret," he said.

Geli caved in. Blood rushed throbbing into her head and, feeling faint, she swallowed back a sob.

De Vos looked down at Stumpff's dead eyes, snuffing contemptuously. "Got to know him, did you? How touching."

Geli looked at him. Defiance had no words for all he didn't know. She felt again the swelling in her throat.

De Vos said, "Funny he didn't let the flunky shoot you. Like you'd be less dead if somebody else did it."

"We'll never know, will we?"

De Vos gave her another look that seemed to want to break out into loathing. "I wouldn't shed a tear for that filth."

She stepped a little closer to the body and looked down at the cherubic face, devoid of sight like fish eyes in a basket. Almost more human now, as if life still moved under his gloves, but never had the chance. In his way, she thought, he had loved her, and she could say it only in a whisper, like a requiem he would laugh off, if he could. Obermeyer lay twisted over there, one arm up on the sofa, the carcass of a jackal. She took a step away from Stumpff. "He never could stay clean enough," she said, "by letting people die but never killing them himself."

"Are you all packed?" De Vos said.

"Yes."

"Then dry your tears and let's get out of here."

PART 2

19

The American Major leaned on his horn. People with bundles tied to bicycles steered, wobbling, to the sides of the road. The jeep bucked over bumps, careered around a bend. Beside the American the British Major grabbed for the door handle and held on. In the back seat Geli reached for Kurt, then took her hand back as they came out of the curve. He hadn't sought to hold her, just made a rigid iron handle of his arm for her to hang onto.

The bright sun shone on a trampled meadow to their right. They passed a dead horse lying in the ditch, still harnessed to its cart. Flies prowled its dully glistening eyes and clung to the ripped hide bloating under stiffened legs. Out in the full sun a girl lay asleep, her straw hat crumpled against her pink cheek. Sometimes a refugee would wave at them from the side of the road. A weary wave, but with a smile. Rottweil was coming up. Majors Haught and Evans had offered them a lift back on the outskirts of Reutlingen. What was going to happen next, Geli didn't know. The jeep swung suddenly leftward, Haught drove a few yards up the narrow street, pulled over and stopped. He was a rangy Texan with a big, kindly face and a way of looking at you that seemed to send back into his mind some request for the words that were to follow in his orderly drawl. You had to give him time to think.

"This must be it," he said.

The shingle swinging outside the neat three-story stucco building read, HOTEL MOHREN.

Major Evans twisted around, smiling at Kurt. "The French commandant's got his command post here. Chap named Darlan. We'll introduce you. Not to worry. Just leave it to us. We'll make sure you don't get off on the wrong foot."

Evans flashed another reassuring smile. He was a slight man with cheerful eyes who looked too young for his rank.

Kurt nodded.

Geli kept quiet. It wasn't her place to say anything. She could be his girlfriend, a relative, they didn't seem to care. They hadn't asked her for any proof of her identity. In time she knew somebody would.

Haught swung his long legs over the side of the jeep, saying, "I see no reason why they shouldn't put you up here for a while, Langsdorff. Let us do the talking. These frogs are kind of funny about guys like you. You know what I mean?"

They all walked into the lobby, Kurt in his rumpled uniform, minus a cap, Geli in tan slacks and a black turtleneck sweater. Heads turned as they came in, eyes prowled the tall man in the SS uniform walking with them, not in handcuffs. French voices chattered in the office behind the registration desk. Halfway up the stairway to the first landing two French officers were haggling in heated voices. Haught led the way up to the front desk.

Behind it a man in the uniform of the French *gendarmerie*

tapped a ledger with a pencil as he watched them. In French he said flintily, "Something I can do for you?" Laying eyes on Kurt, he tightened up on his scowl with a hard squint.

Haught leaned his elbow on the counter. "No offense, pal, but that went right past me."

Kurt stepped forward and in English said, "That's all right, I speak French."

The *gendarme* glared at Kurt. He looked at Evans, switched to English and said brusquely, "Who is this man? Your prisoner?"

"Actually, no," Evans said. "He's in our custody temporarily. We're treating him as a prisoner for his own protection. We'd like to get him into one of your rooms if that's at all possible."

The *gendarme* glowered at Geli. "Who's she?"

Haught leaned a little harder on his elbow, sketching spirals with his fingernail on the pitted counter. "What we'd like to do is have a word with Colonel Darlan about this man. How about you tell us where he's at? Think you can do that for us, partner?"

The *gendarme* looked Kurt up and down as if the next thing he was going to do was spit or hold his nose. "You want a room for this *chien*? This *mauvais*?"

Haught pulled back from the counter, eyes flashing indignantly. With a glance at Evans he said, "What is this shit, anyway, Dan?" He pinned a hard look on the *gendarme*. "For the last time, buddy, this man is in our custody. When you insult him, you insult us."

Stepping back, Kurt held onto his forbearing smile. "You can't blame him, Major. To him I'm a dog. A bad boy. No love lost for the enemy who should be dead."

"Oh, yeah? Translate stupid shit for me so I can tell this guy where to get off."

Kurt made a mildly warning gesture, raising both hands.

Haught slapped the counter, and looked about to lace into the gendarme when Evans spoke up. "Look here, Constable whatever-your-name-is. Our fellow here has a certificate from the military commandant of Reutlingen. Langsdorff, let's see that chit we got back there from Colonel Villon."

Kurt dug into his pocket, pulled out a crumpled square of paper. He peeled it open and tossed it on the counter where it did a pirouette before the gendarme slammed his hand down on it like a fly had done him the courtesy of coming to a fatal standstill.

"Read it aloud," Haught demanded. "Not in French, if you don't mind straining the gut."

Geli almost laughed. She'd had her share of run-ins with the French. Now she felt funny about having to remind herself that she was one of them.

The gendarme shot them all a hot glance before he held the paper under his nose and started to read in a wooden, stingy tone, *"The bearer is not a genuine member of the SS and is not to be treated as such. On the contrary, he is to be treated with every consideration."* The gendarme shrugged and flicked the paper back onto the counter. His English became raw, defiant. "I have no authority to give this man a room. To me, he belongs in prison."

Shaking his head slowly, Haught turned woeful eyes on Evans. "Correct me if I'm wrong, Dan. Did we just come off a cakewalk at Normandy and start picking up German hitchhikers because we were bored?" Haught leaned his full attention across the counter toward the gendarme. In his face pain cranked up disbelief. "Find Darlan for us, or else when we find him ourselves we'll have to tell him how helpful you've been. Then maybe he'll let you carry our friend's bag up to his room. How does that grab you, partner?"

In a soothing yet still crisp voice Evans said, "Yes, if you'd be good enough to point us in the direction of Colonel Darlan, we'll just go on up and have a word with him."

"Room 202," the gendarme said through clenched teeth. "Take the stairs. The elevator is out of order."

Colonel Darlan sat behind a desk in a room that commanded a sweeping view across Rottweil in the direction of the advancing front. He was a stocky man of about sixty with worry carved into his forehead like a Boxer dog's. He was listening to another French officer who was pointing at a map spread out on the desk. He cradled the overwrought furrows of his forehead in one hand, sighed and nodded as the officer's finger shot here and there, pressing on various locations. Awareness of the group of strangers finally brought Darlan's eyes up. "Gentlemen? What can I do for you?"

Evans stepped forward, saluting. "Colonel Darlan?"

"At your service."

"Major Evans, sir. My colleague and I, here – Major Haught – we're attached to the U.S. Third Army. We have a person here we think you'll be quite interested in. Allow me to introduce Kurt Langsdorff. He surrendered to the French commandant in Reutlingen this morning. That would be Colonel Villon. We're doing Villon a bit of a favor by bringing Langsdorff here to you. He had rather a rough go dodging the fanatics on the lookout for deserters to shoot, that's why he hasn't ditched his uniform, you see. He thought we might discuss his being employed in the army security service. We were thinking of the anti-Werewolf force, that sort of thing. Major Haught and I, we've had rather a long chat with him ourselves. To make a long story short, we're convinced that he's as much an enemy of the Nazis as we are. He's got some very important things to tell you about what happened in the Nazi concentration camps. He stands ready to serve as a material witness to bring the guilty parties to justice."

"Guilty parties," Darlan mused. "That's all well and good, Major -"

"Evans, sir."

"Yes, Evans. As you can see, I've got my hands full with the occupation of this area."

"Of course, sir. The thing is, our fellow here is quite worn out, and he has some very important information to discuss with you. We have no authorization to keep him. Our people told us to hand him over to yours. Now if you don't want him -"

Darlan's eyes found Geli. "And the woman? To whom does she belong?"

Haught stepped forward. "Mlle Miroux was with him when we picked them up. They're – as far as we know, quite good friends."

"I see. In no way related, I take it." He looked straight at Geli.

"We have been together since Berlin," she said.

"You're French?"

Beside her, Kurt moved uneasily. He'd been so reticent, almost hostile, since Ubbink and De Vos had left them off, and they had got in with the mobs of refugees moving westward.

"Yes," she said.

"Your name?"

"Miroux," Geli said. "Simone Miroux."

"And you have papers to prove that?"

"Yes."

"You're from -?"

"Provence. I've lived in Germany for some time. My sister, Maxine, lives in Paris. Would you -?"

Darlan waved his hand. "We'll look into that later, if

necessary." Darlan turned a sober look on Haught. "We'd like to take this man off your hands, but I really don't know where we're going to put him."

"Let me point out, sir," Haught said, "that like a lot of other Germans in uniform, he could have tried to disappear into the woodwork. The fact that he hasn't means he's taking a pretty damn big risk, here, and I think we ought to respect that."

Darlan picked up a pencil, let it flop onto the desk under his hand. "The best we can do is to keep him here in, shall we say, honorable captivity, until my security officer catches up to me from Constance. Other accommodations will have to be found for the woman."

"The woman' smarted on Geli's pride. She swallowed and said, "I don't expect to be given special consideration, Colonel."

Darlan raised his eyebrows. "Ah, but special consideration is due. We'll find someplace for you. I'll see to it personally. You won't be left out in the cold."

She lowered her eyes, in silence telling him the cold would be all right with her if that was all there was.

Haught laid his hand on Kurt's shoulder. "Sounds pretty reasonable to me, Langsdorff. Whatta *you* think?"

Kurt searched Haught's face but didn't speak, as if he was ashamed to.

Evans said in a patient voice, "Keeping you here for a few days will give you a chance to finish that report you showed us, Langsdorff. They'll want some sort of testament in black and white, I'm sure, when the time comes."

Kurt's eyes clung to Haught. "Yes, my report. That's all I have except -" He glanced at Geli, then as if mistaken left her standing there, looking more alone himself.

Darlan pulled a pad of paper under the pencil in his left hand and wrote on it. "Very well, take this downstairs and show it to the *gendarme*. He'll assign a room to Herr Langsdorff." He wrote some more on the pad, tore the paper off and handed it to Evans. "Wait in the lobby, Madame, until I find some temporary place for you to stay."

"Beggin' your pardon, sir," Haught said, "but that guy down there behind the desk is not the friendliest cuss in the world."

"He'll obey orders, regardless of his manners. Otherwise he'll answer to me."

"That's good enough for us, sir," Evans said. "Thank you."

Haught blurted in a flighty tone, "I see you're left-handed, sir. I didn't think you folks had any lefties."

"Why wouldn't we?" Darlan said. "We've got dwarf painters."

Haught hacked out a burst of laughter. "Hey, that's good, sir! You got me there!"

Darlan said to Geli, "Once you've finished downstairs, Madame, come back up here to me."

"Yes, all right," she said.

Out in the corridor near the head of the stairway Haught hesitated before stepping off. "So far, Dan, I haven't seen one frog that eats with his left fucking hand. So Colonel know-it-all gives me an art lesson like I just got off the turnip truck from Del Rio."

"You have to do your homework on the French before you criticize them, John. They can't bear playing second fiddle."

Haught took Kurt's arm. "Okay now, Langsdorff. Going on the premise that not all frogs are assholes, we'll see if we can't get you a bath and a change of clothes before we take off. You've got two strikes against you in those boots and pants."

Geli heard them talking like she didn't exist, and maybe she didn't, she thought.

Evans chimed in, "Darlan's not a bad chap, actually. Let

176

your report do the talking for you. That's your ace in the hole. Do that and I don't see why they won't see things your way, precisely as we have."

Kurt didn't smile. Geli felt his coolness, some wedge driven between them. He didn't touch her, make any sign that they were in this thing together, or that, when the time came, she'd be there for him to call upon. He'd been so distant toward her on the long road from Berlin. How often had she got the feeling that love, after all, was too much to ask. She didn't question him. She was afraid to know. Was it his wife? She'd thought of that. The woman he had sued for divorce to protect her, left behind. She'd tried to write it off, seeing the pain in his face, the enormities lost in the life now descending toward the littleness of begging for a room from people who detested Germans. And she was not the bad girl anymore, the spy, but still the person she knew least of all – herself.

The *gendarme* behind the desk read with pursed lips Darlan's note. He assigned a room to Kurt on the third floor, number 313, told him that he was to report here to the *Gendarmerie* three times a day. He would have to wait his turn to bathe on the ground floor. The plumbing upstairs was not in working order. No visitors allowed, without permission.

Geli swallowed, leaving the lump in her throat. They were to be kept apart. She had to find a way around that. But how? Could she risk asking Darlan upstairs?

Kurt turned to her, and she looked up at him, hopes soaring for a moment. By his eyes she couldn't tell what he wanted. She reached for him, he gently took her into his arms and she had only seconds to pray he cared for her before he let go.

She stood back and said, "I'll see you when all this is over."

He didn't nod, said nothing.

Haught's voice broke in. "We'll be taking off now, Simone."

He laid his hand affectionately on Kurt's shoulder. "Don't let these frogs put anything over on you. Get your issue of clean linen and a cake of soap. If this guy balks, report him to Darlan. He'll settle his hash."

"Yes," Kurt said in a strangely meek voice, unlike him. His hand looked limp, too, as he shook with them both, saying goodbye.

They wished Geli good luck.

As soon as they walked out she looked for Kurt, but he was leaning across the counter, waiting to get the *gendarme's* attention. She didn't wait before she said, "Goodbye, Kurt," and marched to the stairway and up to the room where Colonel Darlan was still holding court. She stood there near his desk until his eyes came up, then said, "Shall I wait here for you, Colonel?"

"Ah yes, do that, Madame. You might want to sit over there." Darlan indicated the row of three empty wooden chairs against the wall.

She sat in the chair nearest to the doorway. Maybe she wouldn't feel so alone here, she thought. Something was wrong. As if she'd seen the last of Kurt and he had made the getaway he'd wanted. He'd found a way to ditch her. Yet why had he let her come along with him this far? She'd got De Vos on her side, only to lose him when she'd mourned a Nazi killer. Had Ubbink warned Kurt against her anyway? She would never know unless she asked him. Ask him as if now it was her turn; let Elfriede Bensch, wearing his wedding ring, go to the back of the line, yet all this time it had been her. Simone Miroux was only pretty enough to trample on their vows, for she was here, turning her siren down, so far away was the woman who might hear it if she knew.

20

Colonel Darlan found a place for Geli to stay with the local pastor, named Hecklinger, at the rectory where he lived with his two young daughters. His wife had died of pneumonia in 1942. In the tiny room he set aside for her there was an old typewriter, encased in a dusty cover, on the shelf above the hangers in the closet. She asked the pastor if she might use it for a day or two. Not for herself, but for a friend lodged at the Hotel Mohren. He said the ribbon might have dried out somewhat, but yes, she was welcome to it. It was getting on toward dusk when she walked over to the hotel, lugging the heavy machine.

Boisterous French soldiers crowded the lobby. As she made her way toward the front desk, glimpses of two *gendarmes* showed through the pack of men milling about. They had their hands too full with business there behind the counter to notice her walking toward the stairway.

She kept on going up the stairs, feeling excited, stopped a moment on the first landing to get a better grip on the machine. Nobody yelled out, 'Hey, you!' and finally as she came up onto the third landing, facing 310, she turned leftward into the corridor.

Then she was standing there in front of 313, and thought no, she wouldn't knock. Shifting the typewriter under one arm she tried the knob. It wasn't locked and she went in.

He was sitting at a small pocked wooden desk, cradling his forehead with one hand, a pencil in the other. He looked up and stared at her. She kicked the door shut behind her and started toward him with a big smile, typewriter joggling against her belly.

"Look what I've found for you, Kurt! The pastor where I'm staying lent it to me. Don't worry, I slipped right past them downstairs. Too much of a crowd for anybody to notice. Won't this come in handy? For your report?" She lowered the typewriter onto the rumpled blanket at the foot of the bed.

He scooted around in the chair. "I'm writing it out in French."

"Yes, but typed, they'll find it easier to read. Don't you think?"

He nodded tentatively. "That could be," he said. His face was dour, unsettled, as if she were intruding.

"What's wrong, Kurt? Are you worried about something?"

He looked up at her with a faint shrug. "Worry always seems to tag along with hope."

"Don't think that way. What could go wrong? You heard what Evans had to say about your report."

"I don't know. You've seen the hatred going around here."

"I still say nobody can deny the truth of your report. You're not alone. You've got me to back you up."

As soon as she said it, something swept across his face like a magician's hand, and she thought she could see Elfriede in his eyes, curiously looking on, awaiting her turn. The road

180

ahead took a curve toward her. The other woman he had made a mistake with hung on. He'd keep her around a while longer in case he ran into trouble. Love had been a slip of the flesh, confided to a priest in the confessional. A dream left to fade where it could never have come true, pushed off like a Viking funeral. Nobody would sift through the ashes of the war. A little petulance crept into her voice, "So here it is if you want it," she said. "If nothing else it buys us a few minutes together."

"You're not supposed to be here, you know."

Her heart fell in. "Then I guess we're even. Sorry to see me, then?" She said it with a grin, as if she knew better.

He looked away, shoulders slumping with a sigh. "No, I'm sorry. Thanks for bringing it up. How did you get past them downstairs?"

"Oh, I just walked right past them like I belonged there. It was easy."

He gave her a look tinged with a smile, as much as to say a woman like you doesn't go unnoticed in a crowd.

She felt foolish standing there, and walked past him to the window and looked down across the road at the crippled German *Schwimmwagen* tipped onto its side.

Behind her that typewriter, like something also silenced by the war, sagging into the mattress.

He didn't want it, or her.

In her mind she stared down at Stumpff's dead face. Henk de Vos stood there beside her. She was in Mochalsky's car again, beside Kurt in the back seat, racing to get clear of Berlin. They got out beside a shattered church in some little town, from where they'd have to go on foot, so choked was the road ahead with refugees and military vehicles. Goodbye, Ubbink! Goodbye, Henk! How much had they told him?

Now it was her turn. She whirled on him, thrusting her hands behind her back. "Kurt -"

He turned his head.

She could feel it. Was there any use? Where was he? One foot in his report. She'd outrun her supplies, left the war behind. What right had she to live on borrowed time with him? His future still gaped like a mine field and he had a wife to whom he owed whatever love had not been left for dead. Another woman stood here with him in this borrowed room. That one the Dutchmen had to tell on, so he'd know. Now that he knew, he needn't ask. And if he wouldn't ask, did *she* love him? Or had it only been that woman known as Mlle Miroux?

He was looking at her, as if waiting.

She said, "Have you told your wife what's happened to you, Kurt?"

"No, I couldn't. There was no way to get through."

"But if you could -?"

"I don't know."

"That time you sued her for divorce – did she know why?"

"She wouldn't have understood."

"That's all in ruins now, though, isn't it? Like us." She couldn't bring herself to say, "I know she's on your conscience, now," but let the bait hang out there, praying he would get up and take her in his arms.

He looked at his watch. "Simone, somebody's coming soon to question me. Captain Paul, from Constance."

"I see. You think I'd better not be here when he arrives."

"It might be difficult. He wouldn't let you stay."

"Yes. Well, then -" She couldn't say what she was thinking – that Captain Paul was not here, yet. She was. She went up close to him, laid her hands on his shoulders and looked into his eyes. He stared up at her and she wanted to say would I be here if I didn't love you? He might laugh cruelly in her face. Temptation lined the damning truth with gold and silver. There, too, was the torch that burned a thousand women at the stake. Then it was gone. He didn't move, didn't speak. She didn't want to know. The fears she'd tried to put aside came home to roost: the Dutchmen had got to him. She hated them and said heatedly, "Why don't you just tell me, Kurt. Do you want me to go away?"

A kind of childish bewilderment came into his face.

She couldn't read it.

The door rattled with a hard rapping.

A voice out in the corridor crowed, "Herr Langsdorff! Captain Paul is here!"

The voice belonged to Colonel Darlan.

"I'll go now go," she said. "I'll try to see you in the morning. Wait for me."

He gave her a look she couldn't decipher.

"Langsdorff! Open up! We haven't got all day!"

21

Geli woke up early the next morning to a smell of lilacs gusting in through the open window on the warm July breeze, sweeping the dingy lace curtains in and out. The sun glared on the stucco remains of a blasted wall across the street on which tanks and jeeps kept grinding past, stirring up dust.

She was brushing out her hair when the door creaked and Pastor Hecklinger peeked in, saying, "Excuse me, Madame. A man to see you. May I send him in?"

Her heart soared.

They'd let Kurt out.

"Who is it?" she said.

"Colonel Darlan, Madame."

She kept her hopes up still, and hurried to the door, tying the sash around her dressing gown.

Colonel Darlan came in looking weary and careworn, with bags under his eyes, but managing to smile. "So sorry to bother you, Madame. I have some news." He was looking around for a place to sit.

She pointed at the one chair back against the wall beside the dresser. "Please sit down, Colonel. What news?"

He didn't answer as he sat in the wooden chair with a groan and Geli leaned back against the edge of the bed across from him.

"Yes, first of all, I've come to tell you that you're free to go whenever and wherever you wish – except, of course, back to where you came from. That wouldn't be wise – in the direction of our advancing front." He let his smile linger on her, as if giving her time to take him up on the obvious logic.

"Free to - then the restriction has been lifted?"

"Just that."

"For myself and -?"

"Not for Herr Langsdorff, I'm afraid. That is, not yet."

"What is it, then?"

"You're not being detained for any security reason. You can go now as you please. As for your friend, that might have been up to him, except -" He took a breath and, blinking rapidly, said, "You have certain ties to Herr Langsdorff, we understand that. The nature of which I take it to be personal enough for you to wish to continue on with him. However, I must tell you that, late last night, he was transferred to Constance on the orders of Captain Paul."

A hammer drove up into her head, blood pulsed and swelled there as she waited for the next thing he would say, softening the blow. "You mean somebody just came and got him, and just -?" Her heart burst and tears rushed out.

Darlan got up as she restlessly began to shake her head.

"No, no, Monsieur, I'm all right." She crooked a knuckle under her wet eyes, dug roughly across one cheek and then the other. "What reason did they have for taking him away?"

Darlan lowered himself back into the chair, gripping the

back to ease his fall. "They took him for further interrogation by Commandant Jimmey in Constance."

"But anybody who's read his report can't help but -"

Darlan looked up with a heavy-lidded blink. "That's not up to me, Madame. I read all of his report last night, and I must say it was most impressive. In fact, Captain Paul's opinion of Herr Langsdorff is favorable. Unfortunately, Jimmey, as his superior, has the final say."

"Final say for what?"

"For whether Langsdorff should be perhaps employed by the anti-werewolf force, or detained longer, possibly sent on to Paris."

"Paris? Why there?"

"There is a place in Notre Dame de Champs – an old Renaissance bastion now being used to hold German captives – most of them suspected of war crimes."

"War crimes! But for God's sake, Kurt Langsdorff is anything but that." She made a fist and tilled it roughly once again across her wet cheek.

Darlan wagged a finger at her. "I'm not saying it will go that far. Only that once these wheels begin to turn, they turn very slowly. I've known Jimmey since the start of the war. A very conservative man, which means he trusts his ability to let somebody else take chances. I wouldn't be surprised if they do take Langsdorff's case clear on to Paris."

"But surely somebody, before it goes that far -?"

Darlan was shaking his head fatefully. "You don't know Jimmey. You can't get past him if he's got his mind made up and the authority to do something about it. I outrank him, but in matters of intelligence, out here, he's got the final say. Jesus Christ himself could appear before Jimmey and he'd suspect him of being some escapee from a morality play. Frankly, I got a little hot with him. I told him to think carefully. Langsdorff's report will be extremely interesting for the Secret Service. The man has voluntarily surrendered, and made himself available to supply the names of Nazi officials who bear the responsibility for unspeakable crimes against the Jews. He is – and told me so himself – prepared to sustain those charges in front of an international tribunal. What more do you want? I said to Jimmey. He said that's all well and good, but somebody else, not him, will have to decide this man's fate. By which time it could be too late, I pointed out. I might as well be talking to the wall."

"Colonel, there's no time for me to tell you why, but I have to go after him. We left Berlin in such a hurry. I've come away without all my proper papers."

"But you must have something. You won't get very far without papers of some sort."

"I do still have my old French passport. But I'm alone, and since I'll have to go back through your lines to France, I may need something else if they detain me."

"Such as?"

"A letter of safe passage?"

He looked at her a moment, musing judicially the way a father looks at a daughter who's been bad but he can still love and forgive her.

"I'm going anyway," she said. "One way or another."

Darlan said in a weary voice, "I'll have to think this over. One thing gives me pause."

"Yes?"

"You're French, you say. I should ask you how you came to have French papers in Germany. If there's anything you're running from -"

"Not any more, sir. I'm hanging on for dear life."

He looked down at his knees, looked up again. "I'm a soldier, not a security officer, but I'll see what I can do for you. Come to my office tonight. I'll be there until after midnight."

She took his hand in both of hers and squeezed. "Thank you, Colonel. Thank you with all my heart!"

"I will accept that," he said with a kindly smile.

"I'll see you before midnight, then," she said.

"I'll be waiting."

She stood there by the bed, watching Darlan go out, then went to the window and looked down into the street. A group of children were playing keep-away with a flabby leather ball. The sky became a fan of brilliant pink and yellow behind the shell of a blasted building. A bicycle bell zinged. A small dog nervously skirting the children trotted to the rubble under the wall across the street, sniffed and urinated. Somewhere downstairs a radio was playing. The chansonnier was not a voice she knew, but she remembered the song from a record her mother used to play sometimes at home: *Non, je ne regrette rien.* 'I don't give a damn for the past. I'm starting at zero again. My life, my happiness begins today with you.'

The smell of lilacs seemed to thicken like the presence of a ghost.

22

The brawny sergeant behind the wicket took his time before he looked up at her. His bloodshot eyes were glazed with a kind of dull hostility.

Before Geli could speak, he said, "Go down that way, if you're applying for one of the stenographer's positions." He jabbed his left thumb toward the right.

"I'm not," Geli said. "I'm looking for a man I'm told has been imprisoned here."

The burly man, whose tunic strained across a row of brass buttons, began to shake his head. "Next of kin?"

"No, but I have -"

"Boyfriend," the sergeant stated smugly.

"I only wish to know if you can tell me if this man is here."

"What makes you think he is?"

Geli reached into her purse and pulled out Colonel Darlan's dog-eared letter of safe passage. "This will explain. The name of the man I'm looking for -"

The sergeant snatched the paper through the aperture and began to smooth it out on his side.

Geli hurried to say, "His name is Langsdorff. Kurt Langsdorff. That was given to me in Rottweil by -"

The sergeant rudely pushed the paper back. "Names mean nothing to me unless you're next of kin. Perhaps you don't know that collaborators are still being picked up here in Paris."

"Are you suggesting -?"

"I'm not suggesting anything. Giving you a word of advice."

Geli stuffed the paper back into her purse, feeling hot. She was about to turn away when she tripped on something he had said. "What were you saying about a stenographer's position?"

Breathing stormily, the sergeant pointed toward the left again. "Three doors down that way on your right. I wouldn't bother if you've got no experience."

Those days came back to her when she had learned shorthand in school, got pretty good at it. A thousand years ago, and yet...

"Oh, but I have," she said.

The sergeant made a careless gesture. "You'll find an army of housewives down there in the waiting room. I hope you've brought your knitting."

"Should I come back some other day?"

The sergeant gave her a taste of grudging kindness. "No, you'll miss the boat. These jobs are few and far between. With your looks, you might just have an edge. Officers have a reputation to look after, if you understand what I'm saying."

Geli smiled coyly. "Thanks for the tip," she said.

"Not at all, Madame. Not at all."

She walked down the corridor to a door that stood wide open. There was a hubbub in the room choked with ladies whose eyes came up as soon as she walked in, then cattily followed her, looking her up and down as she made her way to the desk where a secretary sat studying entries in a ledger.

The secretary looked up. "Yes?"

"Would this be where I apply for the stenographer's position?"

"It would. How's your shorthand, *ma chère*?"

Geli gave her head a toss and said, "Better than passable."

"Uh-huh. Well, I hate to say that you're outnumbered, ma chère, but let me have your name. Then you can have a seat, if you can find one."

"Miroux. Simone Miroux."

The woman wrote in the ledger, then scribbled on a small square of paper. "Here's your place in line. Wait till your number is called. Looks to me like standing room only, I'm afraid."

"I understand." Geli took the paper glancing at the number 22, thanked the woman and walked to the back of the room and leaned against the wall.

An hour passed, during which four women were called into the inner office, each one to come back out disconsolately. The hour was getting on toward 6 when the secretary pulled open a drawer, dragged out her purse and a rumpled paper sack. She began to stack and tidy items on her desk. The inner office door opened. An officer stood aside to let a woman pass. The woman said "Merci" gloomily as the officer, nodding, called to the secretary, "That will be all for now, Mlle Daubin."

Groans went up around the room like losers at a horserace.

The officer raised his voice, "Sorry, ladies! Come back in the morning!"

"And lose our place!" one of the women bleated.

The officer was just turning in the doorway when his eyes fell upon Geli. He looked at his watch. Chairs screeched and shoes clattered on the wooden floor. The crowd plodded toward the open doorway. The officer stood watching them as Geli let others go out ahead of her, then all at once he said, "We *could* squeeze one more in, Mlle Daubin. What do you think?"

The secretary stuck out her lower lip, making a helpless gesture. "As you wish, sir."

Geli was about to step into the corridor when the officer called out, "You!"

Several women stopped to look.

The officer's stiffened finger pointed at Geli, and she said, "Me, sir?"

"That's right. How long have you been waiting?"

"I'm not sure, sir. Upwards of an hour."

"Be so kind as to step into my office."

A raucous voice brayed, "I was here before she was!"

The officer ignored the voice, crooking his finger at Geli, who raising an eyebrow at the secretary started toward the officer who stood waiting in his open doorway.

He was a well-built if not a tall man, Geli saw, a few years younger than herself. Not bad-looking either, with dark eyebrows and limpid, intelligent brown eyes. But there was something of the self-important martinet about him – misplaced, she thought, like his pencil-line mustache. It was as if, a few years back, he'd grown it to look older, dapper and dignified as would befit an officer. But then as the years crept up on him he'd left it on, when really, it was time to shave, making him look younger as befits the truth or something more flattering by then.

The small drab office smelled of traces of perfume and pipe smoke.

The officer made his way around his desk, saying, "Please sit down, Mlle -"

"Miroux," Geli said, and smoothing her skirt at the back of her thighs sat on the hard wooden chair.

The officer lowered himself into his sturdier padded chair. "I'm Mattei. You may preface that with Major, but I don't insist. I assume you've left a dossier with Mlle Daubin?"

"No, sir. I'm afraid I've come on rather short notice."

He looked at her, blinking. "You mean -"

"Just that I've only recently learned of the job's availability, sir."

"I see. Of course you wouldn't be here at all if you hadn't come with considerable experience."

"I wouldn't say it was considerable, sir. I haven't been employed in some time. Not since the Germans came in."

"The duration of the Occupation, you mean."

"Yes. I had been working for the Renault factory on Ile Seguin in Billancourt when the Nazis seized it. They wanted me to stay on, but I refused."

"*Did* you. How did that strike them?"

"They told me to go out and have a nice time starving."

Mattei clucked as he rocked a little in his chair. "Not the cheriest sendoff in the world, was it? You don't look the worse for their boorish behavior."

Geli shrugged. "I took up tutoring. They wanted me for that, too, but I said no. That was when we gave them the slip by moving to our tiny place in the Rue de l'Odéon. A rabbit hole where they would have a hard time finding us."

"By *we*, you mean -?"

"Me and my sister, Maxine."

Mattei gazed at her for a long moment, then plunked a pencil on a notepad and pushed it across the desk toward her.

"Take a note, if you don't mind."

Geli stared at him. "Now, sir?"

"If you will."

"You mean in shorthand."

"That's right."

She gulped, but the ultimatum gave her heart, and she reached back in her mind for things she thought she'd never use again. She picked up the pencil. "Ready when you are, sir."

Mattei said, "The quick brown fox jumped over the lazy dog."

She looked up trying not to laugh as Mattei gazed at her evenly. She scribbled on the pad, handed it across to him. He looked down over his knuckles pressed against his lips, slowly began to nod.

"Mmm." Then flung his head back off his fist. "Of course we won't be following the adventures of the quick brown fox beyond this room."

His smirk told her to laugh, and she did. "If I may, sir, what exactly does the job entail, if I should be so lucky as to land it?"

Mattei sat back, getting another creak out of his swivel chair. "My job is to interrogate German prisoners charged with war crimes in preparation for their defenses at trial. Yours would be to transcribe every word that's said during these interrogations, *verbatim*. Think you can handle that?"

"Are you telling me I have the job, sir?"

Mattei smirked. "Well, shall we say on a trial basis without pay to begin with, if you're agreeable, pending the submission of your dossier."

There was a light rapping on the door, followed by Mlle Daubin's muted voice. "I'll be going home now, sir, if there's nothing else."

Mattei sprang out of his chair; it rolled back against the wall.

Geli got up. "Shall I come back tomorrow, sir?"

"Tomorrow? Why yes, do that. Be sure to bring your dossier.

If I'm not here, just leave it with Mlle Daubin. Don't mind the crowd. We still have a few more positions to fill."

Geli hesitated, not liking the kind of smile that lingered on her face. She felt a little bad for being played a favorite, but didn't want to thank Mattei for that. She had nothing to be sorry for. He stood there uneasily, as if expecting something. Or was it just that he couldn't wait for her to hurry up and leave? It all seemed too quick and too impossible. She could always quit if time went by with no trace of Kurt. No trace, though, didn't mean he wasn't here. She took a few steps toward the door. "Of course, sir. I thank you very much for your time."

He waved his hand. "Not a bit of it, Mlle Miroux. Till tomorrow, then."

Geli smiled.

He came around and opened the door for her and she went out.

A few bald light globes shone along the corridor to the foyer as she walked toward the exit. A shade was now drawn on the wicket where the sergeant's face had gruffly glowered out at her. Now for the tram to her little home, to tell her fictitious sister, Maxine, all about it. Then excuse herself to brush up on her shorthand. Can you believe it, Maxine? All these years and I can still write shorthand like it was yesterday. Will wonders never cease?

23

She was a little early that morning. Corporal Dax, one of the jailers, let her into the interrogation room. Major Mattei was not there, yet, although Corporal Dax had brought a prisoner up. She felt uneasy waiting there alone with him, but she didn't say anything. Corporal Dax would be just outside. He'd reminded her of that as he stepped into the hallway, leaving the door ajar. The prisoner sat there looking straight ahead as if she wasn't there. In a way, she wasn't. Who was she but the stenographer?

She draped her sweater on the back of her chair in the corner and looked out at the hazy sky in the open window, through which you could hear the occasional passing of a car down in the street, disturbing the stillness of impending heat. Across the rooftops church bells for matins tolled out over Notre Dame des Champs.

Minutes passed and she began to wonder whether Major Mattei, not always punctual, would be detained again today. How long would she have to sit alone with that rigid sphinx of a human being, the prisoner dredged up from the dungeon below, trapped with his hatred she was all too ready to return? Good thing she was some nonentity to him. The clock on the wall became oppressive with its big hand seeming to stick before it decided to jump onto the next minute.

All at once Mattei breezed in, swinging his briefcase. "Good morning, Mlle Miroux! Late again, I'm afraid." He strode briskly toward the table on the other side of which the prisoner sat.

"Not really, sir," she said. "I came in a bit early."

"Then shall we say we're both on time."

He had begun already to get rather friendly with her, so she said, "Then you're forgiven, sir."

The trace of a smile passed like a fleeting shadow across his face before he reached into his briefcase, pulled out some papers and laid them carefully on the table.

She drew the line at any speculation that might lead her past the woman she appeared to be. The woman who would let him show off as if, for all he knew, she was beginning to like him. Who would let him like her all he pleased, despite the wife he had at home, named Fifi. He fitted on his spectacles, peered over them at the prisoner and then, touching the end of a pencil to his lips, took a few steps toward her, wheeled and paced back.

The young German sat there, a certain arrogance stripped down to the faint smile under his shaved head. Too handsome for his own good, Geli thought.

Mattei stopped suddenly and said in a resounding voice, "Major Roland Mattei conducting inquiry number 1136, in regard to murders and complicity in murder, by order of the Second Standing Military Court, July 19, 1945. Object of the order: Helmut Franz. Name unsubstantiated."

Mattei got into his briefcase and came out with a file and spent some time frowning at the pages as he tore through them. Finally he said, "You've got all that down, Mlle Miroux?"

"Yes, sir."

The prisoner squirmed a little in his chair as Mattei looked gravely down at him over his spectacles, wrinkling his nose to let them slide down off the bridge.

"All right, then, 1136. We've given you some time to think. Are you prepared to revise your statement concerning your identity at this time?"

There was a creaking from the hard wooden chair as the prisoner sat back grasping a handful of fingers in his lap.

"What could there be to change about my own name?"

"For starters, the real one."

The prisoner turned a smirk aside.

Mattei's fingers stiffened on his file. "I didn't hear that, Herr Hauser."

The prisoner's eyes came up, blazing. "Why do you keep calling me Hauser? I'm -"

Mattei inflated his chest, growing the inch it took to assume a judicial air.

"The trousers you were wearing on the night of your capture were of a type not worn by enlisted men in the Wehrmacht, in which you claimed to hold the rank of corporal. Your boots were rather well-kept under the dust and mud you picked up running from our dogs."

The prisoner snuffed in a breath, rolling his eyes. "You're blaming me for polished boots? General von Cholitz would not have tolerated anything less."

"You're not afraid he's going to scold you, are you, Herr Hauser?"

Geli was watching the prisoner when, glancing at Mattei, he slipped her smirk. She lowered her eyes.

"What?" the prisoner whined.

"Let's talk about your trousers for a moment."

"What about them?" the prisoner said moodily.

"I'm sure you'd rather *not* talk about them."

The prisoner blew a restless sigh. "What do I care? There's nothing to add to what's been run into the ground already."

Mattei eyed him over the rims of his spectacles, taking his time. "What I find interesting about these trousers is the nametag stitched to the inside that reads Hauser, S., followed by the letters SS and a serial number."

"So? I've told you. Those trousers didn't belong to me. I borrowed them."

"Because your own didn't fit. Wasn't that it?"

Geli looked up in time to see Mattei's distorted grin that seemed to ask her if it was on right. She quickly looked down at her notepad.

The prisoner said, "In my haste I might have grabbed the wrong pair. I said borrowed because -"

"Sounds better than stolen, doesn't it? All right, why don't we simply say you didn't ask? You just took somebody else's pants."

The prisoner's face flushed red clear up into the welts and stubble on his scalp. "What difference does that make? I admit I wasn't wearing my own trousers."

"There is a difference, though, between the trousers worn by the Wehrmacht, and those more commonly seen on members of the SS."

The prisoner lowered his head, shut his eyes and began to wring his hands.

Mattei gave him a few seconds, watching with a certain relish, Geli thought.

At last the face came up wearing a clown-like mask of supplication. "All right. I was scared. Scared out of my wits. I'd thought of running away, but then I heard that deserters were being shot by our security forces who wouldn't think twice about shooting a stray Wehrmacht soldier, trying to surrender. We'd heard dreadful stories about these lynching commands. God help any soldier walking around alone who met up with them! The SS could talk their way out of such predicaments."

"So you wanted to be wearing the right sort of uniform in order to surrender."

"Yes! That's right!"

"Well, then. Why couldn't you simply remain in your SS uniform until Von Cholitz surrendered the garrison and the danger had passed?"

The prisoner stared at Mattei as if uncomprehending, then said heatedly, "You're trying to trick me. It won't work. I'm not going to lie so you can nail me down with everybody else you've got your mind made up is bad."

"Let me submit to you that you were wearing your own trousers all along. There was never any need for you to change."

"That's a lie!"

"Is it?" Mattei looked down at the papers spread across the table, smiling philosophically as he slid one slightly aside with the tips of his fingers. "Let us for a moment, Herr Hauser, depart from the question of your identity." Mattei tore off his spectacles, fixed eagle eyes on the prisoner. "To what extent, during your assignment under Von Cholitz and the Paris garrison, did you take part in the execution of French partisans?"

The prisoner gaped at Mattei. "Why, I *never* took part in any _"

"You mean to tell me you were never called upon to shoot members of the FFI accused of seditious action against occupying German forces?"

"FFI?"

"The *Forces Françaises de l'Intérieur*, better known to you as

200

partisans. You left a thousand of them dead on the streets of this city. Or did that perhaps escape your notice because you weren't counting?"

"Me? That *I* left -?"

"Unless you politely excused yourself from the reprisals, in which yours and other SS units defending the garrison of Paris were engaged. No exceptions."

Red splotched the prisoner's cheeks, his eyes spread wide open, trapped into mincing horror. "You've got no proof! No proof whatsoever!"

Mattei pulled a grin to one side of his mouth, shaking his head sadly. "That's always interesting to me, Herr Hauser. By the time we get to your compatriots downstairs, I'm sure we'll find a way to persuade a few of them to give you up. We call that cooperation."

The prisoner's eyes strayed. In a tremulous voice he said, "You do know, sir, that as soon as these partisans came out of the woodwork, Parisians were already killing each other right and left."

"Saving you the trouble," Mattei said casually.

"People whose only crime was that they'd got a little too friendly with us."

Mattei eyed him with a kind of pitying amusement. "In other words, certain Parisians can get away with murder, so why not join the crowd?"

The prisoner's face caught fire, he raised a fist, then dropped it loosely on the table. "I'm telling you I stand by who I am! Torture me if you like! I won't fall into line to satisfy your greed to punish those of us who only did our duty!"

"Duty, yes. You wouldn't be German, would you, if you didn't fight to your dying breath for a Fatherland concocted by a madman."

"Slur all you want. You'll never understand."

"Help me to understand what the S stands for after your surname, Hauser?"

"My name is Helmut Franz!"

"And mine is Charles de Gaulle," Mattei said.

The prisoner clapped his arms across his chest, glared sullenly at the table pressing his lips into a thin, tight line.

With a sigh Mattei stood back. He called out loudly, "Corporal Dax!"

The door flew open as if Dax had kept his hand poised on the doorknob. "Sir!"

"Take this man away. Oh, and see to it that he gets a shower before he's brought up here again."

"When would that be, sir?"

"I don't know. We'll let him simmer a while."

Simmer a while, Geli underlined in her mind. That was his method. When might they ever get to Kurt? Or had some other officer taken him on?

"Yes, sir," Dax said, "What I meant was, how soon do you want him to be bathed?"

Mattei looked at him. "What's the point of waiting? That goes for all the others, too."

"Well, sir, we're not equipped down there to do anything like that for *them*."

"What do you mean? No shower room?"

"We do have one, sir, but that's for us, not them."

Mattei stared at Dax, then flirted with a smirk. "Now look here, Dax. If you've got the water and all that – water is water. Plenty to go around."

Dax shrugged. "It hasn't been that way for quite some time, sir. In fact, never."

Mattei shifted his weight and, rocking on his feet, came to a regal standstill. "Who is your superior down there?"

"Lieutenant Giraud, until the other day, sir. Now we've got Lieutenant Dronne."

"Pass along to Dronne that the smell these prisoners bring up here is intolerable. They need to be hosed down, at least. Given something clean to wear."

"All of them, sir?" Dax said.

Mattei squinted at Dax. "You don't mop half a floor, do you, Dax? We're talking hygiene, here, which is as much in your interest as theirs."

"What I'm thinking, sir, is that Lieutenant Dronne, being new to us, is somewhat wet behind the ears, you might say. He may have some trouble convincing our men to share the shower room with the *mauvais*."

The prisoner moved his head, now gazing up at the two men as if his fate was being decided in a kennel. Dax sucked in on a wincing, uneasy smile.

With his canny, intelligent eyes, he seemed in some ways more grown-up than Mattei, Geli thought, making it harder on him to avoid, at times, taking the subordinate role.

"Tell me, Dax," Mattei said, "do you think Lieutenant Dronne will have any problem obeying my order?"

"Well, sir, I'm only saying he could be somewhat at a loss, since sanitary arrangements for the prisoners have never been discussed. They're *them*, you know. Some sort of serious dissension could break out."

"We'll worry about dissension after you pass along my order."

"Of course, sir. I'm confident that Lieutenant Dronne will find a way to -"

"There are no two ways about following an order, Dax."

Dax stood up straight, ramming his arms down rigidly. "Yes, sir."

"Tell Dronne I'll have a word with him if you run into any trouble getting through to him."

Dax shook himself to proper attention, lifting his chin sharply. "I'm sure it won't come to that, sir."

Mattei's eyes softened. His face relaxed. "All right, then. Get this man out of my sight. You might keep in mind that these *mauvais*, as you refer to them, are not so isolated as that epithet implies. They're carriers. You don't want vermin jumping from them onto you like it's a free-for-all. Does that make any sense to you, Dax?"

"Yes, sir, perfect sense."

"Feel free to pass along that line of thinking to Lieutenant Dronne."

"Yes, sir, I will. Shall I – would you like another prisoner brought up now?"

Mattei glanced at his watch. "No. I've got a staff meeting here in a few more minutes." Exhaling stormily, he reached into his briefcase, took out a small notebook and began to riffle through it. "Tomorrow morning we'll have 1074. Time to give him another going over." Mattei clapped the notebook shut.

Dax saluted, went over to the prisoner and helped him out of his chair and hustled him out.

Geli felt their departure struggling with the looks she was wrapped up in as she braced herself to be alone with Major Mattei. Alone again with her eyes set off with too much makeup, the tortoise-shell rimmed spectacles, blond hair straying from hairpins in the hastily done-up pile. Once a stenographer still knowing in her native French the skills of shorthand well enough to be employed. Mlle Simone Miroux, experienced in operating a dictaphone, too. She'd passed the interview with flying colors with a man who not only appreciated her skills, but took a liking to her that she couldn't help but notice had not much to do with shorthand.

"Would you care for a cigarette, Mlle Miroux?" Major Mattei was pulling out a pack from inside his blouse.

"Yes, thank you, Monsieur."

He stepped over toward her, tapping out a clutch of three cigarettes. She took one. He struck a match and she leaned toward the flame. He lit his own with the same match, waved out the flame. "My apologies for the foul odor of the German. He wasn't quite that bad the other day."

"The smell rather reminds me of what they are," she said.

"All of them the same in your book?"

"Their stories change, but essentially the lie doesn't. Whatever it takes to save their own skins."

"Yes. Usually you can see the lie in their eyes while they're trying to fool you. I've learned to read a great deal in a man's eyes."

"It's not my place to look into his eyes. And if it were, I wouldn't. I'd hang them all and be done with it."

"But then you'd never have had this job, and I wouldn't have had the pleasure of knowing you."

She blew smoke through a smile. "I suppose that's true, isn't it?"

Major Mattei's eyes strayed toward the top button of her blouse. "It's difficult to set aside your emotions when you're dealing with these people. But that's what we have to do. Set aside emotions. Justice is tainted by the slightest trace of revenge."

"The Nazis spit on niceties like that for five years. Because of them, my father and one of my brothers are dead."

"I'm terribly sorry to hear that. So are you living alone, now?"

"Well, no. As I believe I've told you, I live with my sister in the Rue de l'Odéon. A tiny place, but we manage. A Nazi officer used to come courting Maxine. He was young and very handsome, like this Hauser. He was always very polite and Maxine liked him, but I made trouble. She's still angry with me. I told her, somebody will say we collaborated. Do you want that to follow you the rest of your life?"

Major Mattei puffed on his cigarette while with his eyes he seemed to caress the downy slope of her nose and the fullness of her lips which, just then, she ran her tongue across. "What about you, Mlle Miroux? How many amorous Nazi hearts might you have had the opportunity to break?"

"Not me, Monsieur. I'd break their heads first."

"Imagine that. Quite different from your sister, then."

"I've got more Italian blood in me than her, Monsieur."

"Italian! Which I suppose accounts for the spirited person you are. I wish I were five or ten years younger. I think it would be nice talking to you in some other place."

"What place?"

"Oh, I don't know. Well lighted, at any event."

She laughed. "How old are you, Monsieur?"

"Me? Too old to be wondering how young you are."

She made her eyes flash with sly appreciation, and looked at him as if the distance between them was torture to him, and the nearness of her held everything she was in some ecstatic dream he dared to think of as the future. A future without the wife he almost never mentioned, Fifi.

He'd said her name once, then stopped talking about her. Now he was standing too close, lingering too long. All at once he said recklessly, "You've been talking to an American officer. Anything serious?"

"Oh, Larry?" She showed a pinch of something with her fingers, cocked her head and made saucy eyes about the possibility.

"What does your sister think of him?" he said.

"Oh! She thinks he's the most beautiful thing in the world, of course! He's going away next month, but he's asked me to marry him. Maxine said to me, 'If you don't, I will.'"

Mattei swallowed. "Imagine that. Too easily swept off her feet, like it was with the German."

"She's only eighteen. The Liberation can be overwhelming to a girl that young. She's absolutely convinced that Prince Charming hails from America. You know she's prettier than I am."

"Water runs uphill, too, Mlle Miroux."

"No, it's true. You ought to see her. I've learned it's better not to ask Larry in when she's home. He likes to look at her, and I don't like being jealous."

"Jealous, eh?"

"Well, not really. He's just the American captain I sometimes hitch a ride with."

"I haven't seen him lately. That is, in the jeep he used to pick you up in."

"Because that's all over, sir. He got his orders to go back to the States. It's just as well. He has a sweetheart back there waiting for him. Her name is Thelma. Isn't that a pretty name? Anyway, I didn't really love him. Just one of those crazy flings, you know."

"Ah." He nodded, smiling at her, but she could see the blood rising into his face. He said, "Never been married, then, Mlle Miroux?"

"I might have been at one time," she said. "Too close for comfort."

He looked down with a strange smile, as if for a place on the floor to empty all the color backed up in his face.

She felt his pulse was in her hand. With a casual air she took a slow drag on her cigarette. "Why is it, sir, that none of the prisoners ever ask about visitors?"

He looked up, a certain pleasure in his eyes like a professor who had all the answers. "They've learned not to. They're not called *isolés* for nothing. Nobody knows they're here. We want to keep it that way."

"Interesting, sir."

Mattei gave her a final inquisitive glance, then began to gather up the papers on his desk. Looking up he said brusquely, "That will be all for today, Mlle Miroux. Report to Captain Chappuis for the remainder of the day. I won't be needing you this afternoon."

"Won't be needing me, Monsieur?"

"That's right. I'll be tied up in a meeting."

"Yes, but you - you'll want me back tomorrow."

"Of course. No reason not to," he said, letting off a nervous chortle as she stared back at him dumbly.

It wasn't that she thought he was the only one. Kurt could be brought before any number of other lawyers, and she'd never know. It was just that this one was the only one she had. The one who'd hired her because...

She'd made him think that she was easy. Not a tart but something of a coquette. Now as if they were in it together she looked for a place to put out the cigarette, but there were no ashtrays. No escape from having known all along his pain of being infatuated with her. I won't be long with him, she thought. No longer than she needed Larry and Maxine and him to hope he had the ghost of a chance with her. Soon she might have to say that Maxine had moved out. We had a quarrel. I live all by myself. If you should ever run across her, she will deny she ever knew me.

"Bright and early then, Mlle Miroux?"

She looked at him as if her mind burned there between her fingers, too, with no place to put it out. "Yes, very good, Monsieur," she said. "Let's hope the next one smells better than the last."

"Ah, well if he doesn't, believe you me some heads are going to roll! You can be sure of that!"

24

Red and yellow autumn leaves were swirling into drifts in the street when the trolley dropped her at *Cherche Midi* early. She climbed the stairs and opened the door to a deserted room, walked over to the window vaguely wondering who it would be this time. There'd been a young woman yesterday, accused of collaboration, who'd broke down crying. Geli couldn't help but feel sorry for her, but was careful not to let it show. She'd only show how much she was supposed to hate the others, coming easier for what they'd done at Tulle, Maille, Ascq, Le Paradis, with their incessant pleas of acting under orders.

She began to lift the sash to let in some of the still cool morning air when shoes slapped the floor behind her. She left the sash alone, turned and said, "Ah, there you are, Monsieur!"

Mattei was out of breath. "I missed my trolley, had to walk. Where's Dax?"

"I don't know."

"So how are you this morning, Mlle Miroux?"

"I'm fine, sir." She started over toward her little school-sized desk. "Getting cool out, with autumn just around the corner."

"Yes," Mattei said absently. His voice took on a sharp note. "Your desk, Mlle Miroux. Did you move it, or was that the janitor?"

"Oh, I hadn't noticed, sir," she lied.

"Really. Then you're still able to hear our voices over here clearly enough."

"Quite clearly, sir. There's no difference at all, but if you -"

"No, no. I thought perhaps the smell of these people brought up had begun to affect you. If anything's been getting done down there, you wouldn't know it."

"No, sir, I wouldn't try to register a complaint by moving my desk. Also I'm getting rather used to -"

"That won't do. I'll have another word with Dax. War criminals or no, there's absolutely no excuse for keeping them in squalor. *And* disobeying an order to do so."

"Yes, sir."

"All right, then. Who do we have this morning?" Mattei hefted two thick folders, dropped them with a thud onto the desk. "To get us started we've got one I have inherited from Captain – sorry, *Major* Guingand, who's been kicked upstairs for - well, I really don't know why. At any rate -"

Mattei had left the door wide open. In the doorway suddenly a violent coughing fit broke out and Corporal Dax was there, saying harshly to somebody behind him, "Control yourself, 1171! Let's not have any nonsense."

Geli hurriedly sat snugly in her little desk. There was a final hack that brought on a retching and she thought at any moment there could be a mess. In the doorway Dax said, "Sorry, sir. I've got 1171 here, if you're ready for him."

"What's the matter with him?"

"Probably the air down there – not too easy on the lungs. Could be a trick, though. You know how they'll try to get away with that."

"Yes. All right, then, bring him in."

Dax stood aside, motioning the prisoner in.

Geli smelled him almost before she saw him, thinking here comes another one, the beaten wraith of a figure shuffling along in a filthy, striped smock, shedding bits of straw. She looked again and suddenly her breath caught in her throat and it was no good running for the cover of her pounding heart.

Dax pulled out the rickety wooden chair, gestured toward it.

The prisoner sat there heavily, tottering on the spindly legs.

Geli brought her eyes up. Not 15 feet away, yet he could not have seen her. No better than a stick of furniture, the stenographer. She was afraid his face would come around and she would have to look down raising one eyebrow at the effrontery of a filthy German. She felt a thickness in her throat and said a silent prayer: Don't look at me, my love!

Dax moved toward the doorway.

"Do you want me to wait, sir?"

"Just outside, Dax, if you would."

"Yes, sir."

There was the sound of the door shutting quietly.

She stared at the side of the sunken, sallow face, remembering his diabetes. Even if he looked, he shouldn't know her. She'd gone heavy on the mascara, as usual, the crimson lipstick, top button of her blouse undone, and she was a blonde, now, hidden behind swallowtail glasses.

Mattei mussed back some pages on the desk.

She was afraid he'd say her name.

"Now then, 1171. Major Guingand has left some comments about you and your report. Quite favorable comments, I might add; however, I prefer to take things from the top. I've spent some time, last night, going over your defense. I'd like to take you back to -"

The prisoner suddenly bent over, hacking into both hands.

Mattei stared at him, then shot a glance at Geli.

She sent back a blank look before she looked down at her pad, ready to get on with it.

The prisoner sat up, clearing his throat. He said in a grating voice, "I'm sorry, sir."

"You're all right now, 1171?"

"Yes, I'll be all right."

Mattei watched him for a moment, then placed a finger on his notes. "I'd like to take you back to 1940, when you made your decision to join the Waffen-SS. Explain to me how, as a devout member of the Confessional Church, you were able to become part of an organization that you had so vehemently opposed."

The prisoner took a sharp breath through his nose, throwing his head back. "The Bishop of Stuttgart -" he began. He coughed and started over. "I'd learned from the Bishop of Stuttgart that mentally sick people were being put to death at Hadamar and Grafeneck. These places on the surface were mental hospitals, but nobody admitted for treatment ever came out. One of the victims was my sister-in-law, Bertha Ebeling, singled out for being feeble-minded, which was untrue. I came to believe that, if I could get inside, I'd have a chance of learning what was going on."

"By inside you mean -?"

"Yes, as it turned out - the SS."

"Just how were you able to pull this off?"

The prisoner's eyes seemed to swim around, looking for something that wasn't there. At last he said, "It came about accidentally. I'd been in prison, Welzheim Concentration camp, for six months, accused of distributing seditious pamphlets in defense of the church, when a man from the SS came in to review my case. When he pointed out that all my father's pleas to get me released had been turned down, I thought all was lost and they'd thrown away the key. But then he told me how he might devise a way out for me if I would listen. Having thoroughly reviewed my work for the church, and the notoriety I'd gained as a Youth Group leader, he went on to tell me that the very things I'd been arrested for made me an ideal candidate for serving in his organization. Namely, the SS. Why waste my talents rotting in a prison cell when I could put the zeal with which I'd served the Church to work for the war effort? His very words were, 'A fanatic like you will make an ideal member of our organization.' I asked him how he proposed to put this over with his superiors, and he just said, 'Leave it to me'"

"The name and rank of this man?"

"*Obersturmbannführer* Wilhelm Stumpff."

Geli swallowed, keeping her head down. Across the space through which this prisoner couldn't know her, she took him into her heart.

"And you did leave it to him," Mattei said.

"Yes. I had my doubts, not knowing how much weight he carried as a relatively low-ranking officer, but it seemed to me my last and only hope for getting out of prison."

"Interesting. In other words your eventual decision to go along with him presented itself as an attractive means of escape – one you could not afford to refuse."

A silence fell.

Geli looked up to see Kurt staring at Mattei before he said, "I believed that, by accepting, I would then be able to follow through with desires I had already thought out."

"Which in the words you stated in your report was to join the SS with the object of spying to further your religious ideals."

"Yes, to carry on an active fight but at the same time learn more about the aims of the Nazis and their secrets."

"Would it be fair to say that the act of getting into the SS would please your father – a judge in Stuttgart and a convinced National Socialist? His maverick son would finally be brought into the fold."

"If that was so," Kurt said, "it simply happened." He spoke more clearly, now, as if the truth depended on it.

Mattei ramped up his caustic tone. "But then of course the pressure would be off. Now that you had come to your senses and could become a member of the Party in good standing."

"I was excluded from the Party in 1939. My father was unsuccessful in his attempt to get me reinstated."

"All the better reason for you to make him proud of you by joining up," Mattei said with a glance at Geli.

She lowered her eyes.

"By letting my father believe what he wanted to, I would then be able to move more freely."

Mattei tore off his spectacles with one hand, used the other to drum his pencil on the desk, as he might knock mud off his shoes. "Let me take you now to November of 1942, when you'd become head of the Technical Disinfection Branch for the SS Hygiene Service in Berlin. You state in your report that you, personally, were chosen to transport the cyanide from one part of Polish territory to another. Why did they pick you to do this when you were stationed in Berlin?"

"That was entirely a matter of chance. My name was put forward by an officer of the Chemical Department to whom the authorities had addressed themselves."

"Why would they send an officer from Berlin to Kolin, in

Czechoslovakia, to pick up the cyanide for transport to Poland, when it would have been so much simpler to instruct an officer already in Poland to do this?"

"I was considered a specialist in cyanide disinfectants."

"Did you receive a written or an oral order for your mission, and what were its terms?"

Geli didn't look but thought he must have sighed, just then, with all this was taking out of him: the truth that didn't have to leave its colors in the depths of where she knew it had been his. She hadn't seen him look her way. Safety felt too dangerous for her to make a sound.

"I received an oral order which was confirmed to me forty-eight hours later by a written order. The terms of the written order were approximately as follows: I order you to procure 260 kilos of potassium cyanide and transport it to a place which will be indicated to you by the driver of vehicle number such and such, assigned to this mission. I chose Kolin because I knew that cyanide was manufactured there by much the same method as it was at Dessau. From the deliberately odd character of the technical questions I asked the foreman at the potash plant in Kolin, the other people working there were able to grasp the enormity of what their product was going to be used for. I did this to get rumors spread among the population. We then set off by truck for the camp near Lublin, called Belzec."

"Yes. The mission during which you state that you were able to dispose of several canisters of cyanide by ordering them buried before you reached your destination. How were you able to accomplish this without arousing suspicion from your superiors?"

"They trusted me because I'd done a good job for them in other areas, one being the purification of drinking water in the SS camps. They weren't inclined to question my expertise in matters they knew nothing about. Being considered an authority on prussic acid and toxic gasses, I could easily have a whole shipment of the cylinders destroyed, giving damage due to decomposition as the cause. That was why I hadn't the slightest scruple in accepting the mission that was put to me."

"So in this instance, how were you able to explain your actions?"

"Through the people at the warehouse in Kolin, I'd learned that the containers of cyanide we would be transporting were old. Their practice was to use up their oldest supplies first. When potassium cyanide ages, it begins to decompose. It can't be safely utilized except as a disinfectant. I had to let some of the containers through, claiming avoidance of waste, so they would take my word for why I buried the rest. On that occasion I accidentally splashed my sleeve with some of the acid, and had to tear it off."

"And you reported this?"

"Yes, by way of explanation to the camp commandant, a man named Wirth. He was not unduly concerned about the incomplete delivery. I got the impression that he would have applauded it if Captain Stumpff had not been there to mourn it. They held opposing ideas about which method should be utilized. Wirth argued for the older diesel exhaust, while Stumpff came down on the side of the more toxic poison Himmler favored."

"We're talking about the same Stumpff whose intercession got you out of Welzheim."

"Yes, as it happened."

"So you were reunited with your benefactor, the very man to whom you owed the start you'd got with the SS three years before."

"Entirely by chance. He was as surprised to see me as I was him."

"Pleasantly?"

"I don't know. In front of Wirth he made no mention of having known me in the past. I thought it best to play along with that."

"Yet both of these men took your word for why you deemed it necessary to dispose of the poison."

"They had no reason not to."

"Almost as if you really were the person you were pretending to be."

"I had to seem to be exactly who they wanted me to be. That was the only way I could go on. Stumpff had a stake in me. Up till then I'd come to think of my involvement with him as a barrier to my past that might otherwise work against me. Now I wasn't so sure."

"Why?"

"He took a very different view of what I'd taken it upon myself to do, but didn't let Wirth know that he was 'disappointed,' giving away our past acquaintance. Wirth put me in for a commendation, while Stumpff berated him for taking lightly any setback in the implementation of Himmler's brainchild."

"With what result?"

"That I could thank the bad blood between these two for getting on Wirth's good side, but Stumpff - from then on I couldn't stop looking over my shoulder for him."

Mattei sucked in his breath, squaring his shoulders. "One thing about this incident sticks in my craw. What did you expect to accomplish by undertaking such an action when you knew it had to be in vain?"

"I didn't know that. I only knew I had to do something."

"Which you were reasonably sure you'd get away with."

"I had to gamble that I would."

"You *did* get away with it, but how many lives do you suppose you saved as a result?"

Geli looked up at Mattei's smug face. She should be pleased: another German taken down a peg. She saw the naked girl she had competed with, that night, for a place beside her shallow grave in Kurt's heart. She gulped a sob, her hand flew to her mouth too late.

Mattei swung his face toward her. "Are you all right, Madame?"

She flashed him a quick twisted smile. "Yes, yes," she whispered impatiently.

"Are you sure?"

She kept her eyes down, nodding as she fluttered a dismissive hand at him. There it was out, now, like a bird from a cage and she kept her face buried in the weight she'd gained, the blowsy clothes, too blonde to be half Italian, eyes smeared behind her glasses. He'd know her voice, but maybe not. Now suddenly she didn't know which one she wanted it to be. She felt ashamed, but fought it back. It shied like a dog she kept telling to go home, but it wouldn't. She heard a page being rustled back.

Mattei cleared his throat. "How much thought, 1171, have you given to the expedience of witnesses?"

Kurt didn't say anything.

She peeked up from under her glasses just as he began to blink as if he couldn't see what he was trying to say.

"Shall I repeat the question, 1171?"

"No, sir. I didn't see much hope of reaching any of the witnesses I could think of."

Mattei took a few steps out around his desk. His voice was unctuous, slithering off his tongue as if he were in court. "Let's give hope a rest for just a moment and get down to brass tacks. In your capacity as the ranking officer on this convoy out of Kolin, you would have had a driver."

"I had a sergeant by the name of Hugo."

"Were you on good terms with him?"

"I liked him, but avoided friendliness. I couldn't afford to let my guard down. He had to think of me as who I seemed to be, so I observed the rule that officers and men were not to fraternize."

"Now when it came to your order to your men to bury the cyanide, there would have been no telling if he'd thought that you were sabotaging your own job."

"If so, it would have gone into the same hole as the cannisters."

"But he *was* there. That much he would remember."

"If you're thinking of him as a witness -"

"Not out of the question, any more than Wirth or Stumpff, who could be only too willing to come forward, since the stakes due to the war are over."

"I don't know what became of Wirth. I was told that Stumpff was killed by partisans."

Geli looked up at the side of his face. De Vos must have said that, she thought. In her mind she saw Stumpff's fat, dead face, pooling blood there on the carpet. That mutual acquaintance dead in the secret separating her from Kurt by fifteen feet.

Mattei blew a sigh. "There remains the question of your wife. You might want to reconsider your instructions to Major Guingand. You're not doing her any favors by refusing to see her. You're going to need her."

"She doesn't know enough to be of any use. I never told her things that the Gestapo could torture out of her in case I was picked up."

"The war is over, 1171. The time for secrecy is over."

"I don't want her to know I'm here," Kurt said adamantly.

"Don't be a fool, Langsdorff. You're digging your own grave!"

All at once Kurt's back heaved, he lurched forward coughing into his fist. With a shudder he threw himself back against the chair and tipped it tottering onto two legs. His hands flew out and slapped the desk and brought the chair back onto all fours with a clump.

Mattei stood there, frozen with a strange fascination. The door swung open, banged against the wall and Corporal Dax came through wide-eyed, crouching in a defensive stance. "Sir! Stand back, sir!"

Geli was on her feet. Then she was on the move.

Kurt had both hands up in front of Dax. She didn't know how close she was to Kurt until she stopped and started to back up, and Kurt was saying to Mattei, "Forgive me, sir. It's only -"

Dax brayed shrilly, "Control yourself, 1171!"

Mattei put up one hand, speaking quietly as if he'd come out of a coma to say, "Where am I?"

"This will be all for today, Dax. You may take the prisoner back down, now."

"You bet I will, sir! Get over here, you -" Dax snatched Kurt by the arm, hauled him out of the chair and hurriedly escorted him out, skidding in the doorway to reach back for the door.

By the time it slammed Mattei was walking toward the window, lighting up a cigarette.

Geli looked down at the smears of mascara on her fingers and slid them along her hips. She was mad and wanted to get out of there. "If that's all, sir -"

"Damn!" Mattei exploded. "I forgot to give Dax that talking-to I – ah, well. Another time." He turned, scissoring his cigarette as he blew smoke through his nose.

"So what did you think of this 1171, Mlle Miroux?"

221

"Think of him? Good Lord, sir. I don't know. I don't listen much, just write."

"I thought you were in distress there for a moment."

"Distress? You don't mean -" She almost laughed out of her nerves strung tight. "Oh, that. I might be coming down with something. You know how sometimes you can't hold back a sneeze."

Mattei nodded perfunctorily as he laid sloe eyes on her.

"What's the matter with you today, Mlle Miroux? You don't seem yourself."

"Why, I don't know, sir. Nothing that I -"

Mattei broke off a brittle smile.

"It *is* deplorable, isn't it, how those creatures down there have to wallow in their own filth as if the darkness and the walls weren't enough. Lieutenant Dronne hasn't heard the last of this."

She looked up, making her eyes go soft. "I do believe this 1171 needs a doctor, sir, more than a shower. He seems to be unwell."

"Think so? Don't tell me you're going soft on them," he said with a kind of runaway smirk.

"Not *them*, sir."

"So then you mean 1171. Him."

"Well, yes. Oh, never mind, Monsieur." She tore her face away with a fey toss of her head, picked up her handbag and started for the door. "I feel exhausted, sir. I'm going if you don't mind."

"Got a ride waiting down there in another jeep, perhaps?"

She stopped abruptly, making herself laugh. It came out shrilly, like a theatrical cackle. "Oh, don't be silly! You think I stick my thumb out for every jeep that comes along?"

Mattei shambled toward her, reddening as he puffed on his

cigarette. He said sheepishly, "These Germans, you know. The lies they think they can get away with. I suppose in some ways it's our fault."

She stared at him. "How so?"

"They know the deck is stacked against them, so they have to go one better than the truth."

"You sound as cynical as I am," Geli said.

He looked at her quizzically, cocking his head. "How *do* you feel, Mlle Miroux, after all you've been through?"

"I don't -"

"Don't tell me you have no opinion, after listening to them day in and day out. Even though it all seems to blur, and you have to throw the whole soup out because you can't find the fly."

"Monsieur, I'm only here to write things down. Whatever I think doesn't matter."

"Don't let excuses hold you back. You haven't in the past."

She tossed her head and forced a little breath of laughter through her nose. "What I'm not getting paid for, Monsieur, is none of my business. But I do wonder sometimes -"

"Yes?"

"Well, those prisoners down there – do you ever torture them?"

He gave her a long look held thinly by a smirk. "That sort of thing is not encouraged, although I can't speak for the jailers. Many of them had relatives murdered by the Nazis. Why?"

"Oh, nothing, sir. Curiosity."

"Ah. Care to elaborate on that?"

"Oh, no. Not here, sir. Not now."

He took a long drag on his cigarette, eyes raking her up and down.

"What about some other place?"

"What for, Monsieur?" she said coyly.

"I'd be glad to show you, if tonight wouldn't be too soon."

In the silence tears stung the back of her eyes and she swallowed, tasting salt. Here Kurt had come and gone, tripped and fallen into her heart like a child she must bear alone.

"Well, I don't know. If you can't get away -"

Maybe Fifi all unknowing, wouldn't really care.

He shrugged. "I work rather late in my office almost every night, you know."

"All work and no play. Hard to get out of the rut, here, *n'est-ce pas?*"

Smoke from his cigarette embraced her like a garland. The scent of it was him, his longing burning up and putting what was left of it around her shoulders.

He said, "There is bistro I know. Quite some distance from the Rue de l'Odéon. Probably too far to walk."

"The farther the better, Monsieur. Just tell me where and what time. I'll be there."

25

They were to meet at the Bistro Dumonde in Montmartre, at 8 o'clock that night. She went home first, so she could dress. She didn't want the two of them to be seen walking the streets together.

She was right on time when she walked in out of the gathering dusk. Two men sat beside each other at the bar. They turned to look at her, eyes prowling, and she returned their smiles.

Mattei was there already, sitting at a table at the back, near the rear door where the light was poor, and as she walked past empty booths her heels clicked on the tiles. He watched her with a faint, slightly wicked smile as she approached him, and she said, "Hello, Monsieur. Been waiting long?"

He got up and pulled a chair out for her. "Not at all. Will you have an absinthe?"

She saw that he was having one in his small glass. A cigarette was burning in the metal ashtray. She let him push the chair in under her, making her a lady in the barman's eyes and those two other men who, every time they looked around, pretended to be just airing their curiosity.

"Yes, that would be nice," she said. "Thank you."

Mattei raised his hand and snapped his fingers. "Philippe! Another absinthe down here!"

"Coming right up!" the barman called out.

Mattei dragged his chair under him, reached for his cigarette and tapped the lopping ash into the sooty tray. "May I offer you a cigarette, Mlle Miroux?"

"No, no. I've been smoking too much, lately. But thank you."

Sitting back, he blew smoke from a fulsome laugh. "You know, I don't really need this, either."

"Don't be silly." She tossed off a saucy smile, let it linger on her lips. "Do you come here often, Monsieur?"

"If you mean with other women, no."

"Sorry, I meant often."

He laughed again, tapping his cigarette over the ashtray unnecessarily. "Every now and then would be more like it."

"Sorry, Monsieur. I shouldn't pry."

Mattei wrung a tepid smile out of his pursed lips. Just then the barman came over and set her absinthe on the table. As soon as he went away Mattei raised his glass. She picked up hers. They clinked.

"Thank you for coming, Monsieur. I hope it's not inconvenient."

"I wouldn't be here if it was," he said cheerily.

She dipped a smile into her glass, the licorice flavor burned going down. He watched her with aroused eyes. She said, "Monsieur, I actually I've come here to apologize for something."

He sat back, throwing one arm back across the chair. "Come, now, this is neither the hour nor the place for apologies."

"No, really, I - I lied to you this morning. That moment when you were concerned about me. I wasn't coughing. It was -"

"That? Think nothing of it. Actually I thought you were distraught, but held my tongue. Sometimes these prisoners come to life when you're just trying to do your job. There's no crime in being human." He sucked on his cigarette, looked at her through smoke.

She kept her eyes on him. "When that happened, I was wondering if you could tell that he was gravely ill."

"The prisoner? Well, none of them are exactly the picture of health, now are they? As far as -"

"I have a confession to make," she said.

Mattei waved his hand. "So you were upset, Mlle Miroux. Forget it, I don't blame you." He raised his glass. "Let's drink to being out of that dreary old bastion. That place can get you down."

Geli left her glass where it was on the table. "I'm trying to say, Monsieur, I've been deceiving you. It's time I put a stop to it."

He stared at her, eyes trying to nudge her like a bug that wanted to go the other way. He began to shake his head, looking at his upraised glass, poised for a sip. "Well, it can't be that bad, Mlle Miroux, really. Go on, then. Get it out of your system. Then I'll tell Philippe to bring us over some of his lovely gruyère from Marseille."

She looked across at him as he wet his lips with absinthe, steadying her eyes as if she were about to read back to him some of her own dictation. "My name is not Simone Miroux. I'm not French, but German. I haven't lived through the war in Paris. I have no sister named Maxine. I made her up."

He stared at her with a fixed, uncertain smile, the way you'd watch a rabid dog for the precise moment when you would have to shoot it. He reached for his dead cigarette in the ashtray with a trembling hand, took it back without the cigarette and covered one hand with the other on the table, clearing his throat. "What reason do you have for telling me this now?"

"I've known Kurt Langsdorff since late in the winter of 1944. We were friends. More than friends, if – if I'd had my way. I couldn't. Forgive me, Monsieur, but I couldn't go on letting you think I had nothing but hatred for all Germans, and wanted them all hung."

There was a sudden tightening around his eyes. "Don't flatter yourself," he said.

"I'm not proud of it, Monsieur."

Mattei swallowed. He looked down at his miniature glass, turning pale. "That's quite a mouthful. What do you want me to do about it?"

"I want to see him, Monsieur. I want him to know I'm here."

Mattei flung his cigarette at the ashtray, missing as it skittered, tumbling across the table and came to rest at the edge. He left it there. "But he must know already. He's seen you."

"He can't have recognized me. I'd know. He would have made some sign. You saw how beaten down he looked. He's gravely ill. It would be like him not to tell you."

Mattei's eyes hardened as if smashed into white heat on an anvil. "What is he to you?"

"It all began in Germany when I was hired to spy on him. I'd worked for the Abwehr in Cairo, but this time they weren't involved. They were kept out of it. It was a private arrangement between myself and – and a -"

Mattei clenched his fist, his red eyes struck out across the table. "God damn it, who are you?"

"My name is Geli Straub," she said breathlessly. "When my husband, a general in the Wehrmacht, was lost in Russia, I became destitute. A way out came along by accident – a deal I made with an officer working for Central Security who wanted me to spy on his protégé. That man was Langsdorff – on the surface every inch a model SS officer. But then in time I found that he was only posing as the kind of Nazi you and I both hate. After that, everything changed. I changed sides. I had enough on him to tell this officer, but I couldn't do it. I couldn't bring myself to sell him out, but I couldn't run, either. One night he confessed to me those things he now so desperately wants you to believe. I knew too much about him to forsake him at that time or any other. Whether he wanted me or not, I left Berlin with him. With the help of two Dutch partisans we got as far as Rottweil, where he surrendered to French forces. French security turned the tables and remanded him to Paris, where I tracked him and – the rest you know. Now you must also know that I can testify to the absolute truthfulness of every word in his report."

Mattei sat back, clutching his glass, arm stiffly braced. "Wanted you," he said. "So that's why you're here."

"No, I -"

"Did you confess to him your real identity before you went with him toward Allied lines?"

"No. I was afraid to. He still doesn't know. Will you - will you let me see him in his cell?"

Mattei jutted out red fury, and slamming down his fist made the ashtray and the glasses and the dead cigarette at the edge of the table jump. "Out of the question! I could have you arrested!"

"Do it, then! And you might be next for letting me slip through your fingers."

He stared, then seemed to crank himself back off his elbows on the table, saying with a sneer, "So that's it. Blackmail."

She hesitated, staring at him. "What are his chances if I disappear?"

"What are they if you don't?"

"You saw how drained of hope he was. No witnesses. Not even his wife. Please let me see him, Monsieur. He's got to know I'm here. If your morals aren't just painted on, try to see me as a woman who wants to save one of your prisoners from the prejudice she once sought to make you think was hers."

Mattei's hand came off his forehead like bandages being peeled off a face disfigured by rash love, mutilated by a siren he'd let play him for a sucker. The pleading in his voice crawled hand over hand. "Were you in love with him?"

She'd left it somewhere in the footlights. A crowd roared and she took the bow, the laurels and the flowers, and love came out glittering in the rave reviews. "I'm sorry if I hurt you, Monsieur."

His face twisted with hate, then just as quickly fell back leaving its dead around the corners of a bitter smile. "If I have you arrested, you'll never see him. If I don't, Colonel Laurent will have my head."

"Not necessarily. There is a way around that. How well do you trust Corporal Dax?"

Mattei began to shake his head. "Nobody goes down there, except the jailers and the doctor. We'd have to do it in the dead of night. I don't know. It's too risky, implicating Dax. To say nothing of the other jailers."

"Swear him to secrecy."

"I won't lie to him. There'll have to be a reason that lets him off the hook if things go wrong. I'd have to make it worth his while."

"You'll think of something," she said.

Mattei's eyes glowed like pulsing embers. "Why should I take that chance and go to jail, too - for what?"

"For a man who needs you desperately."

He stared at her. "If you get what you want, do you think he'll get what *he* wants?"

She searched his face. "He won't leave his wife for me. I don't want him to. I never did."

"Unless you gave him other ideas."

"They couldn't have lasted if I did."

"Now that you're some actress and I got to play the fool."

"Go on, then – arrest me."

"Don't think I wouldn't. For now it seems you've got me over a barrel."

"It's up to you and me to give Kurt hope enough to stay alive."

He lifted his chin a little to look down at her. A haughty look in which she saw him groping for some way out. "When we're found out," he said, "which one of us is going to take the fall?"

"I'll take it all upon myself."

"Will you? Telling them what? You held a gun to my head? The gun of a beautiful woman I let slip through my fingers because I was -" He swallowed hard.

"Monsieur -"

He raised his palm. "Save it. No pity, please."

"It wasn't that," she said.

He shoved his glass away so hard it tipped over, but didn't crack. He left it rolling like a pendulum onto its side.

"Tell me – why did you have to do it this way? Why couldn't you have simply –"

She stared at him as if he ought to know. "There wasn't any other way," she said.

"Damn it, you didn't try."

"Maybe Mlle Miroux told me not to."

"What are you talking about?"

"Suppose I'd walked in off the street and told them I've come

231

all the way from Germany to bear witness to the deeds of a presumed Nazi killer? Or staying French, explain what good I've got to say about a Nazi. Yes, the war is over, but feelings still run high. They'd peg me for a collaborator."

"You didn't try," Mattei said stubbornly.

"Well, then - I'd be your prisoner, wouldn't I?"

He brought his eyes up, smoldering, then with a sigh grabbed his forehead. "God, you've made a fine mess of things!" He picked up his empty glass and righted it on the table. "Give me another day or two."

She said almost in a whisper, "All right," and glanced back toward the bar.

The two men had gone. Philippe began to gather up their empty glasses, then busied himself with something under the bar. Bottles clanked.

Mattei was tapping the table with the nails of one hand. All at once he got up, knocking back his chair and reaching for his wallet. He fished out a few franc notes, tossed them on the table, muttering, "That'll take care of it," then marched off past Phillipe's big unrequited smile.

"Adieu, Monsieur Mattei!" the barman said. "Until we -" His face fell.

At the door Mattei stopped, half-turned toward Geli who was on her feet beside the table. "My car's outside if you need a lift home, Mlle Miroux!" he brayed huffily.

Geli sat still. "No, thank you, Monsieur. I'm sure I'd get you lost."

"I should be so lucky," Mattei said, and went out under the jingle of the bell.

26

Worn slick steps led down into the stench of urine, mold and methane gas cooking in the dim cauldron of a dungeon. Geli took shallow breaths along the narrow corridor, hemmed in by slimy stone walls and passing eyes that sprang, inflamed, to the barred apertures to peer out. Mattei took her arm as Corporal Dax strode briskly ahead, becoming more and more darkly silhouetted by a light on the wall, masked like a fencer's face, down toward the end. Keys jangled, a bolt clanked and Dax swung open the strap-iron door and stood there waiting until they caught up.

"You may go, now, Dax," Mattei said. "Wait for us at your station."

"About how long, sir?"

"Ten minutes at the most."

"Leaving this gate unlocked, sir?"

"Yes."

"If you should run past ten minutes -"

"Unlikely, but if so, don't wait. Come back for us."

"Yes, sir." Dax turned his face toward the gloom inside the cell. "The prisoner seems to be asleep. Shall I wake him for you?"

"Yes, go ahead, Dax. Do that."

Nerves began to jitter along Geli's spine. In that fetid semi-darkness lived the man for whom her love felt suddenly unreal, beyond her reach, so seldom had she touched him, so restless was his place in her heart.

Dax stepped in a short way, ducking his head in under the low entrance. "On your feet, *chien!* You have a visitor!"

Geli cringed at the savage slur, then heard a stirring inside, wood creaking and the crackle of dry straw.

Dax backed out. "I'll go now, sir."

"Thank you, Dax," Mattei said.

Boots clapped Dax to attention, his salute quivered at the elbow. "Sir!"

They stood a moment watching Dax as he grew smaller trudging back through the shadowy ochre light.

Mattei stood aside. "He's all yours, Mlle Miroux."

Geli went in, followed by the clank of the heavy, rusted gate. To the left in the corner she could make out something like a coal shuttle, a foul odor that went with it. In a feeble shaft of moonlight that shone down from a small barred window cut high into the wall, a tall stooped figure in a striped smock rose from the straw-stuffed cot. He began to shuffle toward her, stopped and stood there, eyes peering from the face she wanted it to be, the cobalt blue eyes turned pewter in the half-light. She said, "I wondered if you knew me up there, Kurt, I was so afraid. I'm not afraid, now. Don't you be."

He didn't move.

234

She forced a playful lilt into her voice. "You know you ran out on me back there in Rottweil. When I woke up that morning, you were gone. I knew you couldn't help it. Colonel Darlan told me."

He stared at her as if his eyes were not enough, then reared up making fists, and she saw now that he was sweating and it struck her that the diabetes must have come back on him. She hurried toward him, and how fatally she loved him, wanting to hold him but afraid – this man promised to a girl named Elfriede, kept always to himself behind the locked door of her mind. She plucked her glasses off and shook her hair out, then as if his hand came from some other direction, from Bornichen, she felt his fingers touching her forehead like a blind man, trickling down along her cheek and trembling on her neck behind her ear. She reached around him, coming up on tiptoe. Suddenly he pulled away. "No, I'm so filthy -"

She wouldn't turn him loose, but held on tight, and he stopped bucking and was still. She said in a brusque, commanding tone, "Listen to me, Kurt. We haven't got much time. Mattei knows, now, I've known you since Berlin, but it's all right. I've made a deal with him. In return for letting me keep the promise I made to you in Rottweil, to serve as your material witness, he won't give me away. They could arrest me for impersonating a French stenographer, but not when my only crime is to back up all you've stated in your report. I'm no threat to them because the war is over. That's why, if they have me arrested, they'll go down for letting me slip through the cracks. The Court may never hear or know of me at all, but that won't take away the things I've told Mattei to make me every bit the kind of witness he could call upon. He may never have to use me, but I'm here if he does."

He looked down at her, then turned aside like a long-caged animal afraid of being let out into the wild. A chill gripped her like a cold, dead hand. She tried to pump cheer into her voice. "You mustn't give up, Kurt. Soon you'll be seeing improvements down here in the food. You'll get a shower, something clean to wear. Has the doctor been to see you?"

He shook his head. "They're onto tricks like that – too many Germans claiming to be sick."

She reached for his hand, but it felt limp and cold and she began to wonder whether she'd fallen out of his heart long ago, the day they'd taken him from Rottweil. Given up on her and now Elfriede never had to know. Fear struck down into where she'd once thought she could love him to the end. She took his face in both hands. "Look at me."

His eyes came up as hard as gems, but nothing glittered in them, and she couldn't tell what hid behind them in the dark.

Just then the door clanked.

Mattei looked in, saying, "I'm afraid your time is up. Corporal Dax is here."

She wanted to take Kurt in her arms, but Mattei was standing there, watching like Elfriede's lawyer. He turned away and stepped outside, leaving them alone.

Kurt stood still.

She pulled him close, the smell of him and all so he would know she didn't mind the filth he was ashamed of. "You've got to hold on, Kurt," she said. "You're getting out of here. You'll be going home. Believe that."

"It's all the same to them if I don't last," he said. "They'll find a way to make a liar out of me."

It was as if she'd hit him with a hammer.

Corporal Dax came into the entryway, dangling his keys.

She took Kurt's hand, squeezed and turned away, not looking

back. There would be nothing of his eyes, being lost there in the dark, that would be any good to her until she saw them in the light again, somewhere beyond these terrible walls that seemed to keep her warm for the day she couldn't turn her back on them without the man she never had been sure was real.

27

Geli saw by the light under Mattei's office door that he was working late. She rapped lightly on the door.

There was a sound of movement inside.

She knocked again. "Major Mattei! May I see you a moment?"

More noise, the creaking of a chair.

She wrapped her hand around the knob. "I need to talk to you, Monsieur!"

Chair legs screeched and footsteps thudded toward the door and it flew open. Mattei left it that way as he stalked back to his chair behind his desk, sat in it noisily and began to busy himself with some papers spread out under the lamp.

Geli shut the door. She walked up to his desk and stood there quietly.

He kept on riffling through the papers. Taking another step, she felt the edge of the desk against her thighs, then something caught her eye. A blond young woman in the large, framed photograph, a radiant smile and sparkling eyes, the picture of a woman who knew she was pretty.

Mattei's bark startled her. "Just what is it that you want?"

"I'm sorry, sir. It's been some weeks since you were kind enough to let me see Herr Langsdorff. You no longer bring him up for interrogation."

"What about it?"

"Well, I - can you tell me if the doctor has looked in on him?"

His scowl took on incredulity. "Doctor Trouillet is aware of his condition."

"What's he doing about it?"

Mattei slapped his hand down on the pencil in it. "His best, within limits. There's something wrong with all of them down there, but remember, this is no hospital. Colonel Laurent makes few if any exceptions for preferential treatment."

"How near death does a person have to be?"

Mattei's eyes came up cannily. "I don't make the rules around here."

"What do you do?"

Mattei glared at her, then looked aside airily, as if the spur hadn't dug in.

She softened her voice to say, "Why don't you let me be of help to you, Monsieur?"

"Help how?"

"I don't want to be your enemy."

"Then leave me alone." He gave her a long look, then sat back with a sigh and said, "All right. I go down to visit him from time to time. We chat. He doesn't ask for much. The sanitary situation still leaves something to be desired. You don't get rid of two-hundred years' worth of vermin overnight. Sometimes I take some fruit and cheese - Trioullet's stopgap to getting a request for insulin turned down. I've made him know I'm doing all I can to get him off. Between that and the food, his spirits aren't so bad."

"Has he told you, yet, about Helsinki?"

His eyes came up and narrowed on her cautiously.

"Why?"

"He left it out that time you prompted him for witnesses."

Mattei searched her face. "We never got to that. I found it later on in his report. I had to ask him why he hadn't made much out of it."

"What do you mean?"

"If he was so tormented by the thought that he had saved so few lives, why didn't he invoke Helsinki?"

"Are you asking me, Monsieur?"

"No. I finally got it out of him. Then it was all I could do to talk him out of doing nothing about it."

"I don't -"

"It was his wife. He didn't want her to be brought into it. Apparently, just days before he left Berlin he got through to her by telephone. Whatever other things he told her, Helsinki was the one he thought would stick. He'd kept her in the dark so long, the need for secrecy was over. I tried to make him understand he wasn't sparing her by playing dead. Soon it would be too late. Then what good was his reputation to her if he got convicted when he'd never given her a chance to help?"

"Monsieur!" she blurted, "if he's reluctant to involve her -"

Mattei was shaking his head. "No, no, that's over. He wrote to her. I took his letter to the Americans for delivery. We'll have our witness."

She fought a swelling in her throat to say, "The other two, the Dutch partisans who were the first to hatch the plot -"

"Yes, them. More difficult to locate, but the search is out for them in Holland."

"Did he tell you the hometown of one of them was Lembeck?"

"Ah, yes. Interesting. Friends clear back to the first years of the war, then they all meet again as the unlikeliest of bedfellows."

She stared his way, not seeing him, and the look he gave her slanted one eyebrow over a deep frown.

"Good news, isn't it? Aren't you glad?"

"Why, yes, of course." Geli threw a smile out across the tears backing up in her throat.

"Well then, stop worrying. Things are looking up."

Suddenly she felt flustered. She could only think to say, "Does he ever ask about me?"

Mattei was in the midst of smiling. He looked at her as if she'd spoiled his fun. "He asked me to be sure no harm comes to you."

She looked down at the papers littered on his desk, smiling absently like she would smooth a clean sheet over a dirty bed. She brought her eyes up glistening. "Have you told him who I really am?"

"Oh, no. That would be cheating, wouldn't it? Like I once let you get away with hating every prisoner Dax brought up by preaching justice from my pulpit."

Something came loose and she laughed. "I've put you through the ringer, haven't I?"

He ignored that, glaring at her levelly. "No matter. You can bow out, now."

"I see. Why don't you reassign me?"

"And have all that explaining to do? No, thank you."

She opened her mouth to speak. Nothing came out. She looked down at the picture on his desk. "Your wife there, Monsieur?"

"Yes. We were in Vichy when that was taken."

"She's so pretty."

"She's grown rather shy of being photographed these days."

Geli had only seen her once at the bottom of the stairway - pitifully fat, yet so pretty, catching them together coming down. Roland and the stenographer, and he'd been telling her about the indignities he'd endured at Vichy as Fifi kept on lumbering upward, carrying a basket, and he watched her with a stricken look as if she were a ghost that wouldn't stay buried, all out of breath by the time she reached the top, heaving the words, 'I've brought lunch, dear, it's such a nice day out. Ah, this must be your new stenographer. I've brought enough for three, so you must join us, Mlle Miroux.' And Fifi's hand felt moist, her eyes brimming with the kindness of a woman who knew no better.

"She's so awfully pretty," Geli said with a smile put on like too much perfume.

"Yes, people always say that. Nothing's changed."

Geli eyed him cautiously. "She never -?"

"All that foolishness? It's not the first time, you know. She lets me have my fun, waiting for the day I blow my top and ask her why she has to eat so much, as if that's what the matter is, when really, she left me long ago, in Vichy, when she'd got enough of my self-loathing and decided to get fat instead of looking for another man. A test, until my 'dears' began to sound too dangerously like love, and I could almost hear her say stop sniveling. You're alive, aren't you? Take it like a man. So I did, and now I've only got myself to blame for, well - c'est la vie."

"I'm sorry, Monsieur."

"Don't be. I'm not quite up to real life, most times. I'd rather lie in bed and take the wheel from that American captain of yours, but when we got to your door I wouldn't let you off with just a breezy, gentlemanly farewell. You would invite me in. I'd find your flat quite small, but clean and tidy, smelling of cooking and your hair, when everything else was just a lamp left on somewhere, and it was easy to forgive myself for keeping Fifi in the dark."

"I am sorry, Monsieur."

He sat up, filling his chest with air. "So what now?"

"I won't run, if you can put up with me a little longer."

He sighed, eyes full of wan endurance, then took a breath and said peremptorily, "All right, stop badgering me, now. At this rate I won't get home till after midnight."

Geli turned away and started toward the door.

Mattei's voice beat her to it. "Goodnight, Mlle Miroux. Forgive the stage name, force of habit. Until tomorrow morning."

"Yes, Monsieur. Goodnight." She turned the knob, pulled and went out.

28

The lunch hour came around. Major Mattei went down to the cafeteria as usual. Geli was having a beignet with coffee in the day room when she heard a commotion in the hallway. The door was open.

Wearing new chevrons on his sleeves Sergeant Dax, wide-eyed and out of breath, poked his head in. "Where's Mattei?"

"Why, he's -"

Somebody else ran past behind Dax.

"Never mind, I'll find him!" Dax took off at a fast trot toward the end of the hall and the iron door that opened onto a stairway downward.

Geli hurried into the hallway calling after him, "He went down to the cafeteria!"

Dax raised one hand just as he stepped off onto the stairs.

Across the way a woman she knew only by sight stepped out of her office. She looked this way and that, then at Geli, shrugging her shoulders.

"What's going on?" she said.

"I don't know."

The woman took a few more steps into the hallway. "It's not the first time. Every so often one of the *chiens* down there goes berserk. You know, can't stand the vermin or the food." She hugged herself against the chill. "I suppose I would, too, but I've never murdered anybody for the fun of it. I say they're getting what they asked for. One time we had to borrow a strait jacket from the police station. They had it from before the war. I'm Giselle, by the way."

"Simone Miroux."

"Hello there, Simone." Taking a step back onto the threshold, Giselle looked behind her into the office as if somebody else was there.

"A little excitement doesn't hurt every once in a while. Eh, Simone?"

"I guess we'll find out soon enough what it's all about."

"You think so? For our tender ears?" She raised her eyebrows naughtily. "Who'd care, though, if you shouted from the rooftops? You know how they say the worms crawl in and the worms crawl out. Well, this is a head start for those bastards down there. Their days of drinking up our wine and dragging off our women are over." She twiddled fingers. "*Au revoir*, Simone."

Stepping back behind her door, she swung it shut.

Geli stood there. She turned back into the day room, leaving the door open. The remains of her beignet sat on the plate, her coffee with its milk-slick getting cold. Major Mattei could have rushed past ahead of Dax. He'd left his office, that was all she knew, without inviting her to join him in the cafeteria. That was all right. She would have begged off, anyway. She didn't feel like going back into the interrogation room, just yet, to wait for him alone. She picked up her beignet, pushed the whole thing into her mouth as she leaned over the plate so it would catch the powdered sugar. She was about to take a sip of coffee when there was a tramping in the hallway and a rush of breathless voices in low tones. She kept her back to the doorway, holding her coffee.

The floor behind her creaked, more voices hissed and she turned to see Mattei so close she felt his breath and suddenly she thought he'd been about to touch her. His face was livid, a strange and helpless frenzy pinning his eyes back as they fell from her onto the cup she was holding.

In the doorway Sergeant Dax stood back hesitantly.

She set the cup down and said, "Anything wrong, sir?"

He took her arm and led her back into the corner near the sink. "Mlle Miroux -" His hand came off her shoulder, trembling.

She pulled out a chair, partly to escape him and leaned on it, saying, "Yes? What is it, Monsieur?"

In the doorway Sergeant Dax said, "I'll go now if you don't need me, sir."

"Not yet, Dax. Wait a moment."

Dax slackened his stance uneasily. "Of course, sir."

Mattei swung his face toward Geli like a window suddenly blown open, and it was banging in his eyes, and wouldn't stop. His voice came in like a hot wind she'd felt once bearing the musky scents of the Nile, and the desert swept in, and Reggie stood there in the guttering candlelight, not there at all.

"Something has happened," Mattei said.

In the doorway Dax shifted his feet, glancing behind him as if he didn't want to be there.

A wave swept up out of Geli's stomach. "What is it?" she said.

"Mlle Miroux, the fact is - please, sit down."

"No. I don't want to sit down."

Mattei backed away, looking suddenly alone. He took a breath. "There's been an accident. I'm afraid we've lost a prisoner."

Fear caught in Geli's throat.

Mattei stood there, waiting.

"Why are you telling me?" she cried.

Mattei sucked in another breath. "The prisoner has been identified as 1171."

She stared at him, looking for the lie to fall apart. The number wasn't him. Her hand flew to her mouth. "You mean escaped. A prisoner has escaped!"

"No, Mlle Miroux."

She lunged at him, raising her fists.

Dax took three quick steps toward her. "I am the one who found him, Ma'am. I ran for Dr. Trouillet, but it was too late. There was no sign of foul play. Nothing to be done except -" Dax turned aside, catching his breath.

Geli's fists locked in the air. She screamed insanely. "You couldn't let the Nazi live! You all hated him down there! I want to see him!"

"You can't go down there," Mattei said.

Dax stepped closer to her, said in a quiet, tender voice, "He'd left a letter on his bed, ma'am." Dax began to dig into his pocket.

Mattei cut in sharply. "You took it?"

"Yes, sir. I thought you would want to give it to the Colonel."

Mattei stared at him blankly as Dax slid a glance toward Geli.

"Quite right, Dax."

Dax came out of his pants' pocket with a tightly folded brownish paper.

Mattei took it from him, wrapped his hand around it

247

tenderly as he would clutch a struggling moth. He turned to Geli. "He left this note behind. I think you'd better read it before we have to give it up."

"No!" Geli shrieked. "Take it away!" She doubled over, sobbing.

Mattei took a short sidestep toward Dax, keeping one splayed hand low between himself and Geli. "You'll forget this, Dax. Understood?"

Dax stood stoutly taller. "I have already, sir. I'll leave you now, so there will be no doubt."

"Don't go too far away."

"I'll be just outside, sir."

"Yes."

Dax went out.

The latch caught soundlessly behind him.

Mattei held out the paper.

Geli snatched it from his fingers and flung it to the floor. "No!"

Mattei bent over slowly, picked up the paper and faced her squarely. "If you don't want to read it, I will."

"I don't care!" she cried.

He reached for her arm, she flinched away with a toss of her shoulder. His face tightened with anger as he began to peel open the paper.

"One day his wife may see this. She'll never know he couldn't leave you out. Take it. If you gave a damn about him, do him the courtesy of being the first to read this, as he intended." He grabbed her wrist and and pressed the paper into her palm.

She looked down at the crinkled paper as if it were his ashes, some sound from his last gasp of life, and blood trailed from Kurt's tracks back down into his cell; blood turned against her like a knife that laid her heart bare, and it was false, flown onto the side of his passage to despair. Now it was hers. Hers for now, until Elfriede's tears would fall upon it, too. She brought it closer to her face. It was too close, words smeared in tears as if the echo of his voice was dying out.

With this letter I, Kurt Langsdorff, hereby testify to the reasons for my actions, namely, the ending of my life which will be evident to whomever shall become the bearer of this testament.

I cannot say that the authorities here, assigned to hold and to interrogate me, have not believed me, or have not been sympathetic to my desire to appear before the International Tribunal as a material witness against war criminals. That we Germans being kept here have been strictly segregated from the other inmates leaves little doubt that we are the criminals, and I must honestly admit that I was not prepared for this. To those who know me, and to those responsible for my imprisonment, I can only say that, after all that has happened to me, only emptiness echoes behind these walls in which telling God the truth will never clear me of the cowardice of being able only to plunder the past I can no longer live. There was once a knife-edge path that stood between me and the call to a death I cheated when I watched thousands of innocent people go to their deaths without me.

God's silence is such a terribly long wait. I can only tap and talk as if He will be there on the other side of the wall when, one day, we might escape together.

In her mind now Geli saw him holding the pen that he had somehow got them to lend him. And what it took for him to buy that much more time, hastening the ink across the paper so as not to drag out life before death stopped calling, and hope peeped in to say he had forgotten something.

She looked up. The words flew out as if unbidden. "They killed him! They hated him! *You* hated him!"

Mattei fixed a withering look on her.

The door flew open, Dax lunged in. "Sir! Are you -?"

"It's all right, Dax." Mattei raised his hand against Dax but kept his eyes on Geli. She threw her face into her hands. "Oh, God, I – I didn't mean that!" But she had, and she wanted to run.

Mattei pulled her into his arms and she fought him, but he held her tight, and she began to sob, not knowing where she was except in the middle of a sea and everybody had gone down but her, and Kurt's hand slipped away and they both knew, now, what it was to want to live when you knew that you should be dead.

Two jailers suddenly came into the doorway, spoke breathlessly to Dax. Dax turned to Mattei. "You're needed downstairs, sir. Colonel Laurent is there with Dr. Trouillet. They were asking about the letter."

Mattei stepped away from Geli. "Go down and tell them I'm on my way, Dax."

"Yes, sir."

"And Dax – I'm sending Mlle Miroux home for the rest of the day. She's not available if anybody asks."

"I understand, sir." Dax turned to go, forcing the other two men aside and they began to dog his heels into the corridor.

Geli turned to feel the closeness of Mattei.

Beads of sweat broke from his forehead. He was close enough to smell the heat of her perfumed tears. "I have to go, now," he said. "Let me have the letter. Laurent will never know you've read it. You're going home now, ill. That's all they have to know. No telling how long you may be out. But you won't come back. You're going to have to get out, immediately. Meet me tonight at our bistro in Montmartre. Nine o'clock. If I'm not there on time, wait for me. Your life depends on it."

His saying 'our' bistro struck a strange chord. As if with his embrace, and her collapse into his arms, liberties followed Kurt's obliteration into what might have been with this man if she'd gone on with being Mlle Miroux.

She handed him the paper. "I'll be there," she said.

29

She had stood on this bridge before – centuries ago, it seemed. Not like now. Not in the dark, alone. The water down there combed out in a smoky dream of dying sunlight. Stillness rippled on that great green slab that slid past underneath. It had been noontime, then. People strolling arm in arm. Bustles, parasols and feathered caps in the airless pastel brown, as if the sun was going out. She thought she might have seen them in the movies, but none of them had names. Kurt was not among them. He had not been gone that long. Nobody smiled. She didn't, either, watching them. They were content to be without her. Resigned to being let out for a while into the final hours of the sun. It had been dark, then, but not night. Not like now.

She'd come out onto the Pont des Arts, in what little light twinkled from the spires atop the gallery, shone down onto the damp iron balustrade and found its way in quiet streaks across the water from the darker banks of the stone quays. She hadn't wept since she'd been on her bed in the dark.

She looked down at the river, how the light gleamed on the

swirls across the heaving depths you couldn't see. She shut her eyes and clenched her fists and in her mind she was in Missie Vassilchikov's grand ballroom, watching for who else would notice what she smoked and what she wore, and who her husband was that made her something else to look at, too. He would come home from the party late. Or was it from that place where he'd been shot? He must have died without a thought of her, and she had done that to him so he, too, had died alone. Her eyes came open slowly. The silence of the night went on without her.

She caught a taxi to Montmartre. The bartender, as soon as she walked into the bistro, was drawing the shades - a younger man this time, and as she hurried on along the empty stools, glancing back, he gave her a look as if she'd come in just in time to stop him from closing up.

She said, "You're getting ready to go home, Monsieur?"

The young man gave her a look that sized her up for whether turning her away could be bad for business. "It's been a slow night, Madame."

"I'm expecting a companion. He should be here any moment." Without a watch to glance at, she made imploring eyes instead. "I would hate to miss him."

He ambled around the end of the bar, dragging one hand across the top, and back along the tier of bottles and the mirror in which she saw herself – makeup smeared around her eyes, a woman who'd been crying.

He sighed, and with a wan smile, said, "A drink while you're waiting?"

"Yes, thank you. A glass of Bordeaux, please." She looked down toward the rear exit beyond the latrine. "Last time we sat back there," she said. "So nice and private."

He pulled the cork out of the bottle, reached for a glass

under the bar. "Take your pick tonight, Madame. Privacy whichever way you look."

"You're new, aren't you?"

"No, I come in often to relieve my uncle when he goes to Cherbourg on business."

"I see. What do they call you?"

"I'm Maurice." Then coyly, "I won't be a bartender all my life."

She smiled and looked at him again, his almost girlish pretty face and the hulking, beefy shoulders of an athlete.

"No, you won't. The sky's the limit, isn't it – now that the war is over."

He brought up another glass. "For the gentleman, too?"

"We'd better wait. He likes absinthe."

Maurice poured a soupcon into her glass.

She lifted a sip to her lips. "Quite nice," she said. "I'll just go back and find a place to wait."

He filled her glass, then glanced at his watch and said uneasily, "Begging your pardon, Madame – I'm due to meet a person very soon. Like you!" With the twitch of a smile he told her of the rendezvous with a girl he was afraid might not be there if he was late. "I wouldn't want her to think I'd stood her up," he said.

"Of course, I understand. All I can tell you -"

Just then the bell jingled at the door. Mattei stepped in, looking rumpled in his uniform.

"Ah, he's here!" Geli said.

Maurice stood away from the bar, impatiently preparing to serve the new unwanted customer, looking a little disgruntled that he'd come. Seeing her, Mattei hurried her way. "Sorry I'm late. I haven't been home, yet."

"Oh, then - yes, of course."

Maurice lifted the bottle. "Bordeaux for you, Monsieur?"

Mattei stared at the bottle. His cap was on askew. His tunic bulged sloppily above the belt of his Sam Browne. "A short one, that'll do," he said.

The bartender poured half a glass. Mattei gently took her arm. She thought he was escorting her down to the table at the end again when he stopped beside a booth, gestured toward the seat and waited while she got in. He tossed his cap onto the table before he scooted in across from her. "How are you holding up, Frau Straub?"

Her own name struck like a brazen insult, the real alias, and she looked in vain for the man he used to be, who'd had it bad for her. When he would do almost anything for Mlle Miroux. She'd left the tear-stained mess of makeup under her eyes. Down at the bottom of her heart she felt empty. He was watching her: was she in pain? You can only cry so long.

"I'm doing all right, Monsieur."

He sat back, shaking his head. "Things aren't looking good back at the prison. Laurent is out to find a scapegoat, and the jailers are nervous." He fixed a hard look on her across the table. "You're going to have to get out of Paris right away."

"Oh, but, how soon?"

He reached into the inside pocket of his tunic, pulled out a long brown envelope. "I have here the notice of your resignation. You'll sign it now, and by the time they see it, you'll be gone. They won't think twice about accepting this. With your departure goes any trace of your connection to Herr Langsdorff." He spread out the paper in front of her, lent her his pen.

She had it poised over the paper when she looked up. "What name?" she said.

He shook his head as if she ought to know. "Simone Miroux,

of course. I'll simply tell them you've resigned and won't be coming back."

She scratched the name across the line at the bottom of the page, dropped the pen and fingered her wine glass as she looked up at him again. "There. For the last time," she said, and tried to smile, but courage failed her and she began to feel afraid. Suddenly she knew that she was going to miss him, this man who was now trying to get rid of her, and she said, "I don't know where I'll go."

"You must go back to Germany. Destroy your French papers as soon as you're across the border. Revert to your German citizenship. They're going to ask you what you've been doing in Paris."

"What *have* I been doing?"

"You were called to testify at a military tribunal."

"But if they -"

"I doubt you'll be detained. They'll be too bogged down to bother with a woman who seems unafraid to tell the truth."

"You seem so sure of that."

"I'll give you a note they will accept. They'll have no time or inclination not to."

"So now, you mean I'll just walk off ?"

"Yes, resign and that's the last we'll ever hear of you. I'm the only one who knows what your connection to Herr Langsdorff was. That's how it will remain."

"What about Dax?"

"He'll keep his mouth shut. I've been looking after his interests."

"I liked him," she said.

"Yes, I know. Now, where are your German papers?"

For a moment she was in his office again, being interviewed for a job with the Second Standing Military Court. The questions seemed perfunctory. She knew he was going to hire her. "I've got them in a safe place," she said.

Mattei sat back with a deep sigh, looking suddenly very tired. "Good. I've got a ticket for you."

"A ticket to where?"

"Berlin."

It felt so odd that he no longer cared for her. Or did he care enough to make her go? So odd that she'd hung on to how he'd felt about her. Pride coming in, all tattered but still standing, even on Kurt's grave. Berlin loomed like a death trap.

"Oh, God! Berlin's a rubble heap. My old flat - it can't be mine anymore. Probably not even there." But then she wondered what that was to him. Once she was gone and out of his hair, her fate was in the hands of anybody but him.

He said, "Haven't you some relative? Some former -"

"We had a cottage in Münster. I rarely went there after the war heated up and Gunther was gone. There was a caretaker. I couldn't pay him after the money ran out, so I don't know. Gunther never got around to putting my name on the deed."

"But as his wife and only heir, you could legitimately go there."

"I suppose so, if he's dead. The only person who could tell me if he's still alive is General Guderian."

Mattei nodded. "Was there a will?"

"Yes. Gunther left all his assets to me. Of course I don't know if he's still alive."

"Still I see no reason why you shouldn't go straight to Münster while the tide of the refugee problem is still high and you're not likely to stand out."

She knew these things, but still wanted to rely on him, and said, "Poachers might have taken over."

"Go to the Allied occupation authority. I've heard good

257

things about the Americans. They should be only too glad to kick out any poachers for you."

She thought she heard him saying she'd be pretty enough to get that done, but in his eyes he'd swerved back onto the straight and narrow.

He said, "I've heard Guderian is still alive. The Americans have him locked up at Neustadt. You might have a chance of finding out about your husband if you went there."

"No, I won't go to Neustadt. It's too late for me to know. Right now I - oh, never mind." She looked up, tried to take him in without self-pity. "I'm sorry I deceived you, Monsieur," she said.

He shrugged, then she could see him looking for that waif in her that ran around in circles, ran and ran and couldn't stop until he called a halt. She wanted to give her to him, so he couldn't say goodbye. She said, "Did you ever tell Herr Langsdorff who I was?"

He gave her a long look. "As I recall, you didn't want me to."

She looked down at her glass, rolling the stem between her fingers. "I don't suppose he ever spoke of me."

"You didn't want that either, did you?"

She lowered her eyes again, feeling guilty, as she nodded, for having no more tears to bring up from that place that wouldn't tell her if she had a heart. "No," she said.

He tipped his glass up to his lips, drank sparingly and set the glass back down carefully, clutching the stem.

"For your information, he didn't take his life as a way out of choosing between you and his wife."

She looked up. "Why do you say that?"

"Just so you know."

"If you think I ever sought to steal him from her, God knows

I always knew he was meant for her. Sometimes I feel, though, I killed him."

Mattei looked up sharply. "I don't like the sound of that."

She shrugged, fingering her glass. "Maybe what I mean is I feel worthless, I suppose."

With a trembling hand Mattei picked up his glass and drained it. "One day I'm sure his wife and I will meet. I hope by then I will have cleared his name. I won't give up because he's dead." He looked steadily across at her.

"Suicides," she said, "do you think they're damned to everlasting hell?" She stared back at him through a veil of bitterness.

"Some say so. But what do they know?"

"I thought he had everything to live for," she said.

He sat back suddenly like a fighter ducking a blow. "Yes. I fell for that myself, with all my pride that drove me on until I thought I'd got it in the bag. I promised him what I was never sure I could deliver. The trouble was he bought it. As soon as freedom stared him in the face, he didn't like what he saw."

"I don't understand."

"I didn't see it. Not until it was too late. How hope was turning on him – so obsessed was I with getting him off. I couldn't see that only bought him time enough to know he couldn't take it."

"Monsieur, I can't see any sense to that."

"That's right. Sense was never in the cards. You have to go back to that day when he stood stoically at a death camp watching people shuffle to their death, fighting the urge to die with them. The will to live told him it was useless, even stupid. They would die anyway. His death wouldn't save them. Staying alive, he might save others. So that's what he set out to do, the more dangerous things got to be, the better. He'd tried to get the war to kill him when you came along and bought him some more time. I think he loved you that day he lost track of you in Rottweil. But then, locked up in prison, his wife came back into the picture, even though he'd just as soon be dead to her. Two lovely women – you and her – warm and pulsing in your flesh and blood with all the succor you could beckon him to lie down in and fall asleep – you went with the same bill of goods I sold him with my hope. I didn't know how fatally he knew better. That he was promised to a naked girl, who'd given up her name to '19', the age at which she would be dead in minutes, with the hatred she burned into him before the whips drove her on to where her death left him alive. You helped him at a time when you might have destroyed him, but that, too, went the way of all those things the war forgave. There was no resting on his laurels – however truthful they appeared to be in his report. There was no more war to swim against to keep his head above water. Going home would have to be the lie he'd let his wife believe until the day she found him hanging from a crossbeam, and he couldn't do that to her."

She watched him, not knowing whether he was blaming or forgiving her, and fear struck like a snake, just barely missing. Tears flooded her eyes. "I wonder if I knew that all along."

Mattei was staring at her. "Did you love him?" he said sternly.

Her gaze slanted crazily toward the table. She couldn't find the words and looked up. "I thought I did. No, God help me, I did."

"Then don't ever tell me you were worthless. If it's a flogging you want, I'm afraid I can't oblige." He sounded angry.

She didn't know. The words seemed to condemn her. She reached across and took his hand and held it fast. "I'm going to miss you, Monsieur."

He smiled faintly, looking away. "As long as you don't miss her."

"Who?"

"Mlle Miroux. You'll have to leave her here, you know. Where you're going, you won't be needing her."

She held her eyes on him wistfully. "You still call me that, after all -"

"Hard to break a habit," he said, then broke open in his face as if he'd just awakened from a dream. "All right, enough of that." He began to peel the cuff back from the wrist his watch was on.

She said quickly, "I don't suppose our paths will cross again, but if you ever get to Münster, look me up. You might find me in the directory."

"What are the chances?" he said.

"Yes, to a Frenchman, Germany couldn't be much of a tourist attraction. I'll keep a lookout, though. One day I'll be looking out the window, aimlessly, and there you'll be. All dapper in a suit and hat. No chance I could mistake you for the mailman."

They looked across the table at each other. He had nice eyes, she thought. Words with no sound flew between them like birds that didn't want to lite.

Suddenly he moved, and he was pulling back his cuff again. "God, look at the time! I won't be home till after midnight. Remember, now - there's no need for you to come in tomorrow morning." He reached back and hauled out his billfold. "Here, you'll need some money."

"Oh, but Monsieur -"

"You don't have any, do you?"

By her silence she said no.

He fished out several banknotes, spread them on the table.

Among them was the ticket for Berlin. "You'll need the extra to go on to Münster."

"So this is goodbye."

He looked down at the table.

She thought he was about to lay his hand on the resignation paper, to keep it from her, when he looked up. "You look so different, now. Every bit as pretty as Mlle Miroux. I won't soon forget you."

She felt her loneliness looming in a crowd, then on the train, the passage of a bleak long ride to Berlin. "Will you miss me just a little?" she said.

He gathered her all into his eyes, as if she stood stock still for him to take her photograph.

"I wish there were some way I wouldn't," he said, and tucked the resignation paper under his blouse and shoved his billfold back into his pocket. He reached for his cap and began to slide out, then he was on his feet.

She got out and stood there while he stuffed the wallet back into his pocket. He thrust his hand out, she grasped it firmly and they shook.

"Well, goodbye," he said in a cordial, not quite brittle tone.

"Who knows?" she said.

He smiled, then walked away and she watched him as he stopped to pay Maurice at the bar, then went on briskly and was reaching for the doorknob when his hand dropped, and he half turned. He smiled at her, she smiled back and lifted her hand to wave, but he'd gone out. The second jingle shook as the door shut, and a shadow hunkered, then hurled across the curtain. Tears seemed to come from nowhere, hot and blinding, making the lights swim in the movement of him going, and she was still as they spilled over and ran down like something that would keep her there a little longer, and she knew they were, just for that moment, not all for Kurt.

She didn't want to go. She knew she had to, so Maurice could keep his date.

They were all down there, safe from hearing the whistling and the explosions outside, feeling the ground shudder, but when it stopped, there'd be the all clear. Somebody upstairs, waiting.

The lights behind the bar went out.

Maurice came hurriedly around, shoes clumping. He turned the 'closed' sign outward in the window and rang down the shades. He came over to her, wiping his hands on his apron. "Was there anything else, Madame?"

His eyes shone with the hope that she was through, and she could see his fear of being late by seconds for his rendezvous.

"If she loves you, Maurice, she won't dock you for being late."

"I've got my bike, Madame. That'll get me there in no time."

"Will you be taking her to the cinema? The dance hall?"

He shook his head. "No. We'll just find some secret place and, you know..."

She got into her purse, peeled off 600 francs and pushed them across the table to him. "Here. A little something to light up that secret place of yours."

"Oh no, Madame. I couldn't -"

"If you don't, I'll never come back here, ever again. What would your uncle Philippe say to that?"

He picked up the money shyly. "You're so kind, Madame." He cocked his head at her. "You have an accent. Are you French?"

"Maybe not," she said.

He shrugged. "I couldn't place it. I just heard something."

"Just for that I'm going to tell you I was born in Italy. You

263

could say that, really, I'm Italian. A little German thrown in for flavor."

"Ah, that explains it! May I add, your friend is a very lucky man." He held a lovely smile on her.

"Thank you," she said. "Well, let me get out of here so you can close up. You don't want to keep that girl waiting too much longer. Goodnight, then, Maurice. Until next time." The next time that she knew would never be.

"*Au revoir*, Madame."

She walked straight to the door and went out under the jingle of the bell into the cool embrace of the night. Another light behind her in the shaded window went out. She turned down toward the Place Blanche. She wanted to walk a while before she hailed a taxi to get home in.

Peace fell in all around her, as if the stars up there, immoveable, had been released from prison, and you didn't have to look over your shoulder anymore for the place where death would scream to earth. Maurice would soon be racing through the night toward a restless girl who was too beautiful, too much in love with him to be gone when he got there.

Geli took a breath of the cool air on her face. Where was he? Never to go out into the garden to admire her daffodils and irises, or see the sun so warm against a bright new stucco wall. He had never been hers to have. But she had him, and she always would, there under the menacing harmony of the bombers on their way to the fuel dumps, the bridges and the munition factories, and they were listening for the first bombs like their hearts were falling, too, for the last time.

Made in the USA
Las Vegas, NV
25 May 2023

72528094R00163